# −LIVES−
## *Intertwined*

A NOVEL

## DONNA BROWN

ISBN 978-1-63525-484-6 (Paperback)
ISBN 978-1-63525-485-3 (Digital)

Christian Faith Publishing, Inc.
296 Chestnut Street
Meadville, PA 16335
www.christianfaithpublishing.com

Printed in the United States of America

Home is where the heart is.
Oh why can't I find mine?
With restlessness of spirit,
I'll seek until I find.

*1*945. In a dimly lit New York Army hospital room, a scream jolted Eric Stone from a nightmare. Shaken and awake, he stared at the ceiling until he saw a nurse rush to the soldier in the next bed, give an injection, and try to comfort him. While Eric watched, he thought, *At least God spared me loss of limb.* But tears of remembrance brimmed. Holding his German twin brother while he gasped his last breath had hit Eric as hard as that man's anguish over losing a leg.

The nurse hurried to Eric's side. "Do you need medication?"

He shook his head.

"Are you sure?"

"I'm fine."

"The doctor should be here around nine to release you. Are you glad you'll be home in a few days?"

He mustered a smile. "You bet."

Three hours later, donned in his replacement uniform, Eric stood gazing out the window but turned when the doctor entered.

The physician nodded. "Not a bad fit." He handed Eric a small package. "This came for you . . . from a Col. James Stone. A relative?"

"My uncle." He tore off the brown paper, opened the box, and saw his campaign ribbons and medals.

The doctor raised an eyebrow as he looked at the contents. "No note?"

Eric snorted. "I didn't expect one."

"I take it you two don't get along."

"You got that right." Eric slipped the box into his duffel bag.

"You're not going to put those on?"

Eric shrugged and hoisted the bag to his shoulder. "I will before I get home."

"Remember my orders. For a few months, don't eat rich, greasy, or spicy foods, especially at night."

"I'll remember, sir."

"And please, take it easy. I only discharged you early so you could be home on your twenty-second birthday. Your discharge papers will be sent to your address in Buena Vista, Colorado."

\*    \*    \*

A taxi waited to take Eric to Grand Central Station where he boarded a train. Destination: Denver.

When he arrived Friday, April 20, a bitter wind stung his face as he swung down to the station platform. He buttoned his topcoat, hoisted his duffel bag, and hailed a cab to the bus depot.

"I'd like a one-way ticket to Buena Vista," he told the agent.

"You won't have long to wait. Bus leaves in an hour." He pointed to a table. "Servicemen get free coffee and donuts."

"Thanks."

In the men's room, Eric splashed warm water on his face and blotted it dry with a paper towel. He carefully combed his disheveled blond hair so it covered the long scar that creased his scalp. From the mirror, his bloodshot blue eyes caught an elderly man watching him. Months of impersonating his German twin had made Eric wary of every observant face, every voice inflection. He turned.

The man smiled. His voice reflected friendliness. "Heading home?"

Eric nodded.

"Bet you're glad the war with Germany is almost over. Did you fight in Europe?"

"Yes." To say more would have invited questions.

The old man limped over and laid a fatherly hand on Eric's shoulder. "I fought in World War I." He smiled with empathy. "The worst is over. In time, horrors will fade."

When he lifted his suitcase, Eric said, "Can I carry that for you? It looks heavy."

"It's not far to a terminal bench, and my son will be here soon to handle it. He invited me to live with him and his family . . . thought I was getting too old to live alone. I'm not, but don't tell him. I'm jumping at the chance to spend time with my grandsons before they get too grown up to have fun with me."

"Sure you don't want me to carry your bag?"

"Positive." He winked and whispered in confidence, "It's heavy because I have five-pound weights in here, but keep that our secret."

Eric laughed with him, not sure he believed him, but despite the man's limp, he did look fit.

After the elderly gentleman left, Eric pondered his words about the war. *Can the worst be over? Can time erase nightmares?* Opening a bottle of pain medication, Eric popped two pills, then hoisted his duffle bag. He strolled to the snack table, chose a plain donut, and poured lots of cream into his coffee to lessen its acidity. As he settled on a wooden bench across from the old man, he wondered if it was proper to dunk the donut.

The spry gentleman lifted his donut in recognition, winked, and, as if he had read Eric's mind, immersed the sweet in his coffee.

Chuckling, Eric raised his in a salute and proceeded to do the same. He thought about sitting next to him to see what else they might have in common but saw a family approaching. Two dark-haired boys ran and threw their arms around the old man. In unison, they squealed, "Grandpa."

The joy on their faces sent a stab of pain to Eric's heart. *Dad, you would have made a terrific grandfather.* He pushed aside memories of his father's death and concentrated on watching this wonderful family reunion.

Before they left, the elderly gentleman came over, smiled, and extended his hand. "Remember what I said, young man. In time, horrors will fade."

"I know they will. God helped me get over my father's tragic death twelve years ago."

"But I sense your present memories are more painful."

7

"You're very perceptive."

He slipped an arm around Eric's shoulder and gave him a light hug. "And these, too, will fade."

*Will it take twelve years?*

The bus rolled in on schedule. Exhausted, Eric boarded, shoved his bag in the overhead, and dropped into an empty window seat. Most passengers appeared asleep. He closed his eyes and tried to relax but couldn't. Memories surfaced. Eric relived his twin's death. He shuddered as his mind's eye saw a West Wall pillbox explode. He could feel Erin's mangled, bleeding body cradled in his arms, and hear his last words. "Survive, Eric. Get my things to Mom in Cologne. Tell her I love her."

Eric stared out the window into the night blackness. A pressure cooker of emotions roiled within him, from grief to bitterness. He fought back tears until he recalled a chaplain's advice given after the bloodbath on Omaha Beach. "Shed tears for your comrades. Tears honor them and show your love. Even Jesus wept."

On the semi-dark bus, Eric allowed his tears to flow. He gazed heavenward. *Why, God?*

He clenched his hands in bitterness. Not against God. Not against the Germans but against his uncle—Colonel James Stone.

In remembrance, his hand slipped across his midsection. October 6 at Aachen, a bullet had pierced his stomach and another had deeply creased his scalp. Uncle Jim had visited him in the field hospital—all smiles, no heart.

"Great news, Eric. You have a chance to see your mother and sister in Cologne. Having Erin's belongings is a stroke of luck. You can now impersonate him and perhaps uncover vital information from your stepfather, Colonel von Harmon, who's at German Headquarters. Allied Intelligence has a plan to get you across enemy lines. That head wound will give credence to your faking amnesia. If perchance you're discovered, say you saw Erin's death as an opportunity to see your family."

Eric's fists tightened. *Like always, you weren't concerned about me, how I'd feel. Deceiving Mom and Elizabeth tore me up inside more than the bullet. Did you even take into consideration what the Gestapo might do if they discovered I wasn't Erin?* In February, he was accused of being a spy, and they'd belted him until he'd passed out and later lashed his back. The scars would never fade. Eric breathed deeply and tried to push bitterness aside. *I have to let go. I can't let Aunt Jean and the girls see me like this.*

Eric glanced at his watch—11:35 p.m. In fifteen minutes, he'd be in Buena Vista. He focused his thoughts on the only place he'd called home since his father's death.

The beauty and tranquility of the Colorado Rockies surrounded the sleepy town. To the west and bordering the Continental Divide stood the Sawatch Mountain Range, rising in majestic splendor. Eric envisioned himself in Buena Vista strolling Main Street. He looked into store windows, glanced at the movie theater but lingered at the bakery, inhaling the aroma of fresh bread.

He doubted if much had changed in town or on Uncle Jim's ranch a few miles east—469 acres of lush pasture and stately evergreens, lodgepole pines, cedar, and fir.

When the bus pulled into the depot, Eric smiled, eager to see his family, and determined to start life anew.

Aunt Jean and his cousins overpowered him with hugs and kisses. Nancy, a little older than him, said, "Mom, I'll drive. You sit in back with Eric and Cindy."

Ann, sixteen, hoisted his duffel bag to her shoulder before he could reach down. She grinned with mischief and said in a deep mobster-like voice, "Mister, you're in our hands now."

Eric chuckled. "I'll chance that."

Ten-year-old Cindy latched onto his hand and swung it while they walked to the old Ford station wagon. Seated next to him on the backseat, she gripped his arm and snuggled close.

He kissed her forehead. "Miss me?"

"Uh-huh. Can you take me to Denver to ride the roller coaster and the new rides at Lakeside?"

"Can I unpack first?"

"Not right away, silly. The park's not open. But this summer?"

He nodded and crossed his heart. "One special date for you and me. That's a promise."

Nancy pulled into the gravel driveway, leading to the two-story brick house and stopped by the back door.

In the kitchen, Eric inhaled the mixed aromas of baked goodies. He hoped his aunt hadn't used all her ration coupons on treats for him. He glanced around the room, wondering where they'd hidden his Devil's Food birthday cake, but nonchalantly, he said, "It doesn't look like anything has changed."

Aunt Jean chuckled as she removed her scarf and smoothed her auburn hair. "You must be tired if you haven't noticed more cracks and peeling paint." Her green eyes cast him a welcoming smile. "It's so good to have you home. Would you like a glass of milk and a slice of apple pie before heading upstairs?"

"To taste Bessie's milk again would be pure heaven, but save my pie for breakfast," he said, remembering the doctor's orders.

Ann strolled to the refrigerator. "Would you settle for Priscilla's milk? Bessie is packaged in the Buena Vista food locker."

Eric nodded. Bessie's milk or Priscilla's, it didn't matter. He savored every swallow and carried the glass to the sink.

While Aunt Jean rinsed it, she said, "You sleep as late as you can." She turned. "Do you need anything?"

He saw the concern in her eyes and smiled. "I'm fine."

"You're sure? Jim told me very little about Erin's death or your injuries, only that you'd had a rough time. He's very proud of you, said you could fill in the blanks."

"I'd rather let him tell you. He should be home soon since the war in Europe is almost over." To himself, he added, "I don't plan to be here when he returns."

Cindy pointed to his medals. "Mom says you're a hero. Tell me how you got those."

Before he could speak, Aunt Jean said, "Not tonight. Eric's tired. Besides, he may not want to talk about the war."

"Why not?"

Eric cupped Cindy's chin and leaned down. "Because I saw some terrible things happen, too bad to talk about." He smiled and gave her a hug. "Tomorrow, I want to hear about all the things you've been doing while I've been gone. Okay?"

After Cindy nodded, his aunt tapped her on the shoulder. "Off to bed with you now. We'll be up shortly."

A quick glance around his room showed Eric nothing had changed, except the sheets. The turned back quilt revealed white ones instead of blue. Exhausted, he stripped and put on the flannel pajamas, lying on the bed. Positive he didn't need a sleeping pill, Eric slipped between the sheets and sank into the feather-stuffed mattress that had always provided deep sleep. From the partly opened window, he listened to chirping crickets and an occasional coyote's howl. He closed his eyes and relaxed.

He dropped into a deep peaceful sleep only to be thrown into the throes of a nightmare.

*The Rhine River hurled him downstream—savage red water, littered with dead Germans. Heads bobbed, their grotesque faces twisted in agony. Arms and legs brushed past him, torn broken limbs ripped apart by bullets and bombs. Eric swam with this current of carrion, fighting to keep his head above the raging water.*

*He gritted his teeth, fixed his gaze on a bridge, and struggled to reach the wooden pilings. They exploded, flying apart like matchsticks tossed to the wind. Timber crashed around him, making the dead Germans rise from the water as if determined to kill him in death where they hadn't been able to in life. One, his German twin brother Erin, shouted, "Survive!" Eric fought his way through the bodies and debris to reach a rock. In desperation, he clung to its craggy edge.*

*Jill appeared on the bank, her long blonde hair flowing like tasseled corn. Fairy-like she glided down the embankment and skipped across the slippery rocks as if they were stepping stones. She stopped, reached out, and helped him to his feet, only to let out a shrill laugh and shove him backward.*

Eric cried out and awakened. He sat up, trembling, unable to shake the feeling of being engulfed by the bloody Rhine. Bile rose at the back of his throat. He rolled off the bed, dashed from his room and down the hallway to the bathroom. He didn't have time to pull up the toilet seat. Instead, his left hand clung to the seat while his right clutched his stomach. Eric retched until his throat burned and sank to his knees in exhaustion.

Through tear-blurred eyes, he saw Aunt Jean holding out a glass of water. Eric rinsed his mouth and spat out the water. His aunt ran a washcloth under the spigot, wrung it, and pressed the cold cloth against his forehead. When he dry-heaved, she held the washcloth in place. Afterward, she refilled the glass. Eric rinsed and sat back on his heels in relief.

Aunt Jean moistened the cloth again and handed it to him. Eric buried his face in its cool, soothing dampness while she lowered the toilet lid and flushed. "Better?" she asked, helping him to his feet and gesturing him to sit.

"Yeah." Eric leaned against the tank and closed his eyes, feeling weak, vulnerable, and angry. He was disgusted with himself for awakening his aunt and upset with her for mothering him, but mostly angry with Jill.

"A nightmare?"

He nodded, holding back his welling rage.

"It might help to talk about it."

"I'm okay," he blurted. "It was only a nightmare." Eric stood as much to end the confrontation as to show his aunt he was all right. Her tiny frame seemed to shrink; her green eyes clouded with tears. *Why had he yelled? She wasn't the one who stabbed him in the back while he was knee-deep in gore.* "Aunt Jean, I'm sorry."

"If only your uncle were here. If only you could talk with him." Her eyes begged to help.

Eric gently placed his hands on her shoulders. "I'm sorry I awakened you. Please go back to bed. I'm okay, really I am."

He knew she didn't believe him. His aunt sighed and sent him a wan smile. "Try to get some sleep." She patted his cheek as if he were still the child he'd been when he first came to live with her, his uncle, and three cousins.

Eric watched her leave, shoulders slumped. He chided himself for not holding her to show how much he loved her. But his love was buried too deep to unearth and reveal. Yes, he appreciated all the care she'd showered on him, but right now, he couldn't stand being mothered, and he couldn't show love. *I've got to leave before my mood drags everyone down.*

Eric ran his hand through his hair and told his reflection that stared back with sunken eyes, "War is hell on earth."

He brushed his teeth and went back to bed, but a bitter taste remained in his mouth, the same taste he'd experienced ten years ago. The night after his father's funeral, Eric had vomited, and Aunt Jean had done then what she did tonight. He flipped on the reading light and glanced around. His room seemed to grow larger, and he seemed to shrink as childhood memories flooded back.

## Cologne, Germany

He and his twin brother Erin were six and being torn apart. Martha Stone stayed in Germany with Erin. Daniel Stone had begged her to return with him and Eric to America. His bridge construction job was finished. The boys pleaded with their mother, but she adamantly refused to leave Germany. Twins ripped apart; their family torn asunder. Pain. At six, Eric hadn't understood.

He still didn't. In Cologne a few months ago, he'd asked his mother why she refused to come to America.

She said, "Home is where the heart is. All my family lives here. When I married your father, I thought his heart was here too."

An explanation? Eric tried to put himself in her place. Could he leave the United States? He'd toyed with the idea. His restlessness demanded he do something. He wanted to know his mother and sister better, even his stepfather, Colonel von Harmon, whom he'd come to admire despite his being a Nazi. But return to Germany? His heart wasn't there. Neither did it belong on Uncle Jim's ranch.

Eric turned off his light and scrunched beneath the covers, pondering where he belonged before he fell asleep.

Daylight brought no answer, but he did decide to ride his motorcycle to California. Why? He didn't know. Was it his pioneering spirit whispering, "Go west; head for California," or the prompting voice of Mato, his Hawaiian friend? Born in California but raised in Hawaii, Mato and his family returned to the States shortly before the bombing of Pearl Harbor. As soon as Mato turned eighteen, he joined the army, and the two men became friends during basic training.

His friend talked about settling on the California coast after the war. "I want to teach kids to surf. Maybe the sport will become as popular in the States as it is in Hawaii. Want to join me? I'll teach you too."

Mato had died in Eric's arms on Omaha Beach. His last words: "Guess I won't be riding any more waves."

Eric dashed to the window and threw it wide open. While he drew in gulps of air, he blinked back tears. "My friend, I really wanted to ride the waves with you. Now I can't. But I will go to California. Somehow, I'll learn how to surf."

The hard part was telling Aunt Jean and the girls. They would probably beg him to stay, tell him it was too soon to travel anywhere on his motorcycle. Eric wasn't worried. He had plenty of pain pills, and he would ride his bike every day to make sure he'd have no problems. Eric walked to his desk and studied the calendar. *Sunday, May 13, is Mother's Day. I can't leave before then. I'll leave on Friday, the 18.* He circled the date on his calendar.

Eric took his time descending the stairs. He paused at the landing and fingered the pattern on the large stained glass window—a fully opened, giant red rose. He could hear Aunt Jean singing softly, "There is a place of quiet rest, near to the heart of God. A place where sin cannot molest, near to the heart of God." Eric walked down the last six stairs and waited outside the kitchen door until she finished the song. Quiet rest, he wondered. The war had increased his faith in God but couldn't still his restlessness.

He entered the kitchen and saw two layers of chocolate cake on the counter. Aunt Jean stood to the side, mixing the frosting. "Can I lick the beaters?" he asked. "It's been ages."

"I thought you were asleep." She finished the chocolate icing and handed him the beaters. "I wanted to surprise you."

"I am surprised." Knowing sugar was still hard to come by made his birthday cake an extra special treat. His taste buds reveled as his tongue wove between each coated blade. He couldn't remember anything tasting sweeter. "Where'd you find the sugar?"

"Safeway. I lucked out and got to the market first before the nasty hoarders grabbed all the bags."

"Good for you." From her letters, Eric knew Aunt Jean's pet peeve was people who took more than their fair share of any scarce commodity, thus depriving her household. He turned toward the door when he heard footsteps running down the stairs. It had to be Ann who did everything in high gear.

She glided into the kitchen and frowned. "What are you doing up?"

He grinned, making a big show of licking the frosting. He felt relaxed, almost normal. It was a good feeling to be able to tease her again. *Was I ever sixteen and carefree like Ann?* Her world consisted of boys, jitterbugging, and fun. Her chatter always bubbled with enthusiasm. But right now, he saw her irritation grow as he continued to lick the gooey chocolate. Ann's long red hair seemed to scream a warning as her green eyes flashed.

"Mother! You said he would sleep late. He's spoiling everything."

"Spoiling what? I already know that's my cake. Want me to go back to bed?"

"No. I guess it's not that big a deal. I was only going to decorate it."

Eric hid his surprise. Ann had never been the kitchen-type. She preferred milking the cow and tending the Victory garden. "I'd love to watch," he said with genuine interest.

Ann glowed with pleasure, giving him the impression she was practicing her skills to butter up some other guy. It didn't matter. This cake was his. This birthday was his. Though war-scarred, he was grateful to be alive. *Thank you, Lord.*

Nancy hurried into the kitchen and stared at him. "You're up?"

"Can't keep a good man down," he quipped, wondering if he'd awakened her last night too. Her long auburn hair was piled on the top of her head. Eric thought this latest fashion hairdo ridiculous and aging. Calm and practical like Aunt Jean, she now looked like her.

"I'll fix breakfast," Nancy said.

Breakfast consisted of eggs, sweet rolls, all-you-can-eat bacon, and a piece of pie for him. Eric didn't have the heart to ask how many ration coupons the treat had taken.

Cindy burst into the room and cried out in despair, "You ate it all?"

"Of course not," Nancy said. "Yours is in the oven keeping warm."

"Good." Cindy plopped on a chair, her blonde curls bouncing when she turned toward Eric. "Can I take you to a movie today? I didn't know what to get you for your birthday."

"I'd like that. What's playing?"

"*Road to Utopia* with Bob Hope."

"Sounds great." He rose, ambled to the stove, and poured himself another cup of coffee.

On his way back, Cindy cast him an impish smile. "Could we ride into Buena Vista on your motorcycle?"

He gave her a hug. "You bet, if it's running okay."

Aunt Jean turned from the sink. "I hate to be a killjoy, but the motorcycle is out. Eric can take the truck."

Cindy looked crestfallen. "Why not the motorcycle?"

"You're too young to be on one, and Eric shouldn't be. He just got out of the hospital."

"Aunt Jean, it takes less than twenty minutes to ride into Buena Vista. Cindy will be perfectly safe. I won't go fast, and I won't take chances." When he finally talked his aunt into letting her go, Cindy was ecstatic.

Cindy's squeals of delight showed him she loved every minute whizzing down the road with the wind blowing against her face. In town, during lunch at the Cozy Cafe, she asked, "Can we do this again next Saturday?"

"That's up to your mom. She wasn't too keen about your coming this time."

Cindy's mouth turned down in a pout. "She worries too much."

"With your dad away, she has a lot of responsibility on her shoulders. Managing a ranch and raising a family are not easy tasks."

"I know, but I just wish she'd give me more freedom."

"She will when she sees what a trustworthy young lady you are."

Cindy seemed to be mulling over his words. "Should I try to help out more?"

He nodded. "Doing things before she asks would be a great way to show you're growing up."

Having lunch with Cindy and seeing a movie proved to be a great way to celebrate his homecoming and birthday.

That night after they'd eaten cake and ice cream, Aunt Jean, Nancy, and Ann gave him his present. Tears threatened when he opened the large box and saw the expensive pair of tooled- leather, western boots he'd always wanted. To give himself time to get his emotions under control, he made a show of trying on the boots. Now his wanting to leave those who loved him seemed a terrible sin. How could he do this to them?

After the others went to bed, Eric and Nancy donned jackets and walked outside. Nancy settled onto the oaken porch swing and leaned back, looking content. Eric scooted onto the wide brick porch ledge. He propped his back against the wall and drew his knees to his chest, inhaling the embracing mountain air. He stared westward, picturing the Continental Divide and the ocean miles beyond. He would wend his way there like the streams and rivers meandering to the Pacific.

His army buddies had pegged him as being from California because of his pale blond hair. He never mentioned he was born in Germany or that he had a twin brother, who was probably fighting for the Third Reich. Eric's accent was gone. Uncle Jim had seen to that. He'd forbidden him to speak German and drilled him in English until satisfied Eric sounded 100 percent American. In defiance, Eric clung to his heritage, keeping the language alive by reading again and again the books his father had brought to America. He didn't know then that Uncle Jim would take advantage of his knowledge.

He pushed memories aside and concentrated on his trip—miles of new territory to cover, explore, enjoy. He would be accountable to no one. No time tables. He'd fought for freedom. Now he was free!

Nancy interrupted his elation. "You're leaving, aren't you?" Sadness edged her voice.

Eric met her gaze. "Am I that transparent?"

"No. I saw some maps on your desk when I set clean clothes on your bed, and I noticed May 18 circled on your calendar." Her brow furrowed. "You just got home. Why do you want to leave?"

He shrugged. "Call it the desire to see new places."

"Isn't that what you've been doing these past three years?"

"Jumping from foxhole to foxhole? Crouching behind a tank?" Memories assailed him. Knots of fear crept back as the clamor of battle raged in his mind. Sights and sounds he longed to forget clung like leeches sucking the life out of him. He stood and gasped for air.

Nancy jumped up and threw her arms around him. "Eric, I'm sorry." She held him tight. "It's okay. It's over. You're safe."

Slowly his breathing returned to normal.

"Maybe you should sit down." Nancy gestured toward the swing.

He shook his head. "Think I'll take a walk."

"Eric, please forgive me. What I said was thoughtless."

"Forget it. My memories are just the winds of war blowing through my mind. Someday, I'll learn how to weather them."

"Or how to escape them?" She paused, letting the thought sink in. "Maybe that's why you're restless and feel the need to leave. But we're family, Eric. Let us try to help you. Think about it." She hugged him, said good night, and left.

Eric walked the dirt road leading to the main highway. Why did he feel so much turmoil, when everything around him exhibited peacefulness?

The moon glowed like a heavenly searchlight. It wove among the trees, pointing out gray patches of stubborn snow that clung as tenaciously to the land as Eric's memories did to his mind. Spring had come early to the high country, but new snow could still fall and cover the old, masking its ugliness. Summer would eradicate it altogether. But how can you hide memories? How can you erase them?

Every time he thought about the war, he felt buried beneath an avalanche. How could he escape these claustrophobic feelings? He was riding to California in hopes of learning how to surf, but he sensed he was also searching for something. What? His lost youth?

Happiness? Love? Or a place he could really call home? Would going to California help? Perhaps his search, like Dorothy's of Oz, would end in his own backyard. It didn't matter. Eric only knew for now, he had to get away, to escape being home when Uncle Jim returned.

# CHAPTER 2

On Sunday when his aunt asked him to go to church with them, Eric begged off attending. When he declined the following two Sundays, Aunt Jean said, "You can't avoid the inevitable."

"I know I can't stay away from people. Next Sunday, I promise to attend."

"Because it's Mother's Day?"

"Even if it weren't, I'd go with you."

Her lips drew tight. "I hate seeing you cooped up and moping this morning."

"Mope? It's too nice a day for that. I'm going to take a long walk and enjoy God's creation." When she gave him an "I don't believe you" look, he added, "Aunt Jean, I still need some quiet time to unwind. Okay?"

She nodded. "But no moping."

He held up two right fingers pressed together. "Scout's honor."

"Unwind," he'd told his aunt. The truth was he didn't want to be confined. Surrounded by people on the train and bus had been bad enough, but endurable since he could gaze out a window. Church was a different matter.

Outdoors, Eric strolled the gravel path behind the house to the woods and wended his way to the creek that wove throughout Uncle Jim's property. For a while as he walked along the bank, the nippy morning air invigorated him. After an hour, he grew chilled and retreated to the house.

In the kitchen, he perked coffee and carried a cup to the living room where he tossed logs on glowing fireplace embers. In minutes, flames licked the bark, and he stood in front to enjoy the warmth before settling in an easy chair to read the Sunday *Denver Post.*

Rested and relaxed, he looked up when Aunt Jean and the girls returned from church.

Her face flushed with excitement, his aunt rushed to the radio. "We need to keep this on all day. Talk is that Germany is about to surrender."

The next day, every radio blasted the news: *Germany has surrendered.*

Tuesday, May 8, was declared VE Day, and Aunt Jean lifted her head and hands heavenward. "Praise the Lord. It's over."

"Only in Europe," Nancy reminded her.

Undaunted, his aunt replied, "We're going into town to celebrate. Girls, put on your finest. Eric, dress in your uniform and wear your medals."

He shook his head. "I'd rather celebrate here."

"Then we'll stay home. This calls for Bessie's finest prime rib roast. We'll play games, eat popcorn, toast marshmallows, drink eggnog, and be more festive than we are New Year's Eve. This occasion marks a new chapter in America."

Eric nodded. *Bless you, Aunt Jean. I love all of you. I fought for your freedom, and it means the world to celebrate with you.*

Eric awakened Mother's Day to a depressing, overcast sky. Snow hadn't been predicted, but the dark clouds looked ominous. His gloom deepened while he dressed. He dreaded going to church. How could he stand being on display—people pumping his hand, hugging him, welcoming him home? Only his love for his aunt and his desire to honor her made him submit to the ordeal.

The hand pumping started as soon as they entered the Buena Vista Community Church. Eric put on his best smile and endured. He breathed an inward sigh of relief when he finally slid onto the wooden pew. After the congregation finished singing, the room began to close in on him. In the sanctuary packed with people, he felt as if he were crouched behind a tank, surrounded by his platoon with no place to run. His head rang with the terrifying high-pitched burr of the German MG 42. Eric fought to keep from diving to the floor and rolling under a pew.

Nancy stroked his hand. When he glanced at her, she mouthed, "Okay?"

He nodded and gave her a thanks-for-caring smile.

Eric focused his attention on the pastor who, despite the war news, delivered his usual Mother's Day sermon on the virtuous wife in Proverbs 31. Aunt Jean beamed at the girls and Eric. He gave her a wink. She blushed, but he knew she wasn't offended.

His mind wandered back to his childhood. He thought about his mother. Memories of her remained vague, but those of his brother flowed as warm as the milk from their family cow. He and Erin loved watching their father milk. When they knelt with the kittens for a squirt of the sweet liquid and one of them got sprayed, their squeals of laughter scattered the cats. The barn was their favorite place to play despite the time Eric jumped from the loft into a pile of hay and grazed his thigh on the tines of a pitchfork.

That memory jarred his mind back to the war. The scar left by the wound had given Eric away while he impersonated Erin. His chest constricted, and his breaths came in shallow gasps.

When Nancy stroked his hand again, he didn't dare look at her. Eric focused his eyes on the pastor, forced his mind back to the sermon, and gave a quiet sigh of relief when the service ended.

Outside, he breathed deeply, filling his lungs with cool air. He couldn't get enough.

He knew he couldn't stand being indoors. Once home, he changed into Levis and a maroon flannel shirt. When he tugged on his new boots, guilt assailed him. Would he feel this way every time he pulled them on? Deserting people, whose only crime was caring, was a lousy thing to do. How could he break the news, make them understand, especially Aunt Jean?

Before he went downstairs, Eric tapped on his aunt's door and told her he was going to take a walk. Outside, he felt the release he needed from being cooped up. He strolled through the woods, wondering if Nancy would tell her mother he planned to leave. Instinct told him she wouldn't. Even if he asked her to do it, she would probably say, "Do your own dirty work."

Eric knew he had to tell Aunt Jean, soon.

Monday night after dinner, Nancy and Ann left to attend choir practice. While Eric wiped dishes as Cindy washed, he pondered how to tell Aunt Jeans his plans, but Cindy worked so fast it made it hard to think. He knew she was rushing to get done so she wouldn't miss a second of her favorite radio program—*Lux Radio Theater.* She finished, did a quick clean up, and dashed into the living room.

Aunt Jean entered as he stored the last pan in the lower cabinet. When he straightened, she smiled and grabbed a cookbook from the counter. "There's a new recipe in here I want to try." His aunt slid onto a chair at the table, started thumbing through the book, and frowned. "I knew I should have marked the place."

"I'm sure you'll find it," he said but thought, *Now's my chance.* He poured a cup of coffee, drew in a fortifying breath, and sat opposite her.

She glanced up. "You two sure finished in a hurry."

"You know Cindy. She can be a whiz at washing when she wants to be."

"I hope she made sure the dishes came clean."

Eric laughed to cover his discomfort. "I thought that was the wiper's job."

Aunt Jean closed the book, cradled her hands on top, and regarded him thoughtfully. "I think I did tell you that once, but your mind wasn't on wiping dishes tonight, was it? I've sensed all day, there's something you want to tell me."

Eric shook his head. "I never could pull a sheepskin over your eyes." With his finger, he traced the tablecloth's blue and white checkered squares while he mustered his courage. He lifted his head. Seeing her careworn face almost dissuaded him. "Aunt Jean, I know I haven't been home long but"—he ran his tongue over his dry lips—"I need to get away. I've decided to leave Friday and ride my motorcycle to California."

Eyes wide, she stared at him. "California? Why?"

"I'm restless." He waved his hand toward the mountains. "I feel somewhere out there, I'll find the answers to put my life back together."

His aunt twisted her hands. "If only Jim were here."

"This isn't something he can help me with, Aunt Jean."

"Please don't go. What if you have an accident?"

Eric reached across the table and laid his hand over hers. "God spared my life while I was overseas. He'll take care of me now."

"Yes, He spared your life, but the scars you carry are deeper inside than out. Please stay. Let us help you."

He shook his head. "I need to be alone."

She gazed at him as if she disbelieved what she was hearing. "Have we done something wrong?"

Her words wrenched his heart. "No. All of you have been terrific. No guy could feel more loved. It's . . . it's just that I feel confined. Maybe being imprisoned has something to do with it." He took a deep breath. "I just don't know."

Her brow creased. "Are you planning to return to Germany?"

Eric mulled over the question, wondering if he should go back. There was no sense in returning to Cologne until he could find himself here. He shook his head. "I doubt it. Three years ago, my life was one neat package. War has ripped it apart, and I've got to put the pieces back."

"Eric, please don't rush into this. Give yourself more time to adjust. Besides, you've only been out of the hospital three weeks. You shouldn't be riding a motorcycle that far."

"I was in the hospital mainly to recover from my imprisonment not the bullet I took in the stomach in October. Yes, the doctor told me to watch my diet but gave no other restrictions. I've ridden into Buena Vista every day and had no problems. I no longer need pain medication. I'll be fine, Aunt Jean."

"Please, Eric, don't leave. Let us help you."

Unable to get his point across, he blurted, "I need time alone. Please try to understand." More gently, he added, "You're the only family I have here. You've helped a lot, and I'll miss you. But I've got to be alone."

The light of understanding finally shone from her eyes. "What can I do to help?"

Relief washed over him. "Thanks, Aunt Jean. There's lots of stuff I need to get. I want to camp out if the weather holds."

"You're going to need a warm sleeping bag. I'm sure Ann will lend you hers. What about food?"

"I'll pick up items as I need them."

"Well, I think you need to plan better than that. Leave the food to me."

"Great!"

"You're going to have your hands full getting your motorcycle ready. It still sounds like a threshing machine."

Her about-face change overwhelmed him. "Aunt Jean, I love you. I can't tell you what it means to have your support."

Choked, she said, "I pray your search proves fruitful, Eric, that you'll find all you're seeking."

The next morning, Eric rose early so he could work on his Harley. Ann was already up, waiting for her mare to foal. While she and Eric ate breakfast, he mulled over how to share his plans with her. "I already mentioned my idea to Aunt Jean and Nancy so I'd better tell you before they do. Otherwise, when you find out, you'll probably bop me on the head."

She eyed him with curiosity.

He pursed his lips while he searched for the right words and saw her green eyes cast a warning glare.

"Eric, don't you dare clam up now."

He laughed. "I love it when you start to get angry." In seriousness, he added, "You can't possibly know how much I've missed being able to tease you."

Her gaze softened. "Can't possibly know? While you were gone, I longed to have you here doing just that." She sat back and studied him. "So what are your plans?"

"I intend to ride my motorcycle and camp my way to California then tour the coast."

"That sounds terrific. I've always wanted to see California, sun-bathe on a beach, go to Hollywood, and maybe catch a glimpse of a movie star."

"Want to come?"

"You know that's safe to ask. There's no way I'd get on a motor-cycle. If you decide to take Dad's truck, that's a different story."

They laughed and walked outdoors together. Eric watched her until she reached the barn. After she entered, he knelt in the dirt driveway to work on his motorcycle. At least his Harley was tangible, not elusive like his feelings. For a moment, he stopped and stared at the house, wondering how he could have changed so much.

A few hours later, Cindy rushed out the back door and plopped down near him, hugging her knees. "Where ya goin'? Can I come?"

Eric felt a tug at his heart. He loved his cousin who tagged along whenever she could. "Not this time. I'm going to be gone all summer."

She looked stunned as tears brimmed. "You just got home."

He cupped her chin in his hand. "Hey, big girl, don't cry. I'll be back before winter."

"Why are you going?"

"I've always wanted to see the Pacific Ocean. Between here and the coast are parks I want to camp in, lakes and rivers I want to fish. I'll come back. I promise." He crossed his heart. "We'll go someplace special."

"Lakeside?"

She looked as if she were holding her breath. Cindy had only been to the amusement park in Denver twice. For him to take her meant returning before Labor Day, thus throwing away his no-time-schedule plans, but he didn't have the heart to say no. She was too special. He grinned. "Sure. I already promised earlier to take you there."

Cindy threw her arms around him. "Thank you." She jumped up and raced toward the barn.

*I bet she's eager to tell Ann the good news.*

Satisfied he had appeased all four women, Eric turned his thoughts toward California with a clear conscience. He hoped the warm weather would hold. He didn't mind camping in frigid temperatures, but cold rain or snow could make sleeping out miserable.

Around noon, Ann strode from the barn. Cindy skipped, her face flushed with excitement. "Lulu's ready to have her baby," she announced when they reached him.

"Her foal," Ann corrected.

Cindy frowned. "It's still her baby," she said in defiance, dashed up the back steps, flung open the screen door, and let it bang behind her.

Ann stood with her hands on her hips. "Kids," she said with disgust, "you'd think they'd want to know the correct terms."

"She's only ten, so to her, it's a baby not a foal. Does it matter?"

"You always did take her side. And now you're taking her to Lakeside?"

Knowing Ann loved the amusement park, he said, "Do I detect sour grapes? I think you're jealous. Want to come?"

"So I can play nursemaid?"

"No, I was thinking more along the line of a double date." Interest sparked her eyes when he added, "There's no way Aunt Jean would allow you to go all the way to Denver on a date without a chaperone and—"

"You're asking Steve and me to go with you?"

"Yes."

Her mouth dropped open, and she lowered her eyes as if feeling sheepish. "You always could see right through me, but you used to egg me on and torment me until I wanted to scream." Tears brimmed. "You've changed. War was horrible for you, wasn't it?"

"Weren't you supposed to be calling the vet?"

"It never dawned on me until now what you've been through. I was so happy to have you home I could only talk about the things going on in my life, everything important to me. I never gave you a thought. Forgive me."

"There's nothing to forgive. I welcomed your bubbling enthusiasm. I desperately needed normalcy. Ann, you're the breath of fresh air around here, the promise of summer, and brighter days."

"All these years, I thought you liked Nancy and Cindy better than me."

He shook his head. "I love all of you." He cuffed her lightly on the chin. "I tease you because I enjoy seeing those green eyes flash." He hoped that would end the emotional scene, but Ann threw her arms around him, hugged him, and cried softly.

Touched, he said as matter-of-factly as he could, "You'd better go inside and make sure the vet's coming."

Tears still shimmered as she smiled. "Thank you, Eric. I accept your offer to double date." Wiping her eyes, she walked toward the house.

Eric stared at the closed screen door, amazed at what had passed between them, and at himself for the things he'd said.

Late afternoon, life revolved around the birth of a filly that rose on black wobbly legs and gave a plaintive weak whinny. To Eric, it signified some things were still right with his world.

War had touched them, maybe him the most but as they had made the best of circumstances, so must he. Stronger than ever came the compulsion to ride to California.

He ambled out of the barn, leaving the rest to gawk at the foal. Nancy caught up with him. "Mind if I join you?"

"Not at all. I thought I'd better get back to my Harley. Those repairs won't do themselves."

After a few quiet minutes, she said, "I wish you weren't leaving. Mom's really going to miss you. We all are. Can't you wait until after Dad gets home?"

"That might be all summer. Then it would be too late."

She nodded but looked deep in thought. "I saw Jill in town this morning. She just got home."

He stiffened. "So?"

"She asked about you. I told her you were leaving Friday. She's no longer engaged and would like to see you."

"No longer engaged? Somehow that doesn't surprise me."

"Will you see her?"

He shrugged. "I suppose that's inevitable since we live in the same town."

Nancy's lips drew tight. "You know what I mean. She still loves you."

He snorted. "Loves me? By the time I return, she'll have another fish hooked."

"Eric! It's not like you to be cruel. Can't you forgive and forget?"

"Forgive? Probably. Forget? Never!"

"Why? I know you still love her."

"Love her? No. Whatever love I had, she killed with one neat stroke of a pen."

"But—"

"Drop it, Nancy."

"I was just hoping—"

"That I'd stay?" He shook his head. "I don't want to see Jill, and I don't want to be here when Uncle Jim returns."

She cringed. "Why?"

All of a sudden, he realized why he felt compelled to leave. "I'm not up to confrontations."

"With Dad? Why?" Her words rang loud and clear with disbelief.

Eric didn't know how to explain, but he had to get off his chest what had been eating at him all these years. "I know this is going to sound like I'm ungrateful, but I'm not. I appreciate now more than ever what Uncle Jim did by taking me in but . . . " He bit down on his lip, finding it hard to put his feelings into words. "I don't want him planning the rest of my life. I hated the military school he put me in the fall after I first arrived. Graduating from there and attending Buena Vista High School was like going from jail to freedom. Still, I felt forced by Uncle Jim into doing things I didn't want to do, or things I would have done willingly if he'd only given me a chance to volunteer. I joined the army to escape going to West Point."

Wide-eyed, she stared at him. "I didn't realize." Her brow furrowed. "There's more, isn't there?"

He drew in a deep breath and slowly let it out. "Despite being wounded and sick at heart, I would have willingly volunteered to impersonate Erin if only for the chance to see my family. But Col. James Stone didn't give me a chance . . . didn't even have the decency to ask if I was up to it." Eric clenched his hands as his voice quavered. "I'm grateful, too, for the time I had with Mom and Elizabeth." He bit down on his lip again, trying to get his emotions under control.

"You have to be alone to sort out your feelings, don't you?"

He nodded, thankful she hadn't thrown her arms around him. "It's more than that. I need to find myself. Who am I? Where do I belong? What do I want out of life?"

"Well, riding your motorcycle all the way to California should give you plenty of time to think." She gave him a quick hug. "I hope you find what you're searching for."

# CHAPTER 3

Eric opened his US map and smoothed it across his bedroom desk. For the next two days, he studied different routes, trying to decide which roads to take and what places to see. Every national park and monument beckoned. To keep his promise to Cindy, he'd have to be back before Labor Day. Originally, he'd planned to take his time and tour the entire California coastline. He marked his new course in red. From Buena Vista, he'd head for Salina, Utah, drop south, and go through Las Vegas. He wanted to see Death Valley, perhaps go north to Bishop, and double back to catch Highway 58, which meandered to the coast. From there, he'd decide whether to go south or north.

After dinner Thursday, he spread his map on the table. Aunt Jean and the girls gathered around as he traced the route with his finger. "Well, that's what my little jaunt looks like."

His aunt pursed her lips. "You're going through Las Vegas?"

Eric caught a hint of concern. "That's my plan."

"I don't want you camping near there."

"Why not?"

"That's a wicked place. Camping by yourself you'd be easy prey." She reached on the counter for her purse. "I'll pay for the hotel room."

"That isn't necessary," he said, not accepting the money she offered. "I have plenty."

She folded the bills and stuck them in his shirt pocket. "A little extra money never hurts."

Eric hugged her. "Thanks, Aunt Jean."

During the evening, Cindy wanted to play games, and while Aunt Jean packed his food, Eric and the girls played Monopoly and ate popcorn. Ann chattered away, keeping the conversation cheerful. Around ten, the girls said good night, leaving Eric and Aunt Jean alone. He wanted to get an early start and carried the last of his gear outdoors to stow on his motorcycle.

Aunt Jean followed. "Did you remember to pack your tool box?"

"It's right there." Eric pointed to it under his sleeping bag. He took the small container of food she'd packed and put it in his duffel bag. "What's in here?"

"Just essentials . . . flour, salt, sugar, pancake mix, and oleo for frying your fish. Also, some dried fruit, nuts, and a little venison jerky for times when you want something else."

"Thanks, you're a gem." He put his arms around her. "I love you," he whispered, his voice choked.

"I know." She patted him on the back as if she were soothing a child, but for some reason, he no longer minded. "And I understand," she added.

How could she understand when he didn't? "Thanks for everything," he told her again.

She smiled, but tears glistened. "We're very proud of you. Remember. This will always be your home." She kissed him on the forehead and said good night.

Eric watched her climb the back steps and enter the house. "This will always be your home," she'd said as if he would never return. Was that what she feared? And why was he going, leaving people who loved him, giving up comforts he had longed for while crammed in a foxhole? *Am I putting myself back under the elements just so I can escape confrontations? I must be crazy!*

But a still small voice whispered, "West, West, West."

At five o'clock, Eric's alarm blared. He slapped it off, jumped out of bed, dressed quickly, and hurried downstairs. He entered the kitchen and joined the family, hovering near the wood-burning cook stove. From the oven came the enticing aroma of cinnamon rolls. The tension on the faces around him reminded Eric of the morning he'd caught the train before being shipped out. They'd cried that day.

He prayed they wouldn't cry now. "I can't believe you're all up before me. And breakfast too." He winked at Ann. "Or is that your new perfume I smell?"

Ann laughed. "No, it's sweet rolls. They should be done." Her laughter banished solemnity from the kitchen.

Eric kept his good-byes short. "I'll keep you posted," he said and climbed onto his motorcycle. "See you in August." He waved and sped away, not glancing back for fear they were wiping their eyes. Guilt lingered until he reached the paved road, then a sense of freedom enveloped him. For the first time in his life, he was only accountable to God and himself.

In Buena Vista, he topped off his gas tank and gazed west toward three monumental mountain peaks—Harvard, Princeton, and Yale. When he came to live on the ranch, Aunt Jean pointed out the peaks to him and said, "Those are the names of three famous universities in the United States. How proud your father would be if you were accepted to one of them."

Eric breathed a deep sigh. *She didn't know Uncle Jim was dead set on my attending West Point.* He looked heavenward. "Dad, I hope you're still proud of me."

Memories of his father's death swept over him. He shook them off in the wind as he headed south to Poncho Springs. His sweet roll breakfast, however tasty, hadn't filled him, so he grabbed some scrambled eggs and potatoes at a diner before turning east and taking Highway 50. The sights between Poncho Springs and Grand Junction were almost as familiar to Eric as those around the ranch, but his sense of appreciation for the Colorado Rockies grew as he climbed Monarch Pass and crossed the Continental Divide. He marveled anew at the grandeur around him, snow-capped rugged peaks standing against a cloudless azure sky.

At Delta, east of Grand Junction, he stopped at a market and bought some carrots and two apples before taking the road north to Colorado's Grand Mesa, the world's largest flattop mountain.

That evening, while munching an apple beside a flickering fire, he remembered the week he spent on this mountain with Uncle Jim and the family. His uncle taught him to fish and row a boat.

Eric pondered the crazy stories his uncle told around the campfire. Recalling some made Eric smile. At times, Uncle Jim could make life fun. Eric had to admit he learned a lot from him. His uncle was a top-notch mechanic and taught Eric how to recognize engine problems and make repairs. He taught him how to shoot. By the time Eric was thirteen, he could handle a rifle or revolver with ease and hit the bull's-eye on a target one hundred feet away.

His uncle also gave him hints on how to get along with people—women specifically. After Uncle Jim explained the emotional differences between men and women, he said, "Eric, I want you to remember this when you get married: a woman needs to hear those three little words—I love you."

Eric chuckled. He was only fourteen when his uncle dropped that gem, but afterward, Eric paid attention to how Uncle Jim treated Aunt Jean and her response. He marveled how a man who could be so stern could also be tender.

Eric crawled into his sleeping bag and gazed at the stars. *Was Uncle Jim's sternness his way of shaping me into a man who could take whatever life held? Was giving orders the result of his officer training?* Eric slammed a fist on the ground. *It doesn't matter. He still should have shown some concern before commandeering me to impersonate Erin.*

Eric spent two days in Utah, camping in Bryce Canyon and Zion. The next night, he unrolled his sleeping bag on the south rim of the Grand Canyon. He opted to eat jerky since he wouldn't be in Arizona long enough to get his money's worth from a fishing license. While he chewed pieces of dried venison, he watched the sun set. The canyon blazed with hues of gold, red, and orange. Captivated, Eric walked along the canyon's rim. He wished he had someone with whom he could share this view. A touch of homesickness hit him. He laughed and chided himself, but he couldn't shake the feeling. However short his time had been at the ranch, it was long enough to make him miss his family. And they were his family, more so than those he loved in Germany.

*Why was I so quick to leave? Maybe I should have waited for Uncle Jim and talked things over with him. He fought in two wars. Surely, he could understand my restlessness.* Eric shook his head. He'd bolted just like he had when he joined the army to escape West Point. *Well, right or wrong, I'm too close to California not to continue.*

Eric found comfort sleeping under the stars with the sounds of nature surrounding him. No nightmares. Was there a connection? He gazed heavenward. "Lord, thanks for the good trip. I don't know why I'm restless or what I'm looking for, but please help me find it. And take care of Aunt Jean and the girls, and bring Uncle Jim home soon. They need him."

Eric broke camp the next morning, feeling lighter in spirit. Along the road, he spotted a red and white Burma Shave sign and slowed down. He smiled as he read,

> "WITHIN THIS VALE OF TOIL AND
> SIN, YOUR HEAD GROWS BALD BUT
> NOT YOUR CHIN (BURMA-SHAVE)."

Over the past few days, he'd read these limericks. Most dealt with buying Defense Bonds, and anything reminding him of the war didn't strike him as funny. This sign wasn't particularly witty, but his last good laugh had been long before he shipped out. His laughter erupted now like an awakened volcano. No longer feeling twenty-two bordering on fifty, he let out a whoop and shouted, "Las Vegas, here I come!"

Hours later, he arrived in what his aunt called Sin City. Hotel room prices seemed outrageous. The Y was full, but an attendant recommended a boarding house.

A heavy-set man with thick-rimmed glasses answered the bell.

"I'm looking for a room for the night," Eric told him.

The man snorted. "One night?"

Eric drew himself to his full six-feet. Did he look like a bum because he hadn't shaved? "I just came back from overseas, and I'm camping my way to California."

The man peered at Eric's motorcycle. "And you're passing through to sow a few wild oats." The curl of the man's lip said, "You're like all the rest."

"Do you have a room or not?" Eric snapped.

"Regular hellcat, aren't you? The room's five dollars a day, paid in advance, includes dinner and breakfast. You'll share a bathroom with three others. If you need to wash clothes, there's a laundry tub in the basement. Dinner is at five sharp, breakfast at seven. No drinking. No smoking. Park your Harley in the rear and come and go quietly. Take it or leave it. You can address me as Mr. Larkin."

"I'll take it, Mr. Larkin. My name's Eric Stone."

"After you park your bike in the rear, my wife will let you in the back door."

Mrs. Larkin, standing on the porch watching him, smiled.

Before he secured his bike, Eric asked, "Is this spot okay?"

"Alongside the garage is fine."

His hands full, Eric climbed the porch steps and stopped. "I'm Eric Stone."

"Yes, my husband told me. I'm Mrs. Larkin. Come on in, I'll show you to your room." She held the screen door open.

"Thank you, Mrs. Larkin." She was a tall thin woman, and right away, her welcoming smile put him at ease.

Eric showered and shaved. He retrieved his navy cords and light blue dress shirt from the duffel bag, unrolled them, shook them out, and dressed. His clothes looked rumpled but presentable. In the basement, he washed his soiled shirts, hung them on hangers, and smoothed out the worst wrinkles.

A few minutes before five, he entered the dining room. Mr. Larkin sat at the head of the table, a large, red-checkered napkin draped around his neck. The man caught his gaze. "We're having fried chicken. I hope you're hungry." He snorted. "Seems our other boarders either lost their appetites or their watches. Tomorrow night, we'll have liver!"

Eric suppressed a chuckle. "I happen to like liver," he said, tongue in cheek.

His host gave a raucous laugh. "Well, they don't!"

Mrs. Larkin entered with a heaping platter of fried chicken. She and her husband are as opposite as chicken and liver, Eric mused. Like mouth-watering chicken, she draws people instead of repelling them.

After she set mashed potatoes and peas and tossed salad on the table, she took the seat across from her husband and nodded.

Mr. Larkin bowed his head and recited a quick blessing. From then on, he didn't talk. Just ate.

Mrs. Larkin smiled. "Where are you from, Mr. Stone?"

"Colorado," he said, sinking his teeth into the succulent chicken. When he polished off that piece, she offered him more.

"My husband said you were in the service. What branch?"

He swallowed his food and took a sip of water. "The army." When Mrs. Larkin didn't ask any more questions, he thought, *She must have noticed how hungry I am.* Warm apple pie topped the meal. Eric couldn't believe his good fortune.

That evening, Eric walked the Las Vegas Strip fascinated by the blazing lights that transformed night into day. Every casino beckoned, but he had no desire to play the slot machines. A billboard advertised the Ice Follies. He liked figure skating and thought it would be a decent show, but as soon as the curtain went up, an unsettling feeling came over him. The star performers were terrific, but he couldn't concentrate on their graceful movements. His eyes strayed to the topless background skaters, seeing but not quite believing. Eric stood at the end of the first act and left.

Outside, he took deep breaths, hoping the night air would cool him off. It didn't. He hadn't felt this aroused since his last leave when Jill had pressed him to make love to her. Despite the heat of the moment, he had refrained.

*Brazenly, she'd slipped her hand into his pants' pocket. When he yanked it out, she laughed. "You're afraid," she accused.*

*"We're not married."*

Would making love have changed anything? He walked the three blocks to the boarding house, crawled into bed but couldn't sleep. Loneliness engulfed him. More than ever he realized how lonely he was. He longed for a woman to share his life. *Jill, why Jill? Why did you destroy what we had? If only you had endured our separation a little longer, we would be married, and I wouldn't be sleeping alone and wishing differently.*

The letter she had written was seared in his memory.

Dear John,

I guess that's how I'm supposed to start a letter like this. I put off writing as long as I could. It's not easy to tell the guy I promised to wait for that I just couldn't wait any longer. Someone else has come along, and I accepted his proposal. I gave your ring to Nancy and explained everything. She seems to understand, but I can't really expect you to. Please try to find it in your heart to forgive me. Jill.

Eric clenched his hands. The words still hurt. He'd told Nancy that Jill had destroyed his love with one neat stroke of a pen. Was his love so easy to kill? *Jill, why couldn't you have waited? You're right. I don't understand. I can't forgive. And I'll never forget. Maybe when I get back things will look different. Right now I'm too angry.*

Eric tossed and turned before dropping into a troubled sleep. Two hours later, he awakened from a nightmare still picturing Jill. She stood laughing on the banks of the Rhine as the bridge blew out from under him.

Had he screamed aloud? Eric rose, packed, and wrote a thank-you note to Mr. and Mrs. Larkin. He tiptoed down the hallway to the basement door but hurried downstairs to retrieve his clothes. When he came back up, Mrs. Larkin stood at the head of the steps bundled in a blue robe. "I couldn't sleep," Eric explained, "so I thought I might as well get an early start."

She looked at her watch. "It's not even three thirty." Her face showed motherly concern. "Are you all right? I heard your cry."

"A nightmare."

"The war?"

He nodded. "But I don't want to talk about it."

"I understand. Come with me to the kitchen. I'll pack some fried chicken for you."

"Thanks, but I'm not hungry."

"You will be in an hour, and no place will be open between here and Death Valley."

She was right. The first two towns Eric roared through lay as quiet as ghost towns. The third had an all-night gas station. Eric filled the tank and drove to a small park to eat before proceeding to Death Valley.

At the entrance, he picked up a brochure and rode around neither seeing nor caring. Tired and depressed, he felt as if he had plunged from Death Valley's highest point to the lowest. He needed sleep, but not here. Eric would have liked to camp in Kings Canyon, Sequoia National Park, but he couldn't enter from the east because of the Sierra Nevada Mountain Range. He left Death Valley and headed for Owens Lake.

Beyond the blue water rose Mt. Whitney. The closer Eric came, the more this majestic scene revived him. Unlike Death Valley, this was beauty he could appreciate. No longer sleepy, he decided to follow the Sierra Nevada's north. He liked what he saw. Bishop lay nestled in the valley between California's two highest mountain ranges. Eric bought supplies and a fishing license before setting up camp at Sabrina Lake.

Carrying a fishing pole, he followed a trail around the lake, enjoying the serenity, while he hiked through the woodsy area until he found a good spot to fish. Before sundown, he caught two fair-sized trout, cleaned them, and hiked back to camp. After he cooked and devoured the fish, he wished he'd caught more.

That night, scrunched in his sleeping bag, he promised himself to come back to this area and backpack into the High Sierras. Eric promptly fell into a deep sleep. He never saw the clouds obliterate the stars, never heard the roll of distant thunder. A weatherproof tarp kept the dew off his bike and supplies, but no tent protected him. The first two cracks of thunder and lightning flashes came like a distant battle. He had learned to sleep with noise. The louder the crashes, the closer the battle raged. In a dream, he saw the formidable West Wall fortifications surrounding Aachen, deep belts of elaborately interconnected pillboxes and bunkers.

*One of the pillboxes, supposedly knocked out, sprang to life. Eric's platoon rushed the enemy. The air soon reverberated with the agonizing cries of his wounded comrades. Eric and a handful of men crawled to the pillbox on its blind side. The captain yelled, "Come out and surrender!"*

*"Go to hell!" a muffled voice called in English.*

*The captain nodded to the engineer corporal who carried the satchel of tetryl charges. "Now, Corporal."*

*Eric and the others covered him with fire when he stood and threw the high explosive through the nearest aperture. For a moment, nothing happened. Then violet flames shot out of the opening followed by acrid yellow smoke. The pillbox heaved. Concrete fell from one side, revealing the bloodied mangled body of a blond-haired soldier.*

"No!" Eric screamed as he sat up and wept. Torrents of rain deluged him, matching his tears. He cried out in anguish, "Why, God? He was my brother!"

# CHAPTER 4

Icy rain pelted Eric's face. Shivering in damp clothes, he crawled out of his soaked sleeping bag and rolled it into a tight wad. He needed a place to change and longed for a cup of hot coffee—two impossibilities at the moment. Maybe he could find a diner open in Bishop. He retrieved his dry jacket from under the bike tarp, slipped it on, and secured the tarp around the rest of his gear. "Welcome to sunny California," he mumbled and climbed onto his motorcycle.

Rain lashed him all the way to Bishop where the blazing lights of a diner beckoned like a beacon to a floundering ship. Eric parked as close as he could, grabbed his duffel bag, and dashed inside. Despite the room's overwhelming warmth, he shivered while he walked toward the back booth.

A young dark-haired waitress called, "Coffee?"

"Please." He slid onto a worn leather seat and glanced at the clock. *It's only four? Nothing like getting another early start.*

The waitress approached, her trim hips swinging gracefully. Her smile revealed perfect white teeth. Her eyes said, "You're a special customer." He was the only one, but instinct told him she would give that same winning smile, even if she were harried. She set a steaming mug of coffee on the table. "That's hot," she warned when he picked it up.

"And just what I need." He took two sips. "I thought this was supposed to be the land of sunshine. The stars were twinkling last night when I crawled into my sleeping bag."

She smiled and took an order book from her pocket. "I take it you weren't in a tent."

41

"Right." He studied the menu a moment. "Could you have the cook rustle me up some ham and eggs while I get out of these wet duds?"

"Sure. How would you like your eggs?"

"Over easy."

Eric carried his duffel bag into the men's room and changed. He rolled his soaked clothes in a towel, stuffed the bundle into his bag, and returned to the booth.

The waitress brought his breakfast. "Where are you from?"

"Colorado."

"Did you just get back from overseas?"

"You psychic?"

"No, the duffel bag. And my fiancé recently returned with the same haunted look in his eyes. He said the war was rough."

Eric's lips compressed as he nodded. She gave him a sympathetic smile before she left. He started to eat but set the fork down and stared into space. *Rough? That's putting it mildly.*

Eric found letting out his grief on the mountain enabled him to reflect with less emotional turmoil. The news that the dead German in the pillbox was his twin brother had spread fast throughout his platoon, raising suspicion, followed by questions. Eric's answers evoked sympathy, but war doesn't take time out for grief. D-Day had taught Eric that. He'd lost buddies he'd known better than his brother, but burying Erin left him feeling half-alive. He realized that was when he'd lost his edge. If he'd been alert during the building search at Aachen, the young German soldier would not have had the chance to pull the trigger. *When I did react, I only wounded him. If his gun hadn't jammed, I'd be dead.* What happened next remained a blur. He vaguely recalled two American soldiers entering. *Did the Nazi kid shoot one of them before they killed him?* Trying to remember, Eric closed his eyes. Blood filled his vision.

"Are you all right?" the young waitress asked.

Startled, he looked up. "I'm fine. Just tired."

"You've hardly touched your food."

He shrugged. "Guess it's too early to eat."

She slipped into the seat across from him. "Do you mind?"

"Not at all, but won't you get in trouble?"

She shook her head. "I always take a break before the morning rush."

A gray-haired man ambled from the kitchen carrying a plate of food and a cup of coffee. He set them in front of her, his face non-committal. After he left, she said, "That's my father. He owns this restaurant."

Eric raised an eyebrow. "He's used to you doing this?"

"No, but he's used to me befriending stray cats and dogs."

"And I'm today's bedraggled tomcat?"

"Well, you must admit you did look drenched and dreary when you came in."

Eric chuckled and picked up his fork. "Thank you. You've brightened my day." He started eating. Even though his food was no longer hot, he relished each bite. "Were you engaged before your boyfriend shipped out?"

She nodded. "We talked about marriage but decided to wait . . . let time and separation test our love. We're getting married in June."

"Congratulations."

"What brings you to California?"

"I want to learn how to surf. Should I go north or south when I come to highway 101?

"I don't know much about surfing, but I do know you'd have better luck the farther south you go. The water will still be cold but not frigid."

By the time he left, the rain stopped, and the clouds broke to reveal faint stars on the lightening horizon. The waitress had also suggested he should camp at Lake Isabella near Bakersfield. "I think you'll find plenty of sunshine there."

Her prediction proved true. The sun dried his clothes and sleeping bag while he hiked and fished. Exhausted, he turned in early.

Friday morning, he rode into Bakersfield and decided to get a room at the Y and tour the town. That evening, he took in a movie, *Abbott and Costello in Hollywood.*

Eric awakened early the next morning. He chowed down a huge breakfast before taking off on his motorcycle. "Pacific Ocean, here I come." He whooped and sped toward the coast. Following the wait-ress's suggestion, he turned south at the 101.

Around eleven, he rolled into the town of San Luis Obispo. Yells coming from the high school stadium drew his attention to a baseball game. The sounds stirred pleasant memories. He parked near the Arroyo Grande school bus. The town lay only a few miles from Pismo Beach. For a while, Eric stood behind the chain link fence to watch the game and decided to sit for the last two innings. He slid onto a bleacher on the visitors' side and rooted for Arroyo Grande.

Four cute girls in blue skirts and gold sweaters stood in front of the fans. Three shook crepe-paper pompons and led the crowd in cheers. Eric watched the fourth, a petite young lady with long red-dish-brown hair. Her vivaciousness while tumbling and cart wheeling reminded him of Ann. Eric sat spellbound. She never faltered, never missed a beat. When she finished her routine, the crowd clapped, whistled, and roared their approval. Eric caught her eye and winked. When she smiled in response, his heart quickened. Why?

In the ninth inning, Arroyo Grande broke the tie and won five to four. The jubilant players lifted the girls to their shoulders and paraded them in front of the bleachers. Eric cheered as he raised his hands and clapped when the redhead passed in front of him. "Great job," he yelled.

She flashed him another heartwarming smile.

Eric resisted yelling, "Will you be my pin-up girl?"

After the crowd dispersed, Eric ambled back to his motorcy-cle and rode to a small restaurant he'd seen on the way into town. Thoughts of the girl tumbled through his mind while he ate. He polished off his hamburger and glanced out the window. When the Arroyo Grande school bus passed, his heart pounded. He scrambled to his feet, paid the cashier, and dashed out the door. Why did it seem so all-fire-important to catch up with the bus? What would he do if he saw the redhead again? He'd met plenty of pretty girls. Why should this one seem special?

The bus had reached the main highway before Eric caught up and drew close enough to give a thumbs-up to the students watching him from the rear window. They returned the sign and mouthed, "We're number one."

He pulled alongside to pass, and the young people waved. As if he were still in high school, his carefree spirit returned. He continued to ride beside the bus, dropping back whenever a car came in sight. The students encouraged him by waving and laughing.

Caught behind the bus when it started climbing a steep grade, gagging exhaust fumes made him cough. Eric dropped back. After he found it safe to pass, he sped up and roared ahead. Maybe he'd get the chance to see the redhead on the beach. Glancing back, he waved once more before rounding a sharp curve.

An oncoming car crossed over the double yellow line and headed straight for him. Eric gasped, swerved, and lost control. When his cycle skidded on loose gravel, toppling him, he cried out in pain as his right leg slammed the ground, twisting his ankle. For a moment, he lay too stunned to move. The squeal of brakes and the grinding crunch of metal against metal jarred his senses. Fear raced up his spine. *The bus!* The curve blocked his view, but the air reverberated with screams. He pictured the acrobatic young lady bleeding. *No!*

Eric gritted his teeth while he struggled to stand. His ankle throbbed as if a thousand wasps had stung him. Shaken and unsteady, he hobbled toward the unseen wreckage, not wanting to see but driven by the thought that someone might need help. *God, please don't let that girl be hurt. Let everyone be okay.*

The hysterical screams grew louder. He rounded the curve and gasped. The car must have rammed the bus, sending it out of control. Both had slammed into the hillside. Students scrambled out the back emergency exit. Eric glanced in the car and immediately shut his eyes. Bile rose in his throat. The dead or unconscious driver, trapped amid twisted metal, looked mangled beyond help. *God, please don't let him suffer.*

Heartsick he couldn't help, he limped to the back of the bus. A tall, dark-haired youth was trying to bring order out of chaos. "How bad?" Eric asked.

"Glass shattered everywhere. A lot of the kids are hurt, especially those coming out now." They helped a student gripping his arm, trying to stem the flow of blood. "Roger, how many are still in there?" the tall young man asked.

The injured boy said, "Half a dozen, Jeff."

"You don't look too swift," Jeff said. He glanced at Eric. "Can you help him?"

"Sure."

While Eric assisted the boy to a grassy area, he scanned the other students. Some stood in shock, while others sat on the ground in a daze. Some nursed wounds. He spotted the petite tumbler kneeling and holding a white cloth against a girl's bloody head. *Thank God she's not hurt.* He helped the injured boy lie down. The youth's hand was clammy.

"I need something to prop his feet and keep him warm," Eric shouted. A student tossed him a jacket. Others coming out of their daze asked how they could help.

Eric gave instructions while he hobbled among their schoolmates, checking the injured.

"What about your leg?" a girl asked. "You're hurt."

"I'm okay," he said, but when he followed her gaze, he saw blood oozing from his ripped pants below his knee.

Jeff carried a sobbing girl who had a piece of glass protruding from a gash on her leg. "She's the last," he said and set her down near Eric. "I hope help arrives soon."

Eric drew in a breath and knelt beside her.

The girl reached for the glass. "Get that out," she screamed.

Eric intercepted her hand and shook his head. "I know it hurts, but you'll bleed more if we remove it."

Cars skidded to a stop. Why had it taken so long for people to come? It seemed as if hours had passed, but a glance at his watch showed only minutes.

Two men ran to the students nearest the road. Eric saw a girl point to him and Jeff, and the men dashed over. "We were told you two are in charge. How can we help?" one asked.

"Jeff!" a girl screamed.

Jeff looked toward the cry, turned white, and ran. Eric saw the auburn-haired girl beckoning, her face frantic.

"Take over," Eric told the men. "Don't let her touch the glass," he added and stood when one of them took his place. Ignoring his pain, he hobbled after Jeff.

"Mary!" Jeff cried and reached down to shake the shoulder of a girl with black hair. She didn't respond. Her pale face resembled a porcelain doll, and blood seeped through the cloth held against her forehead.

Tears streamed down the cheeks of the once vivacious tumbler. "Mary was talking to me," she sobbed. "Then she passed out."

Eric said, "Quick! Prop her legs with your jacket. She may be going into shock." He leaned down and held the cloth on Mary's head while the redhead peeled off her jacket. After she wadded it under Mary's legs, she took the compress back.

Mary's stillness unnerved Eric, but when he took her pulse, he found it steady.

Jeff, staring at the blood on Mary's face, stood frozen, his face tinged with green. Eric pointed toward some shrubs and whispered, "Over there."

Jeff dashed for the bushes.

The auburn-haired girl, too intent on helping Mary, didn't notice. Quiet sobs shook her, and Eric's heart melted. After he dropped to his knees, he winced and had to wait a moment for the pain to subside before he said, "Let me hold the compress awhile."

She nodded and sat back on her heels.

"What's your name?" he asked.

"Kathy," she sobbed.

"I'm Eric Stone." How could he comfort her? He knew the agony, the fear, the helpless feeling of not knowing how badly a friend is hurt. He wiped his left hand on his trousers and cupped Kathy's chin. "Mary's pulse is strong." He checked the bleeding, which had almost stopped. "She'll need some stitches to close this gash, but I think she'll be fine."

Kathy searched his face as if she were seeing him for the first time and gave a faint smile.

He winked. "That's better." *You've got the cutest upturned nose I've ever seen. I wish I could make you laugh, make your green eyes dance. Now is not the time to try.*

Her eyes widened as she stared past him toward the road and beckoned. "Dad, over here."

Eric turned to look. A distinguished brown-haired man carrying a doctor's satchel hurried toward them as ambulances and police cars arrived. A wave of relief washed over Eric.

Rushing to Kathy, her father asked, "Are you hurt?"

"No, but Mary is." She pointed to Eric. "This is Eric Stone. He's been helping."

Sharp jabs of pain tore through Eric's right ankle. He gritted his teeth and, with his last reserve of adrenaline, stood.

Kathy's father shook Eric's hand. "Thank you, Mr. Stone. I'll look at your leg next."

"I'm okay. These kids need help first."

The doctor dropped beside Mary and examined her. Eric looked for a place to sit. The back bumper on the bus seemed the only spot. He started to leave.

Kathy touched his arm. "Thank you, Eric."

He nodded and flashed the best smile he could muster before limping across the grassy area. A wave of nausea came over him. He fought it back. Eric saw Jeff running to catch up with him. *Don't spill your guts here*, he ordered himself.

"Captain Dole, our police chief, wants to talk with you," Jeff said.

Eric pointed to the back of the bus. "I'll be over there." He didn't dare open his mouth to say more.

Jeff nodded and left.

Despite the pain, Eric quickened his steps, crossed the road, but didn't stop at the emergency exit. He hobbled around the side, threw up, cursing his own weakness. Close to collapsing, he grabbed the side of the bus for support.

A strong arm went around his waist. "I'm Captain Dole. Let me help you." The captain walked him to the bumper where Eric sat down. "Do you feel up to talking?"

"Can you wait a few minutes?" he asked, retrieving a pack of peppermint gum from his pocket.

"Sure. I'll give you a chance to recuperate."

Eric leaned his head against the doorjamb. His leg burned from ankle to thigh, but he was too exhausted to bend down and look at his injury.

It seemed only seconds before Captain Dole returned. He smiled a good-natured smile that went well with his portly frame, round face, and thick gray hair. "Better?" he asked.

Eric nodded.

The captain's hazel eyes turned serious, inquisitive. "Jeff said you were on the motorcycle, fooling around."

Eric remembered seeing Jeff's face glaring at him through the window. "I wasn't being reckless."

"I'm not accusing you of causing the accident. I just wondered if you could shed some light on why the driver of the car lost control."

"I'd already passed the bus when the car rounded the curve, crossed over the double yellow line, and forced me off the road." After Eric briefly explained, he saw Kathy's father approaching.

Captain Dole smiled. "Dr. Ryan, this is Mr. Stone."

The doctor nodded. "We met earlier. He helped Mary Watkins."

"Everyone I've talked with has mentioned your helping," the captain told Eric. "You really got around. How did you manage on that leg?"

Eric shrugged. "Adrenaline, I guess." He wondered how Captain Dole knew his name. Had he seen it on the duffel bag?

"Your injury is why I'm here," the doctor said. He knelt and cut open Eric's torn pant leg. When Eric winced as the blood-stiffened material pulled from the wound, Dr. Ryan said, "Sorry." From a gash below Eric's knee, fresh rivulets of blood streamed down his leg and into his boot. "How long have you been bleeding? Have you lost a lot of blood?"

Eric gave a feeble laugh. "I don't think I've lost any. It's all in my boot."

The two older men exchanged concerned glances before the doctor cleansed the wound and taped on a compress. "Now let's see if I can slip off your boot so I can check your ankle."

Eric gasped.

Dr. Ryan stopped. His lips drew tight. "I'd better wait until we get you to the hospital. You can ride with Kathy and me." He pointed to a blue Lincoln-Zephyr sedan. "Meet us over there in about ten minutes," he said and hurried back to Kathy.

"Mr. Stone," the captain asked, "where will you be staying so I can get in touch with you?"

"Beats me. With my motorcycle out of commission, I'm in a bind. I'd planned on camping on the beach."

Captain Dole's thumb and forefinger rested thoughtfully against his chin. "There's room and board at my place if you're interested. My wife and I rent our spare room."

"That would be great. Thank you."

"Good. I'll call my wife and let her know. Your gear is in my patrol car. Would you like your duffel bag now, or should I take it to the house?"

Eric couldn't believe how nice the captain acted. "I really don't need anything except a clean shirt. This one's a mess, but—"

"Say no more. One of my men can retrieve a shirt and lay it on the hood of Dr. Ryan's car. Okay?"

"That would be great. Thanks.".

He waited a few minutes before he stood and hobbled to the side of the bus. When he saw Kathy and her father head for the car, he limped toward it. By the time he crossed the road, Kathy had climbed into the front seat. Eric picked up his shirt and ran his hand over the car's front fender. "She's a beauty."

Dr. Ryan said, "Last model off the assembly line before the war shut the factory."

Kathy leaned out the front window and smiled.

"Kathy," Dr. Ryan said, "Mr. Stone is going to ride to the hospital with us."

"Please call me Eric," he said, reaching into the shirt pocket for another piece of gum, hoping it masked his breath. He jammed the wrapper in his pocket.

Kathy watched while he changed. Eric was glad his T-shirt covered his scars

Dr. Ryan held out his hand. "I can put that in the trunk."

"Thanks." Eric rolled the material bloody side in before he gave it to him.

"Ready?" Kathy asked and scooted over to make room for him.

Eric sat and drew in his uninjured leg, but his right leg dangled outside like a dead weight. He had to put both hands under his thigh to lift and pull it in.

Kathy didn't seem to notice. "Welcome aboard."

"How's Mary?"

"Daddy says she'll be fine." She flashed a smile that sent his pulse racing. "Thanks to you,"

Eric found himself wanting to be her personal knight, one willing to fight a fire-breathing dragon to save her.

After her father drove a few miles down the highway, Kathy cast Eric a mischievous smile, laid her head against his shoulder, and closed her eyes. Despite her flirting, Eric sensed she was still Daddy's little girl. He met Dr. Ryan's gaze and said, "She must be exhausted."

Kathy's father nodded, but his compressed lips and furrowed brow suggested he disapproved of her being so forward.

Eric hadn't had a girl this close since Jill. Words from her *Dear John* letter made him clench his hands.

Excitement surged through Kathy, set off by the gentle, soft-spoken man sitting next to her whose flannel shirt smelled of wood smoke. She gave a quiet sigh and kept her eyes closed. She knew she would blush if she opened them, and he looked at her. Kathy pictured Eric. His athletic build equaled Jeff's, but Eric was somewhat taller and very slim. He had the deepest blue eyes she'd ever seen. When he'd lifted her chin to tell her Mary was all right, his gaze had kept her mesmerized.

Dr. Ryan saw Eric clench his hands. What had caused his mood to change? He could have sworn the young man had been enjoying Kathy's flirting. Now his lips were drawn as tightly as his fists. He glanced at Kathy. Was she really asleep?

# CHAPTER 5

Eric rested his head against the car seat and closed his eyes until a slight bump made him open them.

Kathy said, "We're in Arroyo Grande. That's the hospital up ahead."

"Already? I fell asleep? I got up early this morning, but I didn't think I was that tired."

Dr. Ryan parked in the yellow zone in front of a gray brick building. "You two sit tight. I'll be right back." He returned with a couple of nurses pushing wheelchairs.

*Good grief. Wheelchairs?* "I can walk," Eric said, but after Dr. Ryan helped him to his feet, Eric winced and accepted the chair.

"I'll see you inside," Kathy's father said, hurrying toward the entrance.

While the nurses pushed Eric and Kathy side by side, she grinned and quipped, "Me thinkest thou protesteth too much."

"But you didn't object."

"Why should I? It gives us a chance to talk. Besides, I know my father when it comes to hospital policy. You would have found yourself riding whether you wanted to or not."

"Your father's okay. I like him."

"I'm glad." She gave him an I-think-you're-terrific smile.

He liked this outgoing girl who was definitely flirting. *I think I'll stick around Arroyo Grande and get to know Kathy better.*

The nurses parted, wheeling the chairs to different rooms.

"Bye," Kathy said. "See you later."

Eric nodded, unable to come up with a witty reply. He felt as tongue-tied as the horse-head hitching post in his grandmother's front yard. Why had that old relic come to mind? He wondered as the nurse left the room. He visualized being four when their father took the family to America to meet his parents in Colorado. Eric remembered his and Erin's delight in crossing the ocean and watching dolphins playing in the waves. But in Colorado, it was the ranch's hitching post symbolizing bygone days that captivated them—an iron post topped with a brass-ringed horse's head. They played for hours, taking turns clinging to the heavy ring, bracing their feet against the post and pushing back and forth. Later, after they listened on the radio to the *Lone Ranger*, they pretended to be Silver and Scout waiting for their masters to mount them so they could chase the bad guys. Eric shook his head and chuckled. *So long ago.*

Dr. Ryan entered, his hazel eyes gleaming with curiosity. "What are you thinking about?"

Eric laughed. "Just a childhood memory." But he was glad he could remember Erin with laughter.

The doctor remained silent as if waiting for Eric to elaborate. When he didn't, Dr. Ryan said, "It must have been a good one."

"Silly but good."

"Then you're feeling better?"

Was Dr. Ryan referring to pain, or had he sensed Eric's dark mood in the car? "Much better," he said. The answer applied to both. Eric vowed to forget Jill and try to push Erin's death aside. He would dwell on pleasant memories and strive to recapture his youth. Laugh. Joke. Tease. Have fun. Maybe even court a girl.

"I hate to spoil your good mood, but that boot has to come off."

Eric nodded and drew in a sharp breath when the doctor tugged. He gritted his teeth in preparation for the worst but gasped despite his resolve to withstand the pain.

The doctor stopped. "Your foot has swelled so much I'm going to have to slit that leather so I can remove your boot."

"They're new . . . a birthday present from my aunt and cousins. They sacrificed a lot to get these for me. Isn't there another way?"

"Afraid not."

*So much for a terrific birthday gift.*

After Dr. Ryan removed Eric's bloody boot and sock, he cleansed his foot before examining it. "Looks like a pretty bad sprain. I'll tape it after I stitch the gash below your knee." The doctor removed the compress and washed the area. "Do you want me to numb this area before stitching?"

Eric shook his head. "I'm fine."

When Kathy's father finished stitching and taping, he said, "I want you to lie still while I check on Kathy. Afterward, I'll drive you to Capt. Dole's."

"Is Kathy okay?"

"I'm sure she is, but I wanted my partner, Dr. Randolf, to examine her anyway."

Eric ached everywhere. He stared at the ceiling and thought about all that had happened. Aunt Jean would clasp her hands to her breast in horror if she knew how close he'd come to getting killed. He'd better not tell her.

His plight didn't seem all that bad, now that he had a place to stay. He pictured Kathy. She was a tantalizing mixture of girl and woman. From the first moment, something drew him to her. At the accident, he longed to erase her anguish. *Kathy, if I'm around and see you miserable again, I'll do everything in my power to make you smile.*

Eric's mind leaped to a different matter—money. How was he going to pay his medical bills plus his room and board at the Dole's? His service pay had accumulated in the bank. Did he have enough left after all he'd spent on gifts, clothes, and repairing his Harley? He didn't want to ask Aunt Jean for help.

Eric glanced at his watch. *Almost five o'clock. Dr. Ryan's been gone more than a half hour.* He drummed his fingers on the table.

A nurse entered, carrying crutches and leaned them against the wall, out of Eric's reach. "Dr. Ryan will be in soon. Don't even try to get up." She barked like a drill sergeant to a raw recruit.

Determined, Eric sat up, swung his legs over the side of the table and stood. A wave of dizziness made him feel faint.

The nurse grabbed his arm. "Never get up fast after you've lost blood," she chastised.

Dr. Ryan hurried through the doorway. "I'll take over now." He gestured the nurse out. After she left, he said. "She's a little overbearing, but she's right. You can file away her advice for future reference. Won't cost you a cent."

Gradually, the room stopped swimming.

Dr. Ryan brought him the crutches. "Get your equilibrium before you try walking." He grinned. "You don't want to fall flat on your face before your fans."

Eric adjusted the crutches under his armpits. "Fans?"

"Students and parents. You and Jeff are in for a little hero worship."

"Why? We only did what was necessary."

"Maybe so, but when you stop somebody's kid or friend from bleeding to death, you're a hero."

"But I'm not." Eric wondered how he could escape this situation.

Dr. Ryan eyed him as if he were a balking teenager. "Learn to accept praise graciously."

Eric met his gaze and nodded. He'd better heed criticism graciously too. After all, he shouldn't challenge the father of the girl he wanted to date.

Dr. Ryan gave him some pointers on using the crutches and told Eric to walk around the room. "I'll bring the car up front."

Eric hoped they could slip away unnoticed. No such luck. When he entered the corridor, parents and students rushed to thank him. Eric tried to keep a poker face, but he could feel it turning fiery red. He saw Kathy standing near the entrance, grinning. Her eyes danced with mischief while he edged his way toward her as fast as the crowd and his crutches allowed.

She held the hospital door open and escorted him to the car where her father stood waiting. "Don't you enjoy being a hero?"

"I didn't do anything."

"Well, I think you and Jeff were super. I already thanked him. Now it's your turn." She planted a kiss on his cheek. "Thank you."

Though astounded and embarrassed, Eric couldn't help chuckling. He looked at her father. "Anything else I should be prepared for?"

Dr. Ryan frowned at Kathy. "I don't think so."

As if her father's stern tone and look didn't faze her, Kathy said, "We want you to come to dinner tomorrow."

Eric glanced at Dr. Ryan for confirmation. He didn't intend to barge in where he wasn't wanted.

"The Doles have plans for the day," her father said. "You're more than welcome to attend church with us and come to dinner afterward."

Did he dare attend after his claustrophobic experience on Mother's Day? "I'd like to pass on church for now, but having dinner with your family sounds great."

"Good. We'll pick you up around twelve fifteen."

Kathy beamed, making his heart quicken with anticipation. What would tomorrow bring?

On the way to the Dole's, Kathy said, "We live in Pismo Beach not far from the Dole's."

"But you attend Arroyo Grande High School?"

"It's the closest one. Arroyo Grande is the largest town in the area and provides all the major services." She pointed out the high school as they passed and later her church called Chapel by the Sea. "It's an independent Protestant church. Are you Protestant?"

He nodded.

"Good." Her smile of relief told him she considered attending church important. They turned the corner and drove along the cliff highway paralleling the ocean. Kathy pointed to a sprawling home with a manicured lawn and meticulously pruned shrubbery. "That's our house. The Doles live down the road . . . a nice walk, even for someone on crutches."

A brief frown crossed Dr. Ryan's face, again showing his disapproval of her forwardness, but Eric found Kathy's openness just right. The doctor pulled into a circle driveway lined with purple and white petunias. He stopped in front of a modest stucco home. Rose bushes bordered the porch.

Eric opened the car door and accepted Dr. Ryan's assistance. Kathy climbed out, retrieved his crutches from the back seat, and handed them to him. "Thanks," he said.

A middle-aged woman rushed out of the house and down the porch steps. "Kathy, are you all right, child?"

"Fine, Mrs. Dole. Not even a scratch." Kathy accepted a hug.

Mrs. Dole beamed at Eric. "And you're the young man who helped everyone. This town is indebted to you."

*You've got to be kidding. The whole town?* The undeserved praise embarrassed Eric, but he remembered Dr. Ryan's advice and smiled. "I'm happy to meet you, Mrs. Dole."

He reached out, and her warm hands enveloped his. "And I'm pleased to meet you, Mr. Stone."

"Please call me Eric."

Mrs. Dole reminded him of Aunt Jean, but she didn't have his aunt's rugged pioneer look. Mrs. Dole was plump, her hands soft and smooth. Only a few flecks of gray highlighted her dark brown hair.

After Eric said good-bye to Kathy and her father, he followed Mrs. Dole up the porch steps. He stopped midway. A white, silken service banner hung in the window—one gold star, one blue. Two family members had fought in the war. One had died.

"Are you all right?" Mrs. Dole asked.

Eric stared at the banner, unable to speak.

"Our son, Dennis, was killed eight months ago."

"I . . . I'm sorry."

She nodded. Gently placing a hand on his shoulder, she said, "God knows our pain and has comforted us. We trust Him to bring something good from our loss."

*How can Mrs. Dole accept her son's death so serenely? Does she really believe God can bring good from it?* Eric marveled at her quiet strength, but in his mind, no good came from death.

"Come on in," she urged. "Let's get you settled."

In the living room, she gestured toward a blue over-stuffed chair. "You sit and relax. I'll bring you some tea." While Eric laid the crutches on the floor, she turned on the lamp and handed him the paper. "Mr. Dole should be home soon. We're having beef stew tonight."

"Sounds great."

After she left, Eric shifted his position to get more comfortable. It didn't help. Too much had happened in the past few hours, making his head reel as if he'd just stepped off a roller coaster but could still feel its movement.

Gazing at a large family portrait hanging above the fireplace, the gold star came to mind. *Which son died?* Eric averted his gaze, trying to shut out thoughts of death, but one face in the picture haunted him. Where had he seen that young man? He heard a teakettle's whistle, opened the paper to the comics, and tried to appear at ease.

Mrs. Dole entered with a steaming mug. She handed it to him and waited while he took a sip as if wondering if he would like it.

The tea had a pleasant mint taste. "This is good."

"And just what you need to help you relax."

After he emptied the mug, Eric rested his head against the chair and listened to Mrs. Dole humming hymns. She and Aunt Jean probably had a lot in common. When he heard Captain Dole's voice coming from the kitchen, Eric picked up the paper.

The captain lumbered through the doorway. "You're awake," he said, looking surprised. "Dinner's ready. Feel like eating?"

Eric nodded and followed the captain to the dining room table. French doors opened to the deck, and steps descended from it to the beach. He gazed out the window, entranced, marveling at the ocean's beauty. The rays of the setting sun gave the water a fiery glow unlike anything he'd ever seen. "Spectacular."

"We usually eat breakfast on the deck," Mr. Dole said. After he had Eric's attention, he bowed his head and blessed the food.

His tone reminded Eric of his father, and a wave of nostalgia swept over him. After the captain finished, Eric stared out the window.

"Anything wrong?" Capt. Dole asked.

"No. You just reminded me of my dad. He died a long time ago." While they ate, Eric answered the Doles' questions about his parents' separation, but left out the fact that it had occurred in Germany. And he didn't mention the war or Erin's death.

"Have you been able to keep in touch with your family?" Mrs. Dole asked.

"Only by letter."

"Well, now that you're grown, maybe you can visit them."

Eric let the comment ride.

Mr. Dole raised an eyebrow. "Do you play chess?"

"I like the game, but I'm not too sharp."

"Feel up to playing after dinner?"

"Sure."

The captain set up a card table in the living room. Their friendly match was more talk than challenge. In between moves, they discussed Eric's room and board. The captain lowered the rent when Eric volunteered to do yard work. Eric learned his bike had been taken to the police garage, and that the mechanics offered to straighten the frame for free. He couldn't believe how nice people were.

The chess game ended in a stalemate, and Eric leaned back. The family portrait that had stared down at him all through the game could no longer be ignored. When he turned away from it, his eyes met the captain's. "You have a nice-looking family."

"Linda, our youngest, is married and lives in San Francisco. That's where we're going tomorrow. Mark, the one standing next to her, is in the air force. He should be home soon." Sadness filled his eyes. "Dennis was in the First Army. He was killed at Aachen."

"Aachen?" The face in the family portrait and the name came together. Eric broke into a cold sweat. The room closed in on him. "I need to get some air," he gasped, grabbed his crutches, and struggled to stand.

Captain Dole rose to help him, his brow creased with concern. "Let's go onto the deck,"

Outside, Eric took great gulps of air before leaning against the wooden railing next to the captain. He tried to blot Dennis's face from his mind, pictures of it, before and after a rifle blasted away the features. He shuddered.

"It might help to talk about what's bothering you."

Eric turned and met the captain's searching gaze, but words wouldn't come.

"Were you at Aachen?"

Eric nodded. "Wounded there." He stared past the captain, trying to visualize that day. "Everything is fuzzy. I only recently remembered the two soldiers who came to my aid. One, who looked like your son, died during an exchange of gunfire. His buddy sobbed, 'Dennis,' over and over."

"Dennis died October sixth."

Eric sighed. "Same day I was wounded."

The captain leaned against the railing and stared out to sea. "Did he suffer?" he asked, his voice deep with sadness.

Eric's heart ached for the Doles. Choked, he said, "No." Dennis's face flashed before him again. He'd seen so many men mutilated. Why did this one have to have a name and now a family connected to it? *Why now when all I want to do is forget?*

Mr. Dole turned, his mouth drawn, his eyes penetrating. "Did Dennis die a horrible death?"

"He didn't suffer." Eric bit down on his lip. "Maybe I'd better find somewhere else to stay," he mumbled.

"Would living here make you uncomfortable?"

"Yes," Eric blurted. "My presence would be a constant reminder to you and Mrs. Dole of your son's death. I don't want that!"

The captain drew in a breath and let it out slowly. "Something neither of us wants, but evidently, God does." He searched Eric's face. "Do you believe in God? Do you believe He controls our destiny?"

"Yes, but—"

"Stay with us. God must have some reason for guiding you to Arroyo Grande, for bringing us together. Maybe it's so I can help you. I fought in World War I and lost a brother. We weren't twins, but we were close."

"How . . . how'd you find out?"

"From your license plate, I obtained enough information to contact your aunt. She shared all you've been through and the problems you're having. If she'd mentioned where you'd been wounded, I would have only said Dennis was killed in action. Guess God figured it would be best for you to know. Anyway, I told her you'd be staying with us."

Eric turned away from the captain. He stared at the churning waves, battling his own turbulence. Erin's death. Mato's death. Dennis's death. Each brought a wave of despair. *Lord, why did you bring me here? How can I face the Doles every day?* Eric straightened and gazed at the captain. "Your wife may not want me here."

"If she's agreeable, will you stay?"

Despite reservations, he nodded. "But I don't want anyone else knowing about this. Can we keep this to ourselves?"

"Annie's used to keeping confidences."

"Including my being in the service? Sir, I have nightmares about the horrors I've seen. I can't talk about them. I just want to forget."

Captain Dole gave an understanding smile. "You will, but it takes time. Right now, find some fun in your life. Let Sunday be the beginning of brighter days."

Eric nodded, grateful for the reminder he would be seeing Kathy tomorrow.

"You can put your gear in the northeast bedroom—Linda's room," the captain said. "It's a little feminine, but considering the alternative . . . "

*Dennis?* "Feminine will be fine."

*   *   *

Sunday morning at daybreak, Eric awakened from a nightmare. He trembled from its reality, but lying in bed, listening to the waves lapping against the shore, relaxed him. He wished his room faced the ocean so he could see the water as well as hear it.

A door closing told him someone was up. Eric rose, grabbed the crutches, and made his way down the hall to the bathroom where he showered and dressed. He found the Doles on the deck, sipping coffee at a weather-beaten wooden table.

"Good morning," Mrs. Dole said. "You're up early."

"Guess I'm eager to see the ocean at sunrise." He leaned against the railing and inhaled the salty sea air. The tide had gone out, leaving a long stretch of unmarred beach dotted with seashells. He wished he could take a walk and collect some for Cindy. He watched the sun play upon the water; the changing patterns fascinated him.

"Are you hungry?" Mrs. Dole asked.

"I sure am."

"Good, we were just waiting for you." She smiled. "Please feel free to stay with us as long as you want."

"Thank you. I'm used to fending for myself so there's no need to fix my breakfast."

"During the week, you may have to cook for yourself, but Sunday mornings are for eating together."

After she went inside, the captain joined him by the railing. Eric stared out to sea, deep in thought. Everything seemed so peaceful here, but he knew battles raged on the other side of the Pacific.

"You all right?" Capt. Dole asked.

"I'm okay. Did I cry out and wake you up this morning?"

"We were awake, but you sure gave Annie a start. She wanted to rush in and check on you. I told her you were probably having a nightmare. You're under our roof now so be prepared for her to play mother hen. She wants you to stay and feel as I do that God brought you here for a reason."

"I think Dennis was a lucky guy to have you two for parents. I'll stay."

After the Doles left around nine, Eric washed his good plaid shirt in the laundry room sink.

On crutches, it was awkward, but he managed to carry his shirt and blue cords out to the deck, lay the pants over the railing to air, and pin the shirt to the clothesline. He sat at the picnic table to wait and made a mental note to buy lighter-weight trousers and some shorts.

While pressing his shirt, he glanced at the ocean and thought about the homes along the California coast. Until today, he hadn't realized people on the coast felt vulnerable to Japanese air strikes. He'd been in the kitchen with Mrs. Dole, and she explained why they had a blackened piece of plywood above their back door and one two feet in front of it. "The door faces the ocean, and this black tunnel blocks the light." And Eric noticed they didn't use the French doors after dark and kept the black oilcloth shades pulled.

The doorbell rang. Eric unplugged the iron and hobbled to the front door.

Jeff stood on the porch. "Remember me? I'm Jeff Thompson. Mary asked me to drop by and tell you how much she appreciated your helping yesterday." The words delivered flatly conveyed the message that Jeff had done his duty unwillingly.

"Come in. I was pressing a shirt."

Jeff followed him to the laundry room. "I bet you do windows too."

Eric realized it was a jab, not a joke. "You afraid of manual labor?"

"I'd hardly call that *manual*."

"Maybe Kathy'd be willing to do this for me."

Jeff's eyes narrowed. "Don't mess with Kathy."

Eric met his glare. "Isn't Mary your girl?"

"Yes, but Kathy's our friend. You lay one finger on her, and I'll kill you."

Eric wanted to slug Jeff, but three years of shouldering a gun had taught him when to pull the trigger and when not to fire. He put the safety catch on his temper. Something must have happened to provoke Jeff.

"You've no call to lambaste me like this," he said as evenly as he could. "I could have taken the first offer and ridden away from the whole mess yesterday."

"We would have done just fine without you."

"Yeah? You were a big help to Mary."

Jeff reddened. "Just don't mess with Kathy or any other girl in this town."

"I don't intend to," Eric replied. "But I'd like to know what's bothering you."

"You ride a motorcycle." The venom with which he spat the words made Eric's skin crawl. "This town seems to have forgotten what happened here two years ago. I haven't! The only thing in your favor is that you did your level best to help. For that, I'm grateful, but I'll be watching you. This town may have opened up its heart, but I haven't. I'll see myself out."

# CHAPTER 6

S tunned by Jeff's anger, Eric leaned on the crutches and stared at the empty doorway. What could have happened two years ago to make Jeff so bitter? Or was something else behind the attack? *Did I bruise Jeff's ego in front of Kathy when I saw him dashing for the bushes? Kathy was too occupied to notice, but maybe Jeff didn't realize that.*

Eric hobbled out to the deck and rested against the railing. Breathing deeply, he tried to absorb the peacefulness around him, but Jeff's words plagued him. *Forget Jeff! Think about Kathy.*

Eric grabbed his cords and returned to the laundry room for his shirt. While he changed, he pictured Kathy's flirtatious green eyes and relived the warmth of the kiss she'd planted on his cheek. What would today bring? When the doorbell rang, his heart quickened with expectation. Opening the door squelched thoughts of romance.

Kathy stood on the porch biting down on her lip as if she wanted to be any place but there. "Ready?" she asked.

"Be with you in a minute. I need to lock the back door." *What happened to the vivacious girl who kissed me? Did she talk with Jeff? Does she regret inviting me to dinner?* When he returned, Kathy's eyes reflected apprehension. Eric patted his pocket to make sure he had the key before he closed the front door. "It's a beautiful day," he said, trying to keep up with Kathy's quick strides toward the car.

Dr. Ryan stood beside a 1940 Nash station wagon. He introduced Eric to the rest of the family and helped him settle in the front seat next to Mrs. Ryan. Kathy climbed in back with her younger teenage sister, Angela. Jimmy and Tommy, probably around ten and eight, rode on the rear seat.

Eric drew in a quiet breath and tried to relax. It didn't help. During the short ride to her house, silence hung like a guillotine ready to drop. Somewhere between last night and today, he'd lost his shining armor, and it appeared Kathy's change of attitude had tainted the entire family.

Kathy clasped her hands in her lap, unable to escape the fear lurking in the corner of her mind. Yesterday, she had no idea Eric was the motorcyclist who rode beside the bus. The driver of the car who crashed into them had been killed. She assumed Eric had been a passenger. That's what she'd told her father. This morning, when they read the account of the accident in the paper, they were surprised to learn otherwise.

Nothing about Eric resembled the man who raped Mary two years ago, but just seeing a motorcycle panicked Kathy. A shiver of remembrance crawled up her spine. While she and Mary were sunbathing on the beach, Kathy had gone into the house to make sandwiches. Mary's cries for help made her drop everything and run outside. A grunting disheveled man had Mary pinned underneath him. "Leave her alone," Kathy screamed as she scrambled down the cliff steps, grabbing rocks to hurl at him, but her aim fell short.

The man stood, laughing and licking his lips before he turned on her.

She kicked, screamed, and raked her nails across his face. The stench of alcohol on his breath and his putrid body odor had filled her nostrils.

*Stop. Stop thinking about it! Your mom firing the shotgun saved you. That man is behind bars. He can't hurt anyone again. Eric might ride a motorcycle, but he's like the Good Samaritan the pastor talked about this morning. Eric kept Mary from going into shock. When he gazed into my eyes, he made my heart sing.*

Kathy tried to recapture the wonder she'd experienced, but recalling the man she had fought overpowered it.

Dr. Ryan wondered how Kathy would handle her fear.

This morning, after she read the newspaper, she paled. "Eric was the motorcyclist?" she stammered. "Dad, I don't want to see him. Call him. Tell him something's come up. Please!"

He refused, even when Angela and the boys sided with Kathy. Realizing they must face this situation and see it through, he said, "You can't blame one man for another's actions."

Had he made the right decision? It seemed cruel, and it pained his heart to make Kathy face Eric after all she'd been through, but he knew she needed to see Eric was the same man she'd flirted with yesterday. No matter how much that disturbed him, it showed she was getting over Dennis's death. Now she had to lose her fear of men who rode motorcycles.

Dr. Ryan prayed the day would turn out well. He considered himself a shrewd judge of character. Saturday, Eric had risen above his pain to help others. That revealed strong character, but the doctor sensed something about Eric that might be good for Kathy. He would have to let Eric handle the situation. The young man was older than most of the boys Kathy knew, and yesterday, he had displayed gentleness and compassion. Could he sense she needed that now?

Dr. Ryan pulled into the driveway. When the car stopped, Jimmy and Tommy opened the tailgate, jumped out, and started chasing each other before dashing toward the backyard. The doctor hoped they wouldn't pester Eric as they had pestered Dennis. Dr. Ryan hurried to the passenger door to help Eric to his feet. When the young man thanked him, his voice and faint smile reflected concern.

*He has sensed Kathy's mood*, the doctor thought.

Angela scooted off the back seat and handed Eric the crutches. "Thanks," he said, adjusting them, and moved so Mrs. Ryan could get out of the car.

She stood and gasped, "The dog!"

Dr. Ryan turned. Missy, their enormous black and white Great Dane, bounded toward Eric. Before Dr. Ryan could intercept, Eric put his hand out and said firmly, "Sit!"

Missy skidded to a stop and sat. The doctor stared in disbelief. The dog had obeyed! Actually obeyed! Dr. Ryan had been unable to break the animal of leaping and licking him or any other adult male. She would leave children and women alone, but any man became fair game. Dr. Ryan blew out a breath. "Whew, that was close."

The Dane's enormous brown eyes begged the young man for acknowledgment. Unafraid, Eric moved closer and gave the dog a pat on the head. "Well, big boy, what's your name?"

Angela roared with laughter. "She's a girl not a boy. Her name is Missy."

"Missy, I beg your pardon." Eric's eyes twinkled as he bowed as much as the crutches permitted. "Please accept my humble apology." When Missy offered her paw, he took it.

The boys ran up and gazed at Eric in wonder. Dr. Ryan knew they had let the Dane out on purpose. "Boys, take Missy back. You know she's not allowed out front. I'll deal with you later."

"Yes, sir. Come on, Missy," they chimed and raced toward the backyard, the dog leaping beside them.

"I'm sorry," Dr. Ryan said.

Eric adjusted the crutches under his armpits. "No harm done."

Mrs. Ryan clutched her chest. "Dear, you must do something about those boys. They did that on purpose."

"Please," Eric implored, "don't be hard on them. They were only testing me. If I passed, we're off to a good start."

Dr. Ryan nodded. "That may be, but I can't let the matter drop. Their next victim could be injured."

Inside the house, Mrs. Ryan said, "Kathy, show Eric the view from our deck while I check the roast."

When Kathy looked taken aback, the doctor wanted to swat her for making her distaste so obvious.

Kathy's voice squeaked with despair. "Mom, don't you need help in the kitchen or the table set for dinner?"

"No, thank you. Angela can help me."

Dr. Ryan saw the concerned look on Eric's face. *Well, young man, you're on your own.*

Uncomfortable and bewildered, Eric wondered if a skunk would have been more welcomed. He easily kept pace with Kathy's stride. How could he get out of this predicament? Yesterday, he had vowed to make her smile and laugh if she looked miserable again. Today, fulfilling that vow seemed foolish and impossible.

He joined Kathy at the deck railing. The cliff upon which the house stood was higher and steeper than where the Doles lived. The deck stairs led to a large backyard surrounded by a six-foot redwood fence with three strands of barbed wire on top—*to keep the dog in, or to keep intruders out?* The padlocked gate blocking the steep, narrow steps leading to the beach suggested the latter. A hand railing angled the full length of the stairs, emphasizing the danger.

Kathy gazed out to sea, her mouth turned down.

"Nice view," Eric said.

"I like it."

*Would she enjoy the view more it I weren't here?* His head said, *Leave now before you make a fool of yourself.* His heart said, *Go ahead; make her laugh.* "Kathy, look at me." After she turned, he cupped her chin and lifted her head. "Even when you frown, you're adorable."

"What?" She stared as if she hadn't heard him correctly.

"Adorable," he repeated.

Her cheeks reddened, and she turned away, but he continued. "Plus bewitching, cute, delectable, enchanting, fascinating, and gorgeous, even a little heavenly and irresistible."

She faced him. A smile tugged at the corners of her mouth. "Are you going to go through the whole alphabet?"

"Yep."

"Then I think you must be addlepated, befuddled, confused, dumb, egotistic . . . "

"Ouch," he interjected.

Kathy didn't blink an eye as she continued. "Feeble-minded, goose-brained, harebrained, and idiotic." She stopped as if she'd drawn a blank.

"J and K are tough. How about jewel, kissable, lovely, and magnificent?"

She responded, "Jackass, kinky, loco, moronic, and just plain nuts!"

Eric put a mocking hand up to protect himself. "I yield! You've beaten me at my own game and managed to name all my most endearing qualities."

Kathy started laughing. "You really are nuts."

"Sometimes, it helps." He cupped her chin again. "Don't ever let the sparkle in your emerald eyes die again. Friends?" He held out his hand.

Kathy grasped it. "Friends," she sighed. "You did all this just to make me feel better, didn't you?"

"I had to do something."

She suddenly looked contrite, a touch of mist clouding her eyes. "I've really been a brat, haven't I?" Before he could say no, she added, "You've been super. It just happens that you ride a motorcycle, and I have a problem with that."

"I rode one yesterday too."

"But I didn't know until I read the paper this morning."

"First, Jeff, now you. Maybe I'm dense, but I don't get it."

"Jeff talked with you?"

"More like read the riot act. But I can't blame him too much since everything he said was aimed at protecting you." He winked. "Who wouldn't want to protect you?"

A hint of her special smile returned, and he felt his score rise from zero to ten.

"That's sweet," she said. "You really have been super. Can you forgive me?"

"Done." Tongue in cheek, he asked, "What happened to make you and Jeff hate motorcyclists?" Before she turned and stared at the beach, he caught a glimpse of fear that told him more than he wanted to know. Maybe he was wrong. *Oh, God, I hope so.* As he'd felt her anguish yesterday, he now felt her panic. "I'm sorry, I shouldn't have asked. Forgive me, Kathy. Forgive me for stirring up painful memories." He didn't know what else to say. How could he right his blunder?

She faced him, looking more composed. "Forgive you? You had nothing to do with what happened here two years ago. Please forgive my rudeness, and I apologize for Jeff too."

71

"He was only looking out for you. I can't hold that against him. I'd have done the same." He could feel himself lifted and placed once more in her good graces. His score reached one hundred when her you-really-are-terrific smile returned.

Jimmy and Tommy walked onto the deck, looking meek and reluctant. "Dad told us to apologize," Jimmy said.

"Boy was he mad," Tommy added. "He said we were mean to sic the dog on you. We're sorry."

"That's okay. Maybe when I get off these crutches, I can come over and play with Missy, and we can teach her not to jump on anyone."

Jimmy's face lit up with admiration. "That would be great. Most people are scared of her."

Tommy cocked his head. "Do you bowl? We go every week. Could you go with us some time?"

"Sure. After my ankle heals." He smiled at Kathy. "Can we take your sister?"

"She's the one who takes us," Tommy said.

The boys raced back to the living room. "Dad," they yelled, "Eric's says he'll go bowling with us."

"Now you've done it," Kathy said. "You've endeared yourself to them for life, and they'll cling like leeches."

Eric laughed. "I'd rather have them for friends than enemies. They could dream up something worse than turning the dog on me. Besides, I never had a little brother. It will be fun getting to know them."

"Be my guest. Take them home with you. They're a pain."

"You can't mean that. You'd miss them."

She sighed. "You're probably right. Sometimes, they're sweet . . . but not often." She stared past him as if deep in thought before she asked, "Where are you from, Eric?"

"Buena Vista, a small mountain town in Colorado."

Her eyes widened. "What are you doing way out here? One doesn't joyride from Colorado to California on a motorcycle."

"Would you believe I want to learn how to surf? Originally, I planned to tour the entire coastline, but someone told me to go south, that the water north of here is too cold."

She stared at him in disbelief.

"You look astonished. Is my story too hard to believe?"

She shook her head. "No, circumstances are."

Puzzled, he asked, "How so?"

"Your landing here. A few of us ride surfboards. Mary's father makes them for us. If she's up to it, we can visit her this afternoon."

"Why don't you go ahead and let the boys entertain me?"

"And leave you to a fate worse than death? Come with me. I know Mary wants to meet you. In fact I insist."

"Okay." Eric didn't think it was a wise idea, especially if Jeff happened to be there, but he couldn't resist spending the day with Kathy.

During dinner, Dr. Ryan marveled at the miracle Eric had worked. This young man knew how to handle difficult situations. But would he break Kathy's heart when he left?

# CHAPTER 7

After dinner, Eric followed Kathy into the kitchen and leaned against the wall while she talked with Mary on the phone. *I really shouldn't go with Kathy*, he thought when she said, "Jeff will be there too? Super!"

She hung up and, as if reading his mind, said, "No backing out. Jeff is my friend, and I want the two of you to be friends."

"Kathy—"

She raised her hand to stop him. "I won't take no for an answer. When Jeff sees we're friends, he'll—"

"Be mine automatically?" Eric shook his head. "It doesn't work that way. Friendship starts with a willingness to trust."

Her eyes sparked with challenge. "What you're really saying is that you're not willing to trust him."

"I am, but now is not the time."

"When is a good time? Tomorrow, next week, next year? What more neutral ground will you have than today?"

Eric yielded. Maybe with both of them on best behavior, he and Jeff would be able to tolerate each other, if only for Kathy's sake.

\* \* \*

Mary lived in a modest duplex in an older part of town. Her mother answered the door and ushered them into the living room. Mary's injury wasn't serious, but her mother had insisted she rest on the couch with a pillow under her head. Jeff, sitting on the edge of the sofa, stood and glared at Eric.

Kathy quickly stepped between them, leaned down, and gave Mary a hug. "Jeff, introduce Eric to Mary."

Jeff's plastered smile looked close to cracking. "This is the guy who helped you yesterday."

Eric enjoyed Jeff's struggle with the words. *Ouch, that must have hurt.* He smiled at Mary. "I'm pleased to meet you. You sure had us worried."

She showed no awareness of the discord. "Thank you for helping me and the other students. We're grateful."

After Eric and Kathy settled in chairs, he said, "Jeff did every bit as much as I did." *I hope giving Jeff more credit will ease the tension.* An idea struck him. For some reason, Mary's white jeans and fuzzy white sweater reminded him of a dumb joke Cindy had told him. *Dumb enough to break the ice?* "You look much better today," Eric said. "In fact, right now wearing that angora sweater, you remind me of a resting rabbit."

"A what?" all three chimed.

"A resting rabbit. You've never heard the joke?"

Heads shook.

"You know, once there was this farmer who opened his refrigerator and saw a rabbit sitting on the shelf. 'What are you doing in there?' he asked. The rabbit wiggled his nose and said, 'Isn't this a Westinghouse?' The farmer nodded. 'Well,' said the rabbit, 'I'm just westing.'"

Mary giggled politely. Kathy and Jeff exchanged he's-off-his-rocker glances, and Jeff said, "Is that your best shot?"

"You got a better one?"

"Of course. There was a rabbit that started to cross a bridge and was stopped by a troll who said, 'You can't cross unless you give me ten gold pieces.' The rabbit wiggled his nose and said, 'I don't have any money.' The troll replied, 'Then I'm going to turn you into a goon.' The rabbit shrugged. 'Hare today. Goon tomorrow.'"

Mary rolled her eyes. "Jeff, that was bad, really bad."

The joke might have been worse than Eric's, but like the parting of the Red Sea, a path opened for more to follow. Mary became the barometer, forecasting whose was better. The match ended when Mary's mother carried in a tray of sandwiches and lemonade.

Jeff helped Mary sit up and sat next to her. "So what are your plans now that you're here?" he asked Eric.

"I'm not sure, except I'd like to find someone to teach me how to surf."

"Jeff," Kathy drawled, batting her eyes like a southern belle, "since you're the best, you'd be glad to teach him, wouldn't you?"

Jeff nodded, his lips drawn so taut it would have taken a crowbar to pry them apart.

*I'd rather drown on my own*, Eric thought. "It can't be all that hard to learn." Jeff's twisted smile suggested his willingness to let Eric try, and he probably hoped Eric would end belly-up. "First," Eric continued, "I need to buy some swim trunks and summer clothes."

Jeff stiffened like a skunk with its tail raised in alarm. "You're planning to stay the summer?"

"Yes . . . might even settle down here. Seems like a right nice area." *There, let that stick in your craw.* A flash of anger on Jeff's face told Eric his message had been received. He smiled at Kathy. "Is there bus service into town from the Dole's?"

Kathy glanced from Jeff to Eric, her determined expression showing she was bent on carrying out her mission. "No, but Jeff could take you after school. His classes are in the morning. You wouldn't mind, would you?" The spark in her eyes dared Jeff to refuse.

Eric, picturing Jeff as a cooked goose, barely refrained from laughing.

Jeff didn't flinch. "Two hours enough time? I have baseball practice at three."

"Two should be plenty. Thanks."

"I'll pick you up after lunch, say twelve thirty."

"Great."

\*     \*     \*

Monday afternoon, Jeff showed up on time. "Ready?" he asked when Eric opened the car door.

Their eyes locked. Eric had the sensation they were two gun-fighters sizing up each other. "By any chance, you got a six-shooter in the glove compartment and an itchy trigger finger?"

"You're safe. I don't shoot *wounded* varmints."

Eric mulled over the odds of them being friendlier two hours from now—one hundred to one? More like a one thousand to one. He laid the crutches on the back seat of Jeff's 1939 Chevy, scooted onto the front seat, and tried to bring his injured foot inside without making it look difficult.

Jeff's smug expression showed he'd noticed. "Where to?" he asked.

"Any place that has nice but fairly inexpensive clothes. Got a Sears or 'Monkey' Wards?"

"Don't you rich guys buy your clothes at Macy's?"

"Rich? Where'd you get that notion?"

"Your Harley, your expensive boots."

"The boots were a gift, and I earned every penny for my bike."

"Doing what, sharpening Daddy's pencils?"

Eric's hands clenched. "I only wish I'd had the chance, but my father died years ago."

"Then you inherited your money?"

"Not one penny! Only my father's good sense, which is the only thing keeping me from slugging you."

Jeff sneered. "So how *did* you earn your money?"

"Working with my hands . . . mostly mechanics."

"Look at your hands. You're no mechanic."

"I haven't worked the past few months. Maybe I can find a job here."

Jeff's jaw clamped as if he regretted bringing up the subject. He drove Eric to Sears and left him in the men's department while he went to find a present for Mary.

Eric selected three short-sleeved shirts, a pair of lightweight dress pants, and a tie, plus swim trunks, shorts, and some sleeveless pullovers to hide his scars.

Jeff returned while Eric stood in line at the cash register. The woman clerk gazed at Jeff. "Are you skipping school today?"

"No, I only have morning classes."

She beamed at Eric as if she'd just put the two of them together. "I bet you're the young man who helped at the accident."

Eric nodded and laid his clothes across the counter. "I hope you'll accept an out-of-state check?"

"From you? Of course. That's the least we can do for a Good Samaritan."

Jeff's eyes rolled with disgust.

Outside, Eric said, "I take it the clerk knows you."

"Yeah, her son's in my chemistry class, and he goes to Kathy's church. You finished?"

"Would you have time to run me by the hospital?"

"What for?"

"To pay my bill. If it's more than I have in the bank, I need to arrange payments."

"Then you really aren't rich?"

"Definitely not!"

At the hospital, Jeff walked with Eric to the accounting office and waited with him. The clerk finished talking on the phone and smiled. "How may I help you?"

Eric gave her his name. "I need to pay my bill."

She found his folder and opened it. "Your bill has been paid in full."

"Who paid it?"

"I can't give you names, but several people helped."

Eric stood dumfounded. "Thanks is one thing, but this is too much."

"Accept it gracefully," she advised and put the folder away.

Jeff remained silent while they walked to the parking lot.

In the car, Eric asked, "Did you know about this?"

"I suspected."

"I don't feel right about it. What should I do?"

"For all I care, you can refuse to accept the help and insult the whole town."

"Any suggestions on how I can convey my thanks?"

"That's your problem."

*Seems I have several*, Eric thought on the way back to the Dole's. *What next?*

What came next was in the form of a large parcel. Mrs. Dole handed it to him when he entered the house. Eric tore off the brown paper. The covered box pictured western boots. Inside, he saw a pair almost identical to his ruined ones. The enclosed card read: "We're grateful. Please accept these as a token of our thanks."

"First, my medical bills are paid; now this. It's too much. Mrs. Dole, did you know?"

She shook her head. "I'm surprised too."

That evening, Capt. Dole admitted he knew about the boots but not the medical bills. "Our town hasn't been this generous for a long time. They're beholden, son."

Eric blurted, "But it's not right."

"That a town should be grateful?"

"Captain, it's not that I'm ungrateful. When I watched Dr. Ryan cut my boot, it tore me up inside because I knew my aunt and cousins had sacrificed money and ration stamps to buy them. Now people here have shown the same love by replacing my boots and paying my bills. I appreciate that more than words can express, but I'm beginning to feel indebted to them. Would you explain how I feel so we can call this a draw? And please express my gratitude."

Capt. Dole nodded. "I'll handle it."

"Thanks," Eric said in relief.

\*       \*       \*

On Tuesday, Mrs. Dole drove Eric to Dr. Ryan's office and dropped him off. "I'll be back in an hour."

He didn't have to wait long for a nurse to usher him into the examination room.

While Dr. Ryan examined Eric's ankle, his face remained non-committal. Finally, he smiled. "Good, the swelling's down. How does it feel?"

"I've been walking on it some, and it feels fine."

"Then you can dispense with the crutches."

"Is it all right for me to go swimming?"

"Wading is okay, but no swimming until next week, after I take the stitches out of your leg. Besides, in case you haven't noticed, few people swim around here. The water rarely gets warmer than fifty-five degrees."

"But people still surf?"

"Besides Kathy, Mary, and Jeff, probably less than a dozen. All wear modified deep-sea diving suits for warmth. I know how this bunch became interested in surfing. But you? You're from Colorado."

"I had a Hawaiian friend who loved the sport," Eric said.

"You look somewhat bewildered."

"I am. Kathy volunteered Jeff to teach me. If surfing's not popular, where am I going to find gear?"

Dr. Ryan chuckled. "I'm sure Kathy's finagled Jeff to get you a diving suit. His father works at the US Naval Amphibious Training Base. He has access to discarded ripped suits. After being mended, they work great for keeping the kids warm." Dr. Ryan glanced at his watch.

"I don't want to keep you," Eric said.

"I allowed time for talking. Let's go to my office." Seated across from each other at his desk, he said, "Mary's father will probably lend you a surfboard."

"Just like that? He doesn't know me."

"Anyone who wants to learn will get a helping hand from him. Mr. Watkins brought his love of surfing to our shores from his native Hawaii. Crafting boards is his hobby. The family came to America three days before Pearl Harbor was bombed."

"I bet they appreciated being safe in the United States."

"Yes, but we have had scary moments in our area. The Japs haven't entirely left us alone." He opened the lower desk drawer, retrieved a map, and spread it open for Eric to see. His finger pointed to an area north of Morro Bay. "December 23, 1941, shortly after the Watkins settled in Arroyo Grande, a Jap submarine surfaced and chased the *Larry Doheny*, a Richfield oil tanker. A torpedo missed the vessel and exploded on the beach at Cayucos." He moved his finger to Point Estero. "Here, later that night, another submarine sank the

*Montebello*, a Union oil tanker. Despite a hail of gun
crew members survived.

"The sinking shook everyone, especially the
feared Jap bombers would strike next. People took a
seriously, and the Coast Guard only quit patrollin.. ...
horseback in September."

Eric pondered the doctor's words. *Security must have been lax to
allow submarines to get that close, but then, who would have thought the
Japanese would try so soon after bombing Pearl Harbor.*

"Wow!" Eric said when the doctor finished and refolded the
map. "I'm surprised the Japanese were that daring. Thanks for giving
me a rundown on the local history."

"I thought you might want to know the background of the area
before tomorrow."

"What's tomorrow?"

"Memorial Day. The town is going all out to celebrate the end-
ing of the war with Germany. Would you care to join my family for
the parade, ceremony, and picnic?"

"Why are you inviting me? Why do I sense you have an ulterior
motive since you haven't known me long?"

Dr. Ryan chuckled. "And here I thought I was being so shrewd
you wouldn't notice." He sat back in his chair and eyed Eric intently.
"I've known you long enough to realize your being around would be
good for Kathy to keep her from moping Wednesday."

Eric cocked his head. "Why would tomorrow be hard on her?"

"She loved Dennis Dole. They planned to marry."

Eric stared in shock. *Dennis? This is too much, first the Doles, now
Kathy.* "Sir, what makes you think I can brighten her spirits?"

"The way you helped her Sunday overcome being afraid of you
because you ride a motorcycle."

"Sir, I'd like to decline."

"Why?"

"I don't think I can handle this. Fear is far different than grief."

"Eric, you're the first man she's looked at since Dennis died. I
admit I wasn't happy about her flirting. But it pleased me to see she
now could. Would you please try?"

*You don't know what you're asking. Memorial Day will be rough on me too.*

"Please. Do you want her to be miserable? Your being there could make a difference. Besides, you need something to do tomorrow, and there will be a surfing competition. Kathy decided not to compete, but I think she'd enjoy having you sit next to her so she can give you pointers."

"You sure know how to twist a guy's arm."

"Then that's a yes?"

Eric nodded. "What time should I come to your place?"

"Nine."

When Eric left, Mrs. Dole waited out front to drive him back to her house. Eric pondered all that had transpired to bring him to Arroyo Grande. He thought about Mary's family and about her father who brought his love of surfing to this area. *So many lives intertwined by chance. What a coincidence I landed in the right spot and met the right people to help me keep my promise to Mato.*

*Coincidence? Accident?* Aunt Jean would have said it was God's hand. She believed there were no accidents or coincidences in a Christian's life, only incidents God uses to direct our lives. Was she right?

# CHAPTER 8

Apprehensive about Memorial Day, Eric tossed and turned all night. His nightmares centered on Dennis and Kathy. Every bobbing head in the Rhine River looked like Dennis. When Kathy appeared on the bank, Jill shoved her away.

Eric awakened in a cold sweat. He glanced out the window at the lightening horizon, but when he turned on the lamp to see his watch, he realized it was too early for the Doles to be up. Unable to go back to sleep, he rose and showered.

Under the stream of water, he pondered how Kathy would react today. *How will I?* He pictured the first time he saw her. *At the ball field, you tumbled your way into my heart. When you give me your special smile, being near you is the best tonic in the world.* He turned off the water and looked heavenward. "Thank you, Lord, for leading me here. Just knowing Kathy has blessed my life."

While he dressed, he told himself, *Focus on Kathy. She's your key objective. Take advantage of her tears by being a comforting shoulder today and for however long it takes her to get over Dennis.* He stared out the window. Her father had said her flirting indicated she was ready for a new relationship. *Am I the one, or am I only a stepping stone to many?*

"Lord, what do You have in mind? You've thrown me more curves than logic permits. Did You bring me here to help a girl or to find one to have and to hold? Give me wisdom today to do and say the right thing."

To fill in time before having breakfast with the Doles, he sat at the desk and started a letter to Aunt Jean. He'd phoned and assured her he was okay but knew she'd appreciate receiving more details.

May 30, 1945

Dear Aunt Jean, Nancy, Ann, and Cindy,

I'm beginning to believe God led me to Arroyo Grande. I told you about Mato, how we'd planned to come to California so he could teach me to surf. Well, I've met several young people in this area who love the sport, and even have their own competitions. One will be today, and I plan to sit with Kathy Ryan, a terrific girl I've met. She'll explain surfing and give me pointers before I venture out on the waves next week. Her father, Dr. Ryan, is the one who took care of my leg and ankle. The family included me in their picnic lunch today, and I decided to accept their invitation to go to church with them next Sunday.

When Eric heard footsteps, he stopped writing and left his room to join the Doles on the deck. Their thin smiles told him they were probably thinking about Dennis. Did they dread attending the Memorial Day service as much as he did? Despite the painful memories today would bring, Eric felt compelled to overcome them and console Kathy.

Mrs. Dole pushed her half-eaten bowl of cereal aside. "What time are you going to Kathy's?"

"Around nine."

"Don't forget the strawberries in the refrigerator."

Eric grinned. "Yes, Mom."

Captain Dole chuckled even though his eyes lacked their usual mirth. "Annie, he's not a little kid."

"Eric, I'm sorry."

He scrambled to his feet to hug her. "Don't pay any attention to him. You've been great . . . the best mom a guy could have away from home. I appreciate what you've done for me." He cast a grateful smile. "Guess I'd better finish my letter to Aunt Jean. Don't want her sending a posse after me."

Sitting at the bedroom desk, Eric refilled his fountain pen from the inkwell and wiped the excess off the tip. He glanced over what he'd written and added more about Kathy to let his aunt know he'd met someone special. He hoped Nancy or Ann would relay the information to Jill. Maybe she'd quit writing. She'd wasted no time in sending him a letter, one as sensuous as any she'd written while he was overseas. She brought up past situations where she'd aroused him almost to the point of yielding.

> Remember the morning we rowed across the lake to the tiny island and found it deserted? Remember the night we stopped in the park to talk and never knew a police officer was around until his flashlight beam flooded the car? I still haven't worn the white nightgown and negligee I bought for our wedding night. Remember my describing it to you while you were overseas?

He'd never forget that letter. Shivering in a muddy foxhole, aching with longing, he had pictured her gliding toward him with outstretched arms. Did she really believe she could patch their relationship by drumming up past feelings? He glanced at the bottom drawer where her letter lay. Was Jill truly sorry? Did she love him? It didn't matter. It was too late.

He reread what he'd written to Aunt Jean, sealed the envelope, and dropped it in the mailbox on the way to Kathy's. Today would surely be a rough one for her. How rough? He wondered as he walked up the driveway. He shifted his sack of groceries and rang the doorbell.

After Mrs. Ryan greeted him, he followed her to the kitchen and set his bag of picnic items on the table. Jimmy and Tommy started rummaging through the sack.

Jimmy's eyes gleamed. "Oh boy! Strawberries . . . cookies . . . potato chips."

Tommy's face beamed as his head bobbed. "Marshmallows!"

Mrs. Ryan laughed. "You certainly knew what the boys would like."

Eric grinned. "Comes from being one."

"Where on earth did you find marshmallows? They're scarcer than sugar."

"You'll have to thank Mrs. Dole for those. She had them stashed away." Before he could open his mouth to ask where Kathy was, she entered, looking depressed.

"Sorry I wasn't ready, but I see you've been well entertained. We need to leave. I told Mary we'd be at her house by nine thirty." She clipped off the words with less emotion than a broker reading aloud a ticker tape.

*Will spending today with her be a mistake?*

While Kathy drove to Mary's house, Eric tried to think of the best way to help her endure the day and keep his own emotions under control. *Big help I'm going to be. Right now I can't even come up with anything uplifting to say.*

Mary and Jeff waited in the driveway and climbed into the back seat as soon as Kathy stopped the car. Mary did most of the talking on the way to the park where the parade would end. Kathy's stoic expression remained fixed in the car and later while they meandered through the crowd behind their friends.

Jeff pointed to a tree shaded spot. "Let's sit there."

On a blanket, they watched the parade. Mary and Jeff cheered and waved at each float and especially for the Arroyo Grande High School Marching Band. Kathy clapped, but no pleasure shone on her face.

People gathered around for the eleven o'clock ceremony. Families who had lost loved ones in the war were seated on chairs in front of the small stage. Kathy stiffened, and her face paled when the

Doles took their seats. When Eric slipped a consoling arm around her, she glanced at him and bit down on her lip as tears brimmed. *Lord, what more can I do?* he wondered.

The mayor and other community leaders paid tribute to those who had lost their lives on the battlefield and cited feats of heroism. Bereaved families received flags. When the Doles received theirs, Kathy's tears trickled over her cheeks. When she trembled, Eric pulled her closer, not only to comfort her but himself. Knowing the price Dennis and others had paid, he shut his eyes to stem tears of remembrance, but a few slipped through his lashes. He regained his composure and focused his thoughts on how to brighten Kathy's spirits.

After the ceremony, she made no effort to hide her sadness. She looked drained and asked him to drive.

Eric took Mary and Jeff home first so they could change for the afternoon activities. When he pulled into Kathy's driveway and stopped, he handed her the keys. "I'll walk to the Dole's and be back in half an hour." Eric hoped this would give Kathy a chance to relegate thoughts of Dennis to the back of her mind.

"See you soon," she said in a flat voice and turned without so much as a thank you or wave.

*Oh, brother. What have I gotten myself into?*

Half an hour later, he ambled up her walkway and rang the doorbell. Kathy let him in with a smile so faint he had to use his imagination. He cupped her chin and brushed back a fallen lock. "At least, it's a smile."

When tears spilled, her anguish unnerved him. Eric gathered Kathy into his arms and held her tight. "Let it all out," he whispered. "Don't be ashamed to cry for someone you loved and lost. That's why God gave tears." Her crying would let up only to start again. "It's okay. I'm here. Take all the time you need." When he began to wonder how long it would take, she relaxed.

She gazed at him and sighed. "I'm sorry. I didn't want to cry in front of you."

"That's okay." He kissed her forehead before he stood back. "Wasn't it better to have someone hold you?"

"Better for me, but not so good for you."

"Dennis was a lucky guy to have your love. Don't be ashamed to mourn but not forever. He wouldn't want that." Eric longed to spend the day with her. "If you'd rather have only your family and close friends around, I'll understand. There's no need for me to tag along."

She cocked her head. "How'd you know about Dennis?"

"Your father told me."

"What did he say?"

"That you were engaged." He studied her face. "I don't need to horn in on today's activities if it makes you uncomfortable."

"The picnic won't be any fun without you. Please give me a few moments to freshen up and take me for a long walk on the beach before we join the others."

"Sure. I'll wait on the deck."

When Kathy returned, her eyes still looked red and puffy, but she smiled. "I'm ready now."

While they strolled along the beach, Eric put his arm around her waist. Neither made an attempt at conversation over the next half-hour. Finally, Eric broke the silence. "Think we should head back and go to the picnic?"

"Might as well."

At the house, when she handed him the car keys, he knew she was still too upset to drive. *I hope you perk up soon.* He drove to Morro Bay State Park where they found their friends near the eucalyptus trees.

"Where have you two been?" Mary asked. "We've been here over an hour."

"Sorry," Kathy said. "I just didn't feel like hurrying. Have you seen my folks?"

Mary said, "They're on the far side of the picnic area, over by the food. We ate a little as soon as we got here. Dad wants to start our surfing competition at three."

Kathy glanced at her watch. "We'd better hurry."

"Don't eat much," Jeff said. "You and Mary are supposed to ride the waves first."

"I'm not going to compete," Kathy said.

Jeff stared in disbelief. "That means Mary will be the only girl against us six guys."

Mary's eyes pleaded for Kathy to change her mind. "Are you sure?"

"I'm not in the mood."

Mary and Jeff looked disappointed but didn't press.

While Kathy and Eric ate lunch, he asked, "Where are they holding the competition today?"

"Pismo State Beach. That's the best area for surfing."

On the way, they passed Morro Rock, a gold and russet mountain-sized boulder that towered above the sand dunes. "That's one impressive rock, Eric said. "It looks like it's standing guard over the beach."

After she parked, they strolled hand in hand to the water. Kathy pointed. "Let's sit near Mary's parents. They're our judges. In fact, they dreamed up these competitions so they can see how much progress we've made. Even if surfing becomes popular in California, we'll probably never have a real meet in our area because of the cold water. Maybe someday, someone will come up with a cold water body suit that's better than what we have."

"Will Jeff find gear for me?"

With a look of determination, she said, "If he hasn't asked his father yet, I will."

The Watkins sat on lawn chairs, holding clipboards. After Kathy introduced Eric to Mary's father, Mr. Watkins said, "Glad you could join us. I hope you enjoy our little contest." He opened a shoe box. Inside lay a miniature wooden surfer riding a surfboard. Handing it to Eric, he asked, "How do you like what we have for first place?"

"That's some trophy. Much better than a blue ribbon," Eric said, admiring the detail. "Did you make it?"

Mr. Watkins nodded. "Mary loves the larger one I made and asked me to carve smaller ones for our competitions."

"How do you decide who wins this?"

"We take into consideration where the rider catches the wave, the distance of the ride standing, and the skill each one displays."

When Mary started paddling through the waves, Mr. Watkins stopped talking and focused his attention on her.

Eric watched with rapt attention.

When she caught her wave, Kathy pointed out how Mary was crouched low to gain more momentum because the wave was about to collapse. "Oh, no," she groaned when Mary wiped out. "That will cost her, but I'm glad she's not hurt." Mary had no problems with her next wave.

Jeff paddled into the silvery water.

Kathy explained his every move. Eric marveled at his ability. Jeff made riding a wave look as easy as descending a playground slide. Eric longed to be half that good.

On Jeff's second ride, Kathy's voice quivered with excitement, the first show of exuberance Eric had seen in her all day. "Wow! What control! What style!"

Eric caught her enthusiasm. "Jeff looks great."

Kathy beamed and clapped when Jeff received the first place trophy, but she grew quieter and more preoccupied while they drove back to the picnic area to wait for their friends.

While the foursome ate, Mary and Jeff did their best to lift Kathy's spirits. They talked first about surfing, then the Arroyo Grande awards banquet to be held Friday and the upcoming school beach party. Kathy listened and smiled as she nibbled at her food.

When Mary and Jeff left to refill their plates, Eric said, "Not hungry?"

She shook her head. "You're not eating much either."

"I had a huge breakfast," he said, but in truth, her depression had dampened his enthusiasm as well as his appetite.

When their friends returned, Jeff asked, "How soon can I start teaching you to ride the waves? Did today's match make you reconsider? Takes a real man to compete."

Eric grinned. "And Mary almost beat you today."

She beamed at Jeff with adoration. "I'll never beat him."

"I bet you would've today if your head wound hadn't kept you from practicing."

Jeff gave Eric a cock-sure smile. "You're evading my question. Are you going to back out?"

"Not on your life. You may be number one, but sometimes, an underdog tries harder."

The young people walked back to the beach to take part in volleyball games. Eric and Kathy watched from the sidelines. From her downcast expression, he wondered if she were thinking about Dennis. He imagined her envisioning Dennis playing against Jeff and besting him. *I wish I could be out there. Maybe if I stick around long enough, she'll think only of me and spur me on to beat Jeff.*

Around seven o'clock, the community sing began. Kathy leaned against Eric and let her mind drift as she listened to his mellow tenor voice. For a minute, she thought she heard Dennis, but his voice had been deeper. The two men were alike in many ways except Dennis had always been serious. She remembered her mother saying, "What do you see in Dennis? He's so stiff-necked." But Dennis wasn't. He could smile and laugh as readily as the next guy. He just didn't tell jokes or clown around.

Eric glanced down, winked, and gave her a hug.

After the singing ended and their friends left, Eric took her hand while they strolled to the car.

"Did you ever sing in a choir?" she asked.

"Yes, when I was in high school."

"I thought so. You have a beautiful voice. Dennis and I had fun singing in the church choir." Kathy kicked herself for mentioning that fact. *Now he'll realize I have been thinking about Dennis.*

Not cracking a smile, Eric said, "Actually, that wasn't my voice you heard. You see, I've rigged up a little box in my pocket and when I press a button, Caruso's voice belts out those songs, all prerecorded, of course. You just thought it was me, but I felt I should tell you the truth."

"Can't you ever be serious?"

"There's so much disturbing news in the world today, someone needs to play the clown to keep things in balance."

"You puzzle me."

He gave her waist a light squeeze. "That's to keep you guessing."

*He sure has that right.* Sometimes, Kathy didn't mind him kidding around to make her smile, but tonight she wanted him to be serious, more like Dennis. They reached her house and decided to take a walk along the beach instead of going inside and visiting with her family. Kathy leaned close to Eric but recalled the times she and Dennis had made this same walk. Kathy sighed softly.

"Thinking about Dennis?" Eric asked.

She nodded. "Does that bother you?"

"A little, but today's a time for remembering. I've been preoccupied too."

"What about?"

He shrugged. "Just past events."

*Now he's being too solemn.* Kathy wished he would say something to make her laugh. Strolling back to the house and climbing the deck steps, she wondered if he would kiss her. At the top, Kathy turned to face Eric, her heart longing for him to erase Dennis from her thoughts. "I admit I have thought a lot about Dennis, but I've also been thinking about you. You really are a terrific guy."

When Eric took her hands, she pulled his to bring him closer. He stood firm. "Not tonight, Kathy. Not with Dennis between us." He turned away.

"Please don't go. Stay with me." Tears she'd kept in check all afternoon burst forth.

Eric pivoted and gathered her into his arms. When she couldn't stop crying, he led Kathy to a lounge chair and pulled her onto his lap, cradling her as a father would a child.

Dr. Ryan heard a tapping on the window. He knew Kathy and Eric were on the deck since he'd heard her crying, but he had resisted the urge to look through the crack in the curtain. The tapping persisted. He drew back the material and saw Eric holding a sleeping Kathy. Eric put a finger to his lips before pointing to the door. Dr. Ryan opened it and held the screen back as Eric carried Kathy into the house.

Mrs. Ryan rose from the kitchen chair and hurried to Kathy's room. She turned back the covers. With great care, Eric lowered Kathy to the bed and stood back, gazing at her with compassion. Dr. Ryan beckoned Eric to follow him to the living room and offered him a seat.

Eric shook his head. "It's been a rough day. Kathy cried herself to sleep just now, and we were late for the picnic because she was upset. Dennis was a lucky guy."

"Yes, he was, and we all miss him." Dr. Ryan laid a hand on his shoulder and smiled. "But I think you'll find Kathy in a better frame of mind tomorrow."

## CHAPTER 9

Still unnerved, Eric walked back to the Dole's, pondering Kathy's crying spell. Her father had said tomorrow would be better, but Eric didn't know what to make of the redhead tugging at his heart. *Did I misread her? No. She wanted me to kiss her. Why did I have to say not with Dennis between us?* He smacked the side of his head. *You numbskull! You should have taken her into your arms and planted a big one or at least given her a gentle good-night kiss.*

He reached the Dole's, climbed the deck steps, and leaned against the railing to gaze at the ocean bathed in moonlight. Most of the time, the lapping waves calmed his troubled spirit. Tonight, they seemed to say, *You blew it. Did I, or does Kathy realize now she must let go of Dennis and get on with the future?*

With that thought, he entered the house and tiptoed down the hallway to his room. In bed, he lay between the sheets and envisioned how the night could have ended. *How will Kathy feel in the morning? Will she call me? Should I call her? Will I get another chance to kiss her? At least her wanting one gives me hope.*

Eric rose late and found Mrs. Dole dressed in her Sunday best, complete with hat and gloves. "You look spiffy," he told her.

"Why thank you. The department stores in San Luis Obispo are having terrific sales, part of their Memorial Day celebration. I'll be gone all day. There's a ham sandwich in the refrigerator."

"Thanks. Have fun."

"By the way, Dr. Ryan phoned. He wants you to call him at noon."

"What about?"

"He didn't say."

All morning, Eric worked on his motorcycle. The mechanics at the police garage had done a great job on the frame, but it was up to him to make his bike sound as good as it now looked. As he made adjustments, he pondered why Kathy's father had called.

Before noon, his motorcycle no longer sounded like what Aunt Jean called a threshing machine. Satisfied, he went indoors and retrieved the sandwich. *I'd better phone Dr. Ryan first.* He only had to wait a few minutes for the doctor to answer.

"Eric, thank you for calling promptly. I want to apologize for putting you in such an awkward position yesterday."

"Don't sweat it, sir. I hope I helped Kathy. How is she?"

When the doctor said, "She was in tears this morning," Eric glanced out the window at his motorcycle, wondering if he should leave town, until her father added, "But not over Dennis. She's afraid you'll take off on your motorcycle, and she'll never see you again." He paused. "Eric, be up front with me. What are your feelings?"

*Be honest? Okay, here goes.* "I think Kathy is one of the nicest girls I've known. I'd like to pursue a relationship, but I don't feel she's ready for one."

"Maybe. Maybe not. But please call her as soon as she gets home from school."

"I will, sir. Thank you."

Was it too soon to say he'd fallen in love with Kathy? Despite all Jill had done, she still lingered in his mind. Was he lying to himself by saying it was too late for them to renew their relationship?

He woofed down his sandwich and went outdoors to wash greasy smears off his motorcycle. While he polished chrome to a shine, he thought, *Someday, I need to tell Kathy about Jill.* Although Jill's letters lay buried, the words still haunted him. *I should have never opened the envelopes.*

He hopped on his bike took a spin on the coast road and returned to the Dole's, thinking more about Kathy than Jill.

Eric made a minor adjustment on his motorcycle to make it rev more smoothly. As he put the tools away, Jeff pulled into the driveway and stopped but didn't get out of his car. Eric ambled over and put his foot on the running board. "What's up?"

"Nothing. I happened by and saw you, so I decided to stop."

Eric laughed. "Sure you did."

Jeff's face reddened. "Okay, so I didn't. I saw you working on your bike and thought Kathy might be right about you leaving town."

"No, Jeff, as much as that would please you, I'm not."

"Would you believe me if I said I'd like you to stay?"

Eric's mouth dropped open. "Why?"

"If you left, it would break Kathy's heart, and she's suffered enough. She's nuts about you, and that's good enough for me. We may never be friends, but maybe we can tolerate each other for her sake."

"I agree."

Eric watched Jeff drive away. After Omaha Beach, where death beckoned every second, he'd held back from making close ties, but now he felt differently. As Jeff's car disappeared around a corner, Eric thought, *I can live with us tolerating each other, but Jeff, I'd really like to have you for a friend.*

An hour later, he phoned Kathy.

Mrs. Ryan answered. "Yes, Kathy's here."

Eric heard a muted conversation before Kathy, in a tentative voice said, "Hi. Are you mad at me?"

"Of course not, and I have no intention of leaving town."

"Jeff told you?"

"He stopped by and said you were upset."

"Then you wouldn't mind coming over? Jeff and Mary are here. We thought we'd play ping-pong."

"I'll come over on one condition."

"What's that?"

"No more tears."

"I promise. How soon can you be here?"

"Right away."

The purr in her voice enticed him to hurry. His heart raced as fast as the rev of his motorcycle. Kathy stood on the porch before he had time to park. He bounded up the steps. "You must have been watching out the window."

"I wanted a few minutes alone with you." Longing filled her eyes as they searched his.

He blinked in disbelief. "You want me to kiss you? Right now?"

"Am I that transparent?"

"Indeed you are." When he cupped her chin, she threw her arms around his neck and held him so tightly Dennis's ghost couldn't have squeezed between them as she kissed him. "Whoa," he said, stepping back. "The guy's supposed to be in charge. Why do I suddenly feel like putty in your hands?"

"Because that's the way it's supposed to be, silly. You men just think you're in control of this world."

"Is that a challenge?"

Her eyes twinkled. "Take it any way you want."

"I'll concede the first round, but the game is only beginning." He grabbed her around the waist, planted a hard kiss, and opened the door before she had a chance to react. "Want to try for round three?"

"That wasn't fair!"

"You know what they say, 'All's fair in love and war.'"

"How true."

From the way she said it, he knew he'd better stay alert. She would definitely try to get back at him.

Playing ping-pong partners against Mary and Jeff proved challenging, but he and Kathy won three out of five games. While the foursome drank lemonade on the deck, Kathy said, "Jeff and Mary are staying for dinner. Would you like to join us? Dad's firing up the barbecue, and we're having hamburgers."

"Sounds great."

Jeff grinned. "That will give Mary and me a chance to beat you two."

After dinner when they played, Eric and Kathy lost two out of five games, but they didn't mind since it meant the day's match ended in a draw. Eric stayed a few minutes after their friends left.

Kathy said, "Tomorrow night is the school awards banquet. I'd like you to come with us. My treat."

"Sounds great, but I don't have a suit. You're sure it's okay with your parents?"

"It was their suggestion, and it is casual. The banquet starts at five. I'll pick you up after school and give you a tour of the coast. Dad told me he gave you a local history lesson, and I can show you where all the events took place. Afterward, we'll come back here, and the boys can entertain you while I get ready. And Saturday, if you don't have plans, come with me while I run some errands. One will be to Mary's to pick up a surfboard for you. You'll have a chance to see her father's workshop."

"I can't pass that up."

On their tour of the coast Friday, when they passed Morro Rock, Kathy pointed to the buildings south of it. "That's the US Naval Amphibious Training Base where Jeff's dad works." At Cayucos Beach, she showed him the spot where the Japanese torpedo had exploded. "We'll never forget that hair-raising night. Dad was there helping. He told us it was a miracle no one was killed."

Coming back, she seemed subdued as if she were reliving the incident. To get her mind off the war, Eric said, "I really like this area, especially the people. I haven't been here long and already feel at home."

She gave him a mischievous smile. "I'm glad."

That night in the school cafeteria, Eric sat with Kathy's family as she received an award for outstanding academic achievements. Pride shone from their faces. Eric felt privileged to share the moment with them, and his heart overflowed with admiration and tenderness for Kathy. Knowing her had touched him with a special healing. He knew what was happening but felt powerless to fight. The truth was he didn't want to. He wanted to love and be loved in return.

On the way back to her house, Dr. Ryan dropped off Angela to spend the night with a friend.

As soon as they arrived home, Jimmy asked his father, "What game can we play?"

"No games tonight. We plan to have grown-up talk, and we want you and Tommy to play in your room."

The boys' faces turned down in almost identical pouts until Mrs. Ryan said, "As a special treat, I'll bring you a big bowl of popcorn, and you can split a *Dr. Pepper*. Okay?" After they nodded and dashed to their bedroom, she said, "I hope they'll behave so we can talk."

*Did I just witness the boys being bribed? Talk is that important? Why?*

As Mrs. Ryan served pie and coffee in the living room, Eric grew uneasy. Maybe it was the hint of reserve in Mrs. Ryan's manner or the exchanged glances between Kathy's parents, but instinct told Eric they wanted to learn more about him. They knew he'd stayed with his father after his parents divorced and went to Colorado to live with his aunt and uncle after his father died. He'd mentioned his brother and sister but nothing about Germany or that Erin was his twin. Guilt tugged at Eric for being evasive. He prayed no one asked why he wasn't in uniform.

Dr. Ryan wondered about this young man who had the knack of making people smile. Captain Dole had assured him he was an honorable person but would not elaborate. When asked if Eric could be trusted with Kathy, he said, "In my estimation, yes." The policeman was a shrewd judge of character, and the doctor had never known him to be wrong.

*Eric seems like a nice young man, and Kathy sure likes him. Once, Dennis received her special smile, now Eric does. Maybe tonight we'll learn more about him.* "So you grew up in Colorado. Do you intend to be a rancher like your uncle?"

"I haven't decided."

Dr. Ryan sat back and listened with interest when Eric began talking about his childhood. His words, like an artist's brush, painted vivid descriptions. The doctor could picture the Colorado Rockies, even the ranch. Some of Eric's experiences made the family laugh. *Strange, Eric doesn't talk about his uncle, father, or mother. He's only mentioned his brother once when he talked about them playing on the hitching post at their grandmothers.* It was then Dr. Ryan caught a glimpse of sorrow in Eric's eyes, a mistiness quickly masked. *What painful memory caused this?*

The more he listened, the more he realized Eric was manipulating conversation to be entertaining not informative. Why? What was he trying to hide? *Who are you, young man? Monday when I take out your stitches, you and I are going to have a long talk. I want straight answers before my daughter falls in love with you—if it's not too late.*

After Eric left, Kathy leaned on the deck railing and listened to the waves crashing against the cliff wall. While she drove home from the banquet, Eric had slipped his arm around her shoulders, and the car drifted. "Steady," he'd said, grasping the wheel with his other hand, his cheek brushing hers. "I didn't mean to startle you," he added, giving her a gentle hug.

She'd longed for a sign he cared, and his actions today left no doubt in her mind. Kathy heard the French doors open and turned to see her mother.

"Shouldn't you be turning in? It's almost midnight," she said, joining Kathy at the railing.

"I know, but it's so beautiful out here. I want to drink it all in."

Her mother laughed. "Fog is beautiful?"

"Tonight, it is."

"Do I detect stardust in your eyes?"

Kathy sighed. "Isn't he wonderful? I could have listened to him all night."

"He does have a way with words. Has he been sweet-talking you?"

"Of course not! Why do you suppose he's traveling around the country? I can't help wondering why he's not in the service, but I'm afraid to ask for fear he's 4F. One of Jeff's friends became bitter when he was rejected."

"Maybe Eric's recovering from a serious illness. This would explain why he's so thin and pale."

"It wouldn't be right for me to ask, would it?"

"No. When he's ready to share his personal life, he will."

"If he had a tan like Jeff, he'd be the most handsome guy in Arroyo Grande."

Her mother laughed. "When you invite him to spend Sunday on the beach with us, make sure he keeps lotion on so he doesn't fry."

Too wound up to sleep, Kathy reluctantly went indoors. She sat on the window seat in her room and thought about Eric. *Oh, my mystery man, there's so much I want to know about you.*

Dr. Ryan looked up from his book when his wife came into the living room. "Something wrong?"

She sat on the arm of his chair. "I'm afraid Kathy's falling in love."

*       *       *

Saturday afternoon, Eric waited for Kathy on the Dole's front porch. He glanced at his watch for the fourth time—almost one. *She's not all that late.* When he saw the Ryan's station wagon, Eric dashed down the steps and climbed in as soon as the car stopped.

"Sorry, I'm late," she said. "I had to change a flat. These reconditioned tires are the pits." She pointed to the C sticker on the windshield. "This allows Dad to buy more gas, but nothing enables doctors to purchase new tires."

Kathy's vivacious rambling tickled him. *She was so different from Jill, not a snobbish bone in her body.*

Kathy started to turn the key in the ignition but stopped. She cocked her head and stared at him. "What's so funny? Didn't you think I could change a tire?"

"Far from it. You are the most capable young woman I've dated." *Jill would have died before touching anything dirty.*

"Then what amused you?"

"You misread me. I was watching you and listening with pure enjoyment." When her brows came together with skepticism, he added, "I guess changing a tire on this monstrous station wagon does surprise me a little." He winked. "But I like able-bodied women."

"Dennis did too." She turned the key. "Since you're from Colorado, it surprises me that you've heard about surfing."

"I mentioned this to your father, but I guess he didn't tell you. I had a Hawaiian friend who loved surfing. He predicted the sport would become as popular in California as it is in the Islands and Australia. He was quite a guy."

"Was?"

He drew in a breath. "He was killed on Omaha Beach."

Kathy bit down on her lip and started the car. "Dennis died at Aachen."

Eric nodded. "Mr. Dole told me."

She focused her eyes straight ahead and silently drove down the tree-lined road.

Eric wanted to kick himself. Why couldn't he have just said he had a Hawaiian friend? "What's on the agenda?" he asked, trying to dispel her thoughts.

"What?"

"Where are we headed?"

"To Mary's, to pick up a surfboard. Her father said you can use an old one he has." Her face remained deadpan, but at least she'd come out of her trance. She gestured toward the back of the car. "First, I have to drop off those smashed tin cans at Tommy's school. There's a contest to see who can collect the most for the war effort. Then it's to Hinkle's Market. They set five pounds of sugar aside as a favor to Dad for saving Mrs. Hinkle's life. On the way home, I have to stop at the meat locker to drop off a can of bacon grease Mom saved and pick up some meat. Dad bought fifty pounds of frozen beef the army sold after VE day." Her face brightened. "You get steak tonight if you stay for dinner."

"I can't pass that up."

After they finished their errands, Kathy drove to the Watkins. Mary, sitting on the porch, stood and hurried down the walkway to greet them. "Hi," she said, "you missed Dad by ten minutes. He came home between jobs."

"I was hoping to watch him work," Eric said. "I'd like to see him make a surfboard."

"Follow me around back," Mary said. "Dad's shop is in the garage, but he hasn't made a board in months. His landscaping business keeps him busy dawn to dusk. Maybe this fall, he'll get back to his hobby."

They followed her into a partitioned section of the garage that housed Mr. Watkins's workshop. Eric glanced around the sawdust-strewn room. Slabs of balsa wood lay on a table. The smell of varnish and wood permeated the area. "This is great work," Eric said, running his hands over an unvarnished board lying on the workbench.

"Dad's experimenting with different finishes. Balsa makes great lightweight surfboards, but the material gets waterlogged. The board he has for you is over here." She pointed to a large well-worn surfboard that looked as if it weighed over fifty pounds. "This is the one Dennis used while he was learning. It's a Thomas Blake hollow board. They're not as popular as they used to be, but they're fast and sturdy."

Kathy ran her hand lovingly over the surface. "I'd forgotten your father loaned this to Dennis."

Eric tried to shrug off Dennis having used it, but like a tiny sliver, it lodged under his skin, lessening his enthusiasm.

Mary gave Eric an understanding smile. "Before you leave," she said, "don't let me forget to give you the diving suit. It's in a box on the porch. Jeff's mother mended the rips and cleaned it up the best she could."

Eric picked up the surfboard, and Kathy carried the box to the station wagon. After they put the items in back, Eric said, "What now?"

"Dad suggested I show you the Cal Poly campus. Would you like to see it?"

"Sure."

They drove to San Luis Obispo and toured the tree-studded campus. Eric gazed around in surprise—no red brick, ivy-covered buildings stood here. Unlike those pictured in movies, these halls of learning wore drab yellow stucco, but their red tile roofs gave them old-world charm. One with a spire housed a clock. It towered over the campus as if to monitor the footsteps of all within its view.

Before they headed home, Kathy stopped at a drug store. At the counter, they sipped cherry phosphates. "Are you planning to attend Cal Poly this fall?" Eric asked.

Her eyes misted. "Dennis and I were going to but . . . " She shrugged. "Now it doesn't seem important."

*Dennis again. Can't we discuss anything today without his name popping up?* "I can't wait until Monday to try out my surfboard. I'd like to see what I can accomplish before the rest of you come down after school."

An hour before dinner, they returned to the house and played ping-pong. Usually, she matched him volley for volley. Today, her reflexes seemed slow, making him feel her mind was still on Dennis. He wished she'd laugh and give him her I-think-you're-special smile, but he sensed that was on hold.

*Maybe I'm kidding myself that I can take Dennis's place. Maybe Kathy and I aren't meant to be. Nancy and Ann had mood swings, but I'm beginning to have doubts about Kathy's. How can a gal throw her arms around you one moment and later shove you into the pits?*

During dinner, Eric realized that Dr. Ryan wasn't his friendly self either. Was his attitude a reflection of Kathy's?

When her mother started talking about the annual church beach barbecue, Kathy smacked her head and turned to Eric. "I invited Mary and Jeff, but I forgot to mention it to you. Everyone migrates to the beach after church even though we don't eat until five. Dinner is followed by a short evening service around a huge bonfire. I'd love for you to come. Will you?"

"Sure . . . sounds like fun."

While Kathy and Angela were in the kitchen doing the dishes, Eric sat in the living room with Dr. Ryan who asked, "Mind if I change your Monday appointment to eleven thirty? After I remove your stitches, I'd like to take you to lunch."

"Sounds great," Eric said, but sensed Dr. Ryan had something on his mind. Did he want him to back off from courting Kathy?

# CHAPTER 10

Sunday morning while Eric ate breakfast with the Doles, he stared out the dining room window. "That fog's so thick I can't see beyond the deck."

"It will burn off," the captain assured him. "There will be plenty of sunshine this afternoon."

*No way will this fog lift,* Eric thought while he waited on the porch for Kathy's car to pierce the cloud of vapor. When she invited him to attend church, he accepted, but his past bouts of claustrophobia made him leery. He never knew when thinking about the war or feeling confined would bring on an attack.

Like an airplane emerging from a cloud bank, Dr. Ryan's Lincoln Zephyr appeared in the driveway and stopped in front of the house. Eric dashed down the steps, climbed in, and winked at Kathy. "Think you can find your way in this pea soup?"

"I've had lots of practice. Colorado may not have much fog, but we're used to it on the coast."

As if to prove her words correct, the church parking lot was full; the sanctuary, packed. Eric stiffened with apprehension. He remembered Mother's Day. In case he had to leave, he guided Kathy toward two empty last row seats and slipped his hand over hers while they exchanged smiles.

Their closeness relaxed him but not for long. The first song *Onward Christian Soldiers* made him break into a cold sweat.

The pastor, dressed casual in a short sleeve shirt, smiled as he took his place at the pulpit. "Since I was called out of town last week, I missed our Memorial Day service honoring military personnel, especially those who have given their lives in defense of freedom. I've asked the choir to repeat last Sunday's music selections."

The choir sang a medley of patriotic songs while a Boy Scout troop marched in with the American flag. Everyone stood, and the congregation joined the choir in singing *The Battle Hymn of the Republic.*

Eric, too choked to open his mouth, didn't know how much more he could take. When tears streamed from Kathy's eyes, he fought to stem his. After they sat, he offered her his handkerchief. She blotted her face and wrapped her hands around the white linen as if she needed to hold something.

In a hoarse voice, the pastor said, "We want to honor all our veterans and those in the military. Would you please stand."

Guilt plagued Eric when he didn't rise. He clapped with the congregation but felt as if he were denying his own birthright. *I've got to put the war behind me. I need to talk about my bitter memories.* When the pastor prayed, Eric's soul cried, *Lord, help me.* He blinked back tears and tried to regain his composure.

After the prayer, Kathy dabbed her eyes and clutched the hand-kerchief with tight fists. Compassion for her overcame Eric's anguish. He put his arm around her, drawing her close. Kathy cast a faint smile, but her lower lip quivered.

Eric blocked out the sermon with thoughts of Kathy and gave a quiet sigh when the service ended. He had endured. Outside, introductions were brief as everyone seemed eager to get away.

Eric was glad to see the blue sky, but Kathy seemed shrouded in fog while she drove him to the Dole's. "Want to talk about it?" he asked in a gentle voice.

"I'm sorry. If I'd known the pastor was going to repeat last Sunday's patriotic service, I never would have invited you. Today, I didn't want anything reminding me of Dennis."

"The service must have been hard for you."

She nodded. "But I didn't want Dennis coming between us."

"Nor did I, but it's hard to forget those we've lost."

"I noticed the Memorial Day observance as well as today's upset you too. Did you lose anyone close?"

He nodded. "My brother."

"I'm sorry."

"It's a lousy war. I feel for you and the Doles. I wish I could have known Dennis. He must have been a great guy." He gazed out the window, knowing he should use this opening to tell her he'd just returned from fighting. His lips compressed tighter. He couldn't tell her about Dennis. Not yet and never in detail.

Kathy pulled into the Doles' circular driveway and stopped in front of the porch. She searched his face. "Instead of touring the coast, are you sorry you ended up in Arroyo Grande?"

"Not in the least."

"I'm glad. See you at lunch."

He gave her hands a gentle squeeze. "I'll hurry and get ready."

In his bedroom, Eric changed into blue shorts, tugged on a light blue sleeveless pullover, and tucked it in securely so it wouldn't flip up and reveal his scars.

Mrs. Dole met him at the front door and handed him a beach towel and suntan lotion. "Use this freely," she admonished. "I want no lobsters in my house tonight."

Eric grinned and saluted. "Aye, aye, Captain."

She laughed and shooed him out the door. "Have fun."

Eric walked to Kathy's with mixed emotions. He looked forward to spending the afternoon on the beach, but he couldn't shake the depression brought on by the church service. Her having lost the man she loved presented a problem. What should he do? His heart longed to rush in and sweep her off her feet. His head said, *Go easy.*

Jill had prodded him to speed up their relationship. She wanted him to marry her before he went overseas. She wanted a child, and his refusal angered her. Maybe if they'd married and had a baby, she would've remained faithful. Did she still love him? Did it matter?

As he approached Kathy's house, he realized the two women were as different as a kid's swimming pool and an ocean—one shallow, one deep. Right now, he wanted the ocean, but he'd wade in, take things slow. *Kathy may have Dennis on her mind and may be depressed. I'll try to make her laugh.*

Eric hurried up the porch steps, rang the bell, and drew in a breath when Kathy appeared. Over her swimsuit, she wore a skimpy white cover-up tied with a turquoise ribbon. "Am I too early?" he asked, imagining how she would look when she removed the cover up.

"Of course not. Come in. Mom has tuna sandwiches on the table to tide us over until the barbecue."

While they ate, Kathy's brothers begged to walk with them instead of riding with her parents. Eric was glad she refused to let them come. This would be their only chance to be alone. Her quietness during lunch gave him the impression she was still feeling down, and he longed to bring a smile to her face.

Dr. Ryan said, "Eric, before you and Kathy leave I need to recheck the stitches in your leg." After doing so, he nodded with satisfaction. "You've healed so fast, I could probably take these out now, but I think I'll wait until tomorrow's appointment. Have a good time at the beach."

The boys followed Eric and Kathy outdoors. "Please let us go with you," Jimmy pleaded.

"We'll be good," Tommy said.

Kathy put her hands on her hips. "I already said no. Mom and Dad are ready to leave now. You'll get there much sooner going with them."

The boys stood on the deck, sulking.

Eric followed Kathy down the steep cliff steps. Her auburn ponytail bounced as she descended. When she turned and waited for Eric at the bottom, he stopped and studied her. The ribbon around her waist had come untied, allowing the wind to blow open her cover-up, revealing a two piece, turquoise swimsuit that accentuated every curve.

"Hurry up, slowpoke," she called.

Eric took his time. When he reached her, he grinned.

"What are you scheming?" she asked.

"Not a thing."

She cocked her head and eyed him with suspicion. "What are you thinking?"

"In one word? Knockout."

"What?" she laughed.

"Knockout. I know I said kissable last Sunday but now, *knockout* applies."

A hint of color tinged her cheeks. While she retied the ribbon, a mischievous smile crept across her face. "Does that mean I'm no longer kissable?"

Eric tried to mask his surprise and knew he'd failed when her eyes danced with laughter. Like a kitten toying with a mouse, she'd caught him off guard and was enjoying the moment. Eric wanted to grab and kiss her long and hard. Propriety dictated otherwise since they stood in full view of the house. Was that why Kathy felt safe in giving him such an open invitation?

He put his finger to his lips and stared past her as if deep in thought before he shrugged. "I guess since I said earlier you were kissable, you still are." He took her hand and kissed it in gallant fashion. In his best Rhett Butler voice, he said, "Ms. Kathy, would you dare ask me that tonight when no one can see us?"

She fluttered her eyelashes and said in a falsetto voice, "Sir, to ask would make me appear forward."

Eric laughed. *And I was worried you might stay depressed? Today is definitely going to be a good day. Tonight? I can hardly wait.* He put his arm around her waist as they strolled on the beach toward the barbecue area. Kathy lapsed into silence. Her sudden quietness puzzled him. What was she thinking? He stopped, picked up a seashell, and hurled it to skim the waves.

"Eric, when you told Jeff last Sunday you might settle down here, were you just egging him on?"

"At the time, yes, but I really think I could be happy living here."

"Haven't you been happy elsewhere?"

He hesitated, searching for the right words. "Over the past three years, I haven't stayed in one spot for long. In May, my restlessness compelled me to leave home. I don't feel restless now. Maybe I'm finally growing up." He chuckled. "It's about time, I guess."

She tilted her head. "How old are you?"

"Twenty-two."

Kathy raised an eyebrow. "And you've been traveling from place to place for three years?"

He nodded.

"How do you support yourself?"

"I'm a good mechanic."

"Would you like to open your own garage?"

"Not really. I couldn't stand being cooped up every day. I want to go to college and study agriculture and animal husbandry or maybe forestry. I like being outdoors."

"Then why not do it?"

He picked up a handful of seashells and flung them one by one toward the rolling waves.

"Eric?"

He brushed off his hands and turned. "Why not do it?" he repeated. "Because I'm just taking one day at a time."

"Why?"

He picked up another shell, stared at it, and tossed it aside. "Like you, marriage figured into my future. If things had gone according to my plans, I'd probably be on my honeymoon."

"What happened?"

"She dumped me for another guy."

"While you were traveling?"

He wished she'd quit probing. "Yes," he said more forcefully than he intended.

Kathy cringed. "Maybe she got tired of waiting."

"Would you have waited for Dennis?"

"Yes, but he was overseas. That's different!"

"Not really, but let's drop the subject. I came to California to forget and have fun. I'll race you to the barbecue area."

Kathy and Eric loped side by side, neither running nor trying to outdo the other, but thoughts raced through Kathy's mind. *I must forget Dennis today. I'm not going to embarrass myself by crying in front of Eric.*

When they reached the shaded picnic area, Jimmy and Tommy rushed toward them, grabbed Eric's hands, and pulled him toward the water.

"What took you so long?" Jimmy asked Eric.

"We want to go wading," Tommy said.

Eric cast Kathy a feigned look of fright. "Help! They're planning to drown me."

She laughed as the boys dragged him to the water's edge. With a quick yank, he broke free and turned on them, chasing each one, pretending he couldn't catch them. They squealed with delight.

*Eric likes children. He'll make a good father. He likes to clown around but he can be serious.* She recalled how his eyes reflected internal pain when he mentioned his brother and talked about Jill. Was emotional turmoil the cause of his restlessness? Would he ever get over it? Could he really be content here? *I hope so. I long for him to stay.*

Kathy walked to her parents' station wagon and retrieved an old blanket. She carried it back to the beach, spread it out over the sand, and sat.

Eric left the boys playing in the water, tucked his pullover under his trunks, and flopped beside her. "What kind of a woman are you? I begged you to save me!" He clutched his chest and gasped, "You're heartless." He keeled over and closed his eyes.

"You are positively nuts," Kathy said.

He opened one eye. "No tears? Beware, when you least expect it, you'll meet your fate."

Kathy started laughing.

Eric rolled over and came to his knees. "You think I'm kidding." He bounded to his feet, and before she could resist, he picked her up and carried her toward the waves.

"Eric, put me down!"

"Believe me, I intend to."

"Please, I don't want to get wet now."

"Too late, my sweet Kathy. You've laughed once too often." He carried her until the water reached his knees and dropped her, but she landed on her feet.

"You beast," she laughed and playfully pushed him backward.

"Beauty and the Beast . . . that always was a good combination." He scooped her into his arms, carried her to the blanket, and gently set her on it. He plopped beside her and held out the suntan lotion. "Would my Beauty please spread this on my neck and shoulders?"

She extended her fingers but cocked her head. "Why should I?"

"Because Beauty is always kind to the poor beast."

Kathy laughed and accepted the bottle. She smoothed the lotion on the back of his neck and over his shoulders. *Why doesn't he go bare-chested like the other guys? Does he wear a tank top to protect him from the sun, or could he be hiding a tattoo?*

From the corner of her eye, Kathy saw her brothers creeping toward them with pails of water and knew they were going to empty them on Eric. She fought back a giggle but laughed when two buckets of water poured over him.

Eric sprang to life. Dripping wet, he came to his knees and shook himself like a lion, growled, and crawled menacingly toward Tommy who was laughing so hard he couldn't run away.

Jimmy came to his rescue. He climbed onto Eric's back and kicked him in the ribs. "Giddy-up."

Eric tossed him off by rolling over. Tommy started to pounce on his stomach. To Kathy's surprise, Eric grabbed him by the waist and sat up. "Fun's over," he said in a harsh voice. "Time to play by yourselves." Her brothers, shocked and puzzled, backed away. "Look," Eric said, "I didn't mean to sound so gruff. I guess you've worn me out." Smiling he added, "We'll have some more fun later. Okay?" They nodded and ran toward the water.

Looking downcast, he stared after them before returning to the blanket.

Kathy brushed the sand off his shoulders Sensing, he was upset, she said, "I told you they could be pests. Sometimes, they get under my skin too."

"But I acted so mean."

"Don't worry," she said, pouring suntan lotion on his shoulders. "They'll forget before this sinks in." She puzzled over his reaction. He'd looked alarmed as if he were afraid of being hurt. *Is he recovering from an accident? I wish I had the nerve to ask so I could silence Jeff.* During school lunch hour, Jeff constantly voiced his doubts about Eric's credibility, implying Eric might be a draft-dodger. Dennis had been Jeff's best friend, and she knew it irked Jeff to see her falling for Eric, but he had no right to say disparaging things. So far, she'd managed to keep him from asking Eric why he wasn't in uniform.

Eric winced. "Easy, that's not bread you're kneading."

"Sorry, I guess I got carried away."

He turned to face her, sitting Indian-fashion. "Far, far away. What's on your mind?"

"I was thinking about you and Jeff, hoping you'd hit it off better today."

"Oh."

"What is it with you two anyway?"

"Ask him. He's the one with the chip on his shoulder." He raised an eyebrow. "Hasn't he given you a clue?"

Kathy sighed. "Dennis and Jeff were close friends. I think Jeff resents your taking Dennis's place."

His eyes widened. "Have I?"

Her own words shocked her. For a moment, she stared past him, unable to reaffirm them. "You're beginning to."

She expected him to smile, maybe say something witty or romantic. Instead, his forehead furrowed. "Is that all he resents?"

Almost in a whisper she added, "He resents your not being in uniform."

He took her hands in his. "Does that bother you?"

"No," Kathy said, wishing she could erase the concern she saw in his eyes.

"I'm glad." He stared at the blanket a moment before searching her face. "The past three years have been hard on me, Kathy . . . too rough to share with you now. Can you accept that?"

"Of course, I can."

Tension drained from his face. "Thank you. I'll try to get along with Jeff when he and Mary get here."

His thumbs massaged the back of her hands causing unsettling feelings to surface. Could Eric sense how his closeness and intense smile were affecting her? She saw Mary and Jeff running toward them. Relieved to escape Eric's scrutiny, she pulled her hands free and waved.

Mary beckoned. "Come on. The volleyball game's about ready to start."

Kathy glanced at Eric. "Do you want to play?"

"Sure. My ankle's strong enough now."

Jeff and Eric acknowledged each other with a nod, their faces showing no trace of antagonism. Kathy took that as a good omen.

While two of Jeff's friends drew the boundaries in the sand, he asked Eric, "Do you want to play on the same side or the opposite?"

With Jeff throwing the gauntlet, Kathy knew, even before Eric answered, they would be playing opposite their friends. The two men, pitted against each other several times, returned volley for volley. Their intense expressions showed determination to outdo the other. The games were close, but Jeff and Mary's team won two out of three.

After the teams broke up, Jeff said to Eric, "Well, old man, do you want a rematch?"

Eric raised an eyebrow. "Old man? You just had the edge because I'd already played hard with Jimmy and Tommy. How are you at basketball?"

Mary beamed. "Why, Jeff's the best player on the team."

"Well now," Eric said, "how about a little one-on-one sometime next week?"

"You're on. Is this for fun, or do you want to make it interesting?"

"Since you put it that way, how about the loser taking the winner and the girls to dinner and a movie?"

"Sounds fair. Where would you girls like Eric to take us?"

"Pretty cocky, aren't you?" Eric interjected. "Old man, you said. Would you like to eat your words Thursday or Friday?"

"I can whip you Thursday just as easily as Friday but why not save Friday for dinner and the movie?"

Laughter tugged at the corners of Eric's mouth. "Good, that way, you won't find your words ruining your appetite."

Jeff had no comeback, and Kathy relaxed. The two men might never be friends but through competition, maybe they'd learn to respect each other.

After the evening church service, Eric walked her home, his arm around her waist. The moon shed enough light to pinpoint the water's edge but not enough for Kathy to see Eric's face clearly. What was he thinking? When would he kiss her?

When they reached the cliff steps leading to her house, Eric said, "Thank you for inviting me. I don't know when I've enjoyed myself more."

"I had fun too." Kathy grew so tense she wanted to scream. Why was he taking so long to kiss her?

"Kathy." He stopped and drew in a breath. "More than anything, I want to kiss you, but it wouldn't be fair. I told you about Jill, but I didn't tell you she wrote and said she broke up with the other guy and wants to see me when I return. My feelings for her are still mixed. I wouldn't hurt you for the world."

Kathy stood stunned, confused. *What am I supposed to do?* Letting her heart dictate, she put her arms around his neck, gave him a quick kiss, and released him. She trembled and held her breath as she pulled back to judge his reaction. Had she made the right move?

Both surprise and pleasure registered on Eric's face. He embraced her, brushing her lips with his before kissing her fully. "I don't know what possessed you," he whispered, "but thank you. I have a feeling by the time summer ends, there will be nothing in Colorado to keep me there when I return in August."

"Do you have to go back?" Her voice quavered despite her attempt to remain calm.

"I promised Cindy I'd take her to the amusement park in Denver before school starts, and my sister, Nancy is getting married this fall."

"Will you see Jill?" The words caught in her throat.

He nodded. "She'll be in the wedding party. But August is a long time away." He gathered her into his arms, kissed her again, and murmured, "I hope you sleep well. I know I will."

When Kathy glided into the living room, her mother looked up and smiled. "You must have had a good time today."

"Marvelous. He's wonderful."

Her father frowned. "Kathy, please don't let your heart get the best of you. We know very little about Eric. I don't want you to get hurt."

"I know all I need to know, Daddy." In a dream-like state, Kathy walked to her room. Sitting on the window seat, she picked up her favorite teddy bear and hugged it. She had three months to make Eric forget Jill, who had hurt him deeply. She glanced at Dennis's picture on her dresser with a twinge of guilt. She would never forget Dennis. Maybe Jill deserved to be forgotten, but Dennis didn't. *Oh, Dennis, I know you will understand.*

# CHAPTER 11

**M**onday morning, Eric glanced at his watch before strolling to the kitchen. He had plenty of time for a second cup of coffee.

Mrs. Dole entered with the mail, sniffing an envelope. "Here's another sweet scented letter for you."

Eric's face grew hot. *What must she think about my courting Kathy and getting perfumed letters from another girl?* "I don't intend to answer."

"Maybe you should to let the young lady know how you feel."

"She jilted me while I was overseas."

"I see." Her brow wrinkled as she went back to sorting the mail.

Eric sensed she wanted to say more but wouldn't pry. He laid the pink floral envelope on the table and finished his coffee.

In his room, he dropped the unopened letter in the lower bureau drawer. Why couldn't life be simple? When he had proposed to Jill, he envisioned fighting for freedom and rushing home to her waiting arms. He glared at the chest of drawers, pivoted, and strode from the room. He had an appointment to keep with Dr. Ryan.

Arriving early, he sat in the waiting room, thumbed through a magazine and tossed it back on the stack. Unable to relax, Eric strolled to the window and stared at the cars zooming on the beach highway as fast as the thoughts whizzing through his mind. *What does the doctor want to discuss? My intentions? Did Mrs. Dole say something to him about my receiving love letters?*

A nurse interrupted his thoughts. "Mr. Stone, the doctor will see you now."

His heart thumping, Eric followed her to the examination room.

Dr. Ryan's face revealed nothing when he came through the doorway, but his first question confirmed Eric's suspicion he had something on his mind. "Do you object to having a heart-to-heart talk after lunch?"

Eric met his gaze. "You want to know my intentions?"

"Among other things."

"Such as?"

"Your evasiveness."

"Oh." Eric stiffened. The ensuing silence seemed ready to strangle him. "I haven't done anything criminal."

Kathy's father smiled. "If you had, Captain Dole wouldn't have you staying with them." He raised an eyebrow. "On the other hand . . ."

Eric lowered his head. Guilt had plagued him since Erin's death. He held himself responsible. True, he hadn't tossed the explosives, but he had prayed for the German defender to be blown to bits. His brother's death brought the sharp realization that whenever he pulled a trigger, he might kill someone else's loved one.

Dr. Ryan put his hands on Eric's shoulders. "What's wrong?"

Eric longed to share all he'd been through, but the words wouldn't come. Finally, he whispered, "I was in the war." The room closed in on him like his prison cell. He broke into a cold sweat, and his hands grew clammy as he backed away. "I need air."

"Let's go for a walk. I can take out your stitches later."

Eric sucked in cool air until he regained his composure.

"Better," the doctor asked while they walked.

Eric nodded.

"Feel like eating? There's a place around the corner that has *out-side* tables."

Eric caught the emphasis and wondered if Dr. Ryan had diagnosed his problem. "Sure," he said, forcing a smile.

Students finishing lunch break milled around the stand but left before he and the doctor placed their order. A white-haired man cleared and wiped their table. "Those students are good kids, but they sure leave a mess. You'd think they'd never heard of a trash can," he snorted, hurried back inside, and returned with a tray of hamburgers and two coffees.

Dr. Ryan took a sip of coffee before he picked up his hamburger. "These are the best. I think you'll see why the kids flock here. I predict a bright future for these little stands."

Eric nodded. "This burger is good."

"What branch of service were you in?"

"The army."

"The problem that hit you in my office, have you experienced it before?"

"Ever since I came home in April."

"Have you talked with a psychiatrist?"

"No," Eric blurted. "It only happens when I think about the war."

"I imagine the service Sunday must have been as hard on you as it was on Kathy."

Eric drew in a breath and slowly let it out. "Maybe harder. I saw too many killed. My Hawaiian friend died in my arms on Omaha Beach, and three months later, I lost my brother." He bit down on his lip. "I don't want to think about the war, let alone talk about it. And I don't want Kathy or anyone else to know."

The doctor's expression turned to one of a disapproving father. "You're not giving Kathy or her friends much credit for being able to understand how you feel."

"Maybe so, but right now I can't deal with it."

"So you're going to continue living a lie. You didn't stand Sunday with other servicemen."

"And I felt like a traitor, but that would have invited questions."

"To which you could have simply said, 'I can't talk about the war.'"

"Maybe so. Now to admit I was fighting will demand explanations."

"Am I demanding any?"

"No, but you're not Jeff or his buddies. If you insisted, I could make myself give you answers. I can talk to your generation better than mine."

"How come?"

Eric stared into space as he wondered how to convey his thoughts without going into detail. He met the doctor's gaze. "My father's job required him to move often. Maybe if I'd been able to stay in a school long enough to make friends, I wouldn't have a problem. As it was, kids teased me because my speech differed from theirs, so I learned to keep my mouth shut."

"This happened all through school?"

"Until I entered high school. By then, I could speak clearly, but I couldn't open up to my peers, not even close friends. I know I should be up-front with everyone, but the war scraped my emotions raw. I need more time to put the horrors behind me."

"Were you able to talk to your uncle?"

"Talk to Col. James Stone, an army career man? He only barks orders!"

Dr. Ryan raised an eyebrow. "I take it you don't get along."

Eric inhaled slowly as he gathered his thoughts. "I was ten when my father and I went hiking. A rock tumbled off a cliff and killed him." He took in a fortifying breath. "After the funeral, my uncle said, 'No more tears. Real men don't cry.' That fall, he shipped me off to a boys' school. I've only bucked my uncle once. I refused to spend my high school years away from the ranch. Aunt Jean sided with me until Uncle Jim relented and said, 'I guess you do need some coed schooling before attending West Point.' That did it. As soon as I graduated, I enlisted."

"Aren't you being a little harsh? He was probably doing his best to raise you. Was he home most of the time?"

"No."

"Maybe he felt an all-woman environment wouldn't develop the manly qualities he wanted to see in you. A lot of boys long to attend West Point, but you didn't. Was it because that's where he went?"

Eric nodded. "I sound pretty spiteful, don't I?" he said without a trace of remorse.

Dr. Ryan cocked his head. "There's more, isn't there?"

"Yeah, there's more, but nothing I want to share."

"Fair enough. I would like to ask a personal question. You said your uncle refused to let you cry. How have you handled the death of your brother and friend?"

"Have I shed tears? Yes. After Omaha Beach, the chaplain visited each foxhole and told us not to hold in our emotions. 'Shed tears for your fallen comrades. They show love and respect.'"

"A very wise man. I'm glad you've been able to grieve. That helps with the healing process." Dr. Ryan took a sip of coffee. "Kathy said you're a mechanic. Is that how you plan to support yourself?"

"Temporarily. I want to go to college, maybe study agriculture or forestry. Right now, I'm taking one day at a time. I've got some living to do."

"I've been trying to get Kathy to register at Cal Poly, but she keeps putting it off. They have a good Ag program."

"Are you trying to entice me or Kathy?"

"How serious are you about her?"

"Serious enough to stick around in hopes she can forget Dennis."

"She's young, Eric, and she's had two tragic experiences."

Eric wondered if he was referring to the motorcyclist as one of them, but the doctor didn't elaborate as he continued.

"Kathy still has upsetting days, but she no longer has crying spells like she had six months ago." He gazed at Eric with fatherly concern. "To be frank, you're both a little mixed up."

Eric laughed dryly. "Maybe that's why we've hit it off so well."

Dr. Ryan's brow furrowed. "I wish you'd share what's troubling you. I'm a good listener." When Eric didn't respond, he added, "I know readjusting to civilian life takes time, and I won't mention what you've told me, but I think you should tell Kathy." He glanced at his watch. "We'd better head back and get those stitches out. Kathy said you want to get your feet wet, surfing."

"I'd love to be able to ride in upright today, but I'll be satisfied if I can learn how to handle the board and paddle through the waves."

After the doctor removed the stitches, he said, "Forgive me for bringing up the war, but surfing is strenuous even for those in A-1 shape." He paused. "Were you wounded?"

Eric's grip tightened on the edge of the examination table as he nodded.

"How long ago and how severely?"

Eric slid off the table. "Early October, but I'm fine now," he said more forcibly than he intended.

Dr. Ryan rolled his eyes. "Relax. I only brought it up because I want you to take it easy out there today. And please, hold onto that surfboard. I'd hate to see you get hurt."

"Forgive me for raising my voice. I appreciate your concern and will remember your advice." He extended his hand. "Thanks for lunch, for everything."

The doctor's eyes searched his. "If you really care about Kathy, will you promise me something?"

"Like what?"

"See a doctor friend of mine if your emotional problems haven't eased by summer's end."

"Knowing Kathy and talking with you and Captain Dole have helped immensely, but yes, I promise to see your friend. You be the judge when."

Dr. Ryan watched the door swing shut behind Eric. *I wonder what else has contributed to the bitterness you have toward your uncle. What's really eating you? Many emotions can make a man tight-lipped— anger, fear, pain. I sense you're dealing with the whole gamut. Maybe I've made some progress in gaining your trust, but when will you open up and share all that's bothering you? I'm glad you promised to get help.*

Eric rode his motorcycle back to the Dole's, wishing he hadn't spouted off. After all, the doctor was only looking out for his welfare. *I can't believe I promised to see a shrink. But for Kathy's sake, I will, if I can't get a handle on my emotions.*

He parked his motorcycle in the Dole's backyard and dashed into the house to change his clothes. From the box Mary had given him, he retrieved the modified diving suit. The arms and legs of the rubberized khaki material had been shortened so he could move freely but still stay warm. As he tugged it up over his shorts and T-shirt, he wondered if Jeff had chosen the worst one he could find?

Mrs. Dole drove him to the area where he planned to meet the others. "I'll pick you up at five," she said.

Eric hoped to make substantial progress before Kathy, Mary, and Jeff arrived. He carried the board to the water's edge and studied the waves, trying to get a feel for them. He marveled how they swelled, curled, and broke. Eric envisioned riding over the crest and knew it would be one of the crowning points of his life.

When his friends had paddled through the waves, the feat looked relatively easy. His attempts proved futile. Stretched out on the board, he paddled hard, but the wall of water pushed him back. He managed to keep the surfboard from being wrenched from his grasp, but that gave him little consolation. Exhausted, he rested and studied the only other surfer on the beach and realized he'd been lying too far forward. He also noticed how that fellow raised up slightly.

On his next try, Eric pushed through the waves. Elated, he turned the board, rode back to shore lying prone, and paddled out again. This time, he tried to stand but lost his balance. Back on shore, the other surfer yelled, "Get up quicker."

Eric followed his advice and managed to stand a few seconds before he spilled. He paddled back, exhilarated and eager to try again. He looked up to see his friends watching. *Blast it. Why couldn't I have ridden in upright?*

Kathy stuck her board in the sand and ran to meet him. "Great job!" she said as if he'd won first place. "I told Jeff you could do it. He said you wouldn't even make it past the waves today, but I knew you'd do better than that." She beamed. "I'm proud of you."

"Thanks, but don't make any bets on how soon I can ride, standing."

"But you were up. You're a natural. Look how much you accomplished in only a few hours. And you didn't even need me."

"Are you offering your help?"

"You bet I am." She cast Jeff a side glance. "We'll show him he's not the only natural-born surfer."

Eric's stomach muscles ached too much to take her up on her offer. "Right now, I'll sit and watch you. Maybe I can pick up some pointers." He also watched Mary and Jeff, marveling how they sprang to their feet the minute the wave lifted them. No hesitation. No struggling to keep their balance. Each had complete control.

When Mrs. Dole pulled into the parking lot, Kathy said, "I'll walk to the truck with you. Will you come over tonight?"

"Don't you need to study for finals?"

"Not tonight but Tuesday and Wednesday, I will. I have two tough ones, so I won't be able do any surfing."

"Then I'll come over tonight since I won't see you until Thursday. I'll miss you."

She cast him a mischievous smile and quipped. "Absence makes the heart grow fonder."

"And that's what you want?"

They'd reached the truck, and she only grinned before turning her attention to Mrs. Dole. "Hi, Eric's doing great. I bet by Thursday, he'll be a surfer."

All evening, Kathy remained the bubbly girl he'd come to love, and when he kissed her, she entwined her arms around his neck and prolonged their embrace. Eric enjoyed the moment, but he didn't kid himself that Dennis was out of the picture.

Kathy sat on the edge of her bed, feeling a pang of guilt for falling in love so soon. *Dennis, please try to understand. No amount of tears will bring you back. I'll always love you, but I need someone's arms I can feel, someone whose lips are warm and exciting. Please try to understand.*

Eric returned to the Dole's, retrieved the newspaper from the coffee table, and scanned the used car section.

Captain Dole walked into the living room and settled in his easy chair. "Looking for anything in particular?"

"A cheap truck to carry my surfboard."

"Is Mr. Watkins selling it to you?"

"No."

"Why waste money on an old pick-up? Use mine. Hephzibah mostly sits in the garage. She might enjoy watching you surf."

Eric laughed. "Hephzibah?"

"Yes, the other woman in my life. You've never named a car?"

"Never."

"Would you allow Hephzibah the honor of serving you?"

"How can I refuse? I'll take good care of her and make sure she's well fed."

Free to come and go, Tuesday and Wednesday, Eric spent every moment trying to master the art of surfing. Wednesday, when Kathy stopped by after school to see his progress, he could only stand for a few minutes.

"Better," she said. "Keep practicing. You'll get the hang of it. Wish I could stay and watch, but I have two big finals tomorrow."

After she left, instead of quitting as he had intended, Eric spent more time on the water until every muscle screamed for mercy. He returned to the Dole's exhausted and famished.

"You look ready to drop," Mrs. Dole said.

"Nothing a hot bath and a hot meal won't cure."

"Do you like Mexican food?"

"I've only had chili."

"Would you like to come with us to a place in San Luis Obispo that has an outstanding Mexican buffet?"

"Sounds great."

*   *   *

Upon entering the restaurant, one whiff sent Eric's taste buds into fast-forward. He didn't know where to start or when to quit. When he finally settled back in his chair feeling like a contented bear ready for hibernation, Mr. Dole chuckled and said, "Annie, I do believe he likes Mexican food."

"That was terrific," Eric said, "I'm stuffed."

Back at the house with a full belly and exhausted from his extra hours on the water, Eric retired early. For a while, he lay awake thinking about seeing Kathy tomorrow. He had his day planned. He'd spend a few hours surfing in the afternoon before resting up for his evening basketball match with Jeff. He wanted to be in top form since Mary and Kathy would be watching. Mentally, he played one-on-one with Jeff until he fell asleep.

A nightmare gripped him.

*Tanks rumbled into the town of Aachen. Eric ran crouched behind one, his rifle poised, his nerves taut. He dashed toward a bombed-scarred stucco building, froze outside the doorway. Rushing in, his rifle spewed as it swept around the room.*

*Despite the deafening din echoing in his ears, he heard the scrape of a boot above the stairs. As if his rifle had a will of its own, the gun swung toward the sound, but Eric's finger refused to pull the trigger. The German soldier staring down at him looked barely out of puberty. His eyes, glazed with fear, seemed oddly misplaced on the plump rosy cheeked face, which should have been concentrating on shooting marbles, not a rifle. The boy pulled the trigger. Eric reeled when the bullet struck his head. The youthful German dashed down the stairs and fired before Eric could recover. Another searing pain ripped Eric's midsection, blazing a trail so fierce a muted cry rose in his throat.*

Eric awakened with a start and grabbed his stomach. His pain was real, abdominal pain so excruciating he broke into a cold sweat. He rolled slowly out of bed and tried to walk it off but doubled over, clutching his stomach. It was as if someone had closed a vise on his guts. He staggered down the hall to the bathroom, hoping relieving himself would help. It didn't.

He had ached yesterday from his surfing workout, but not like this! Could he have re-injured himself? An hour passed before the pain eased enough for him to find a comfortable position in bed, but he couldn't go back to sleep.

Over and over, his mind replayed the same scene—the German kid wounding him, the boy's gun jamming, and Eric recovering enough to shoot to disable him. *I couldn't kill him. He didn't look much older than Cindy.* Eric remembered the relief he felt when two American soldiers entered the building. Dennis's face remained etched in his memory before blood obliterated the features.

Sudden realization hit. Sitting bolt upright, Eric cried out, "God, tell me I'm not responsible for Dennis's death because I spared that kid's life!" Even though a voice in his head said, *You are not responsible,* Eric couldn't shake the guilt wedged in his heart.

He tried rationalizing it away, but a small finger remained pointed at him. Eric pushed it away. *God would not be that cruel. If I were responsible, God would not have led me to Arroyo Grande to fall in love with Kathy, or would He have me boarding with the Doles.* Eric leaned back against the headboard, trying to remember the details his mind had shut out. Until he could recall every detail, he would never know the truth. "Lord, help me remember."

By morning, he convinced himself to leave everything in God's hands. More certain he was not the blame for Dennis's death, he pushed feelings of guilt aside. However, although less severe, he couldn't ignore his stomach cramps.

At eight o'clock, he called Dr. Ryan's office for an appointment. "You're in luck," the receptionist said, "he has a cancellation. Can you be here at ten?"

"Yes."

## CHAPTER 12

E ric sat at the weathered picnic table and watched Mrs. Dole hang the washing. His stomach still bothered him, but he couldn't tell if it was due to last night's problem or if it ached from not having eaten.

Mrs. Dole stretched the last sheet on the clothesline, picked up the wicker basket, and climbed the deck steps. "Feeling better?" she asked, watching him sip water.

"Being up and moving have helped immensely. I think I'm getting hungry, but I can't be sure. Maybe I should call and cancel that appointment."

Her brow creased. "No. Yesterday I worried about your spending all day surfing, and I won't rest easy until I know you didn't re-injure yourself. I pray you haven't."

"Me too." He grinned and winked. "I'd hate to have to *hang* up that surfboard just when I'm getting the *hang* of it." He hoped his acting as if he no longer had a problem would ease her mind.

She rolled her eyes. "I can see you're feeling friskier, but you must keep that appointment."

In the examination room, Eric stared out the window, unable to quell his concern.

Dr. Ryan strode through the doorway. "Good morning. I was surprised to see you listed on my schedule. What's the problem?"

Eric related his symptoms and told him about his previous stomach wound.

After asking a few questions, the doctor said, "Guess I'd better check you over. Take off your shirt."

Eric hesitated before slipping it over his head, but he knew he couldn't stop the inevitable. As he laid his shirt on the back of a chair, he purposely turned so the doctor could see his scars. When he again faced him and saw the man's eyes widen, he said, "The Gestapo did this before I was imprisoned."

With a light touch, Dr. Ryan ran his fingers over the crisscrossed marks. "Your back hasn't been healed very long. Did they give the allotted forty lashes?"

Eric shrugged and stretched out on the table.

"I see why you always wear a shirt on the beach. When were you tortured?"

"Middle of January."

Empathy shone from the doctor's eyes a moment before his face turned noncommittal while he probed Eric's midsection for tender spots. "As far as I can tell, you're fine. You mentioned your last checkup was in April. What were the army doctor's instructions?"

"To eat light for the next two or three months and to keep greasy and spicy foods to a minimum."

"And what did you eat yesterday?"

"The Doles took me to a Mexican buffet in San Luis Obispo."

"The Greasy Tortilla?"

"I don't think that was the name."

"It's nickname, a place known for fried, spicy food."

Eric gazed at him sheepishly. "And I ate everything I shouldn't have, which means I was having a plain old-fashioned bellyache last night. Boy, do I feel dumb."

"At least you had sense enough not to ignore symptoms that could have been serious." He smiled. "I think if you only have soup for lunch, you'll fare just fine."

After Eric put on his shirt, he noticed Dr. Ryan's inquisitive expression. "Is there something you want to ask?"

"Why the dietary restrictions? If you were wounded in October, why are you still having stomach problems? Did the Gestapo do more than lash your back?"

"They beat the stuffing out of me, belted me blow after blow until they could no longer revive me after I'd pass out." Eric swallowed hard. "I came to, suspended by my wrists from rafters."

"That's when the lashings began?"

Eric nodded, breathing deeply to quell claustrophobic feelings ready to engulf him.

"Let's go sit in the courtyard."

Eric had seen the French doors leading to the patio and fought the impulse to rush past the doctor to reach them first.

After they took seats on a wrought-iron bench, Dr. Ryan said, "You're doing better about opening up. If we sit out here, would you be able to confide in me and tell me the whole story?"

Eric nodded, knowing he would avoid his part in Dennis's death, but he did want to unburden his heart. *Where do I begin?* "My father was a civil engineer who built bridges, and the company sent him to Germany where he met Mom. My twin brother Erin and I were born in Cologne."

"So when your parents divorced, your mother stayed there while your father returned to America with you?"

He nodded. "My brother fought for the Third Reich." Eric briefly told him about Erin's death. "Later, I was wounded at Aachen." Before the doctor could ask if he had known Dennis, Eric said, "Along with my stomach wound, a bullet creased my skull." He lifted a portion of hair on top to show the long, thin scar.

"I noticed that when we met and wondered how it happened."

"It didn't do much damage but did give me headaches and lent credence to my pretending amnesia." When Dr. Ryan's eyes widened, he added, "Uncle Jim volunteered me to impersonate Erin and spy for Allied Intelligence."

"Do I detect bitterness?"

"Dr. Ryan, I was flat on my back in pain, and he never asked how I felt, or did he give me a chance to volunteer. He just gave orders. In the field hospital, I was isolated from the other wounded and drilled on my German as well as procedures for passing along information. How they knew I'd be hospitalized in Cologne and later assigned to German Headquarters still puzzles me. They kept me in bed for three weeks. Even then, I didn't feel strong enough to be slipped behind enemy lines, but good old Uncle Jim assured everyone I was ready." Eric explained how they'd smuggled him across enemy lines and left him. "My biggest hurdle was convincing the Germans I'd been wounded, captured, treated at a field hospital, and managed to escape, all the while pretending amnesia. I said the Americans had called me Captain von Harmon.

"When my mother and sister visited me in the Cologne hospital, it shook me to the core, and it took all my willpower not to throw my arms around them when they kissed me. Meeting my stepfather, Colonel von Harmon, terrified me until I realized he really thought I was Erin."

After he finished relating the rest, Dr. Ryan said, "I think I understand you better now. When were you freed from prison?"

"The first of March. A week before the Allies took Cologne, my stepfather managed to get me out. He knew the Allies would be there soon and wanted me home to protect Mom and Elizabeth. He said, 'I know the mindset of an invading army when they find women.'"

"You said Allied Intelligence got you across enemy lines and left you. Didn't that raise a red flag? After all, you had a serious wound."

"My story was the two men who escaped with me took off."

"I guess I'd buy that." Dr. Ryan studied Eric a moment. "I surmise your imprisonment is the cause of your claustrophobia, and this question will be difficult. Were you in solitary confinement?"

Eric nodded. Despite being in a courtyard where a breeze carried the scent of roses and dispersed the fountain's misty spray, concrete walls dropped around him. He squeezed his eyes, trying to make the walls go away.

The doctor laid a hand on his shoulder. "Open your eyes, Eric. Look at the blue sky. Feel the cool fountain water misting across your face." When Eric didn't respond, he said in a firm, insistent voice, "Eric, look up."

Breathing hard, he lifted his eyes heavenward and gulped fresh air as the walls receded. He pressed his head against the tree behind their bench. "Whew."

"I take it my question took you back to that cell. Can you tell me about it? How long were you confined?"

Eric drew in a breath and slowly let it out. "Less than a month, but it was pitch-black and underground, a cement cell with a hole in the floor to drain the water after hosing."

"They hosed it down while you were in it?"

Eric nodded. "They gave me food and water, but I lay doubled up in pain and could only envision the rats getting fat. My stepfather came every day to clean me up, force me to drink warm broth, and put salve on my back. I owe my life to him."

"Thank you for sharing. I know how hard it must have been, but you're doing better about opening up. Now it's time to let Kathy, Mary, and Jeff know you were in the war."

"Not yet. And would you please keep all I've told you confidential."

"Until you need someone to pull you out of the pit you're digging?"

Eric frowned. "Look, I'll know when it's the right time to tell my friends."

"I doubt that, but I'll keep mum."

About twenty minutes after Eric returned to the Dole's, Jeff pulled into the driveway and climbed out of his car. *Has he come by to make sure I'll show up for our one-on-one match? How can I tactfully reschedule it?* To stall for time, he said, "Want to take a spin on my Harley? I need to get some shaving cream. I forgot to stop on the way home from the doctor's office." Eric mentally kicked himself for divulging the information.

"Doctor's office? Something wrong?"

"I woke up with stomach cramps and thought I might have hurt myself surfing."

"Did you?"

"Dr. Ryan said I didn't."

"Then what was wrong?"

Eric wished Jeff hadn't asked, but he couldn't lie. "Promise not to laugh?"

Jeff nodded.

132

"I ate too much Mexican food yesterday."

Jeff roared, and Eric glared at him.

"I'm sorry, but I couldn't help myself." Jeff stopped, his mouth half open, as if he had more to say.

Eric waited for him to continue.

"The truth is, I dropped by hoping you'd back out. I'm not really up to a match this afternoon." He looked reluctant but added, "My ulcer gave me fits last night."

*An ulcer? At his age? He's under that much pressure?* "Do the girls know you're hurting?"

Jeff shook his head. "Would you be willing to cancel our match without letting them know why?"

"I'm not sure how we can manage but I'm all for it. And hey, I can keep a secret if you can. Shake?"

"Shake."

After Jeff left, Eric rode to the drug store for shaving cream. When he returned, Mrs. Dole told him Kathy wanted him to call.

She answered the phone on the first ring. "Hi, Jeff and Mary are here. We thought we'd play ping-pong."

"Jeff wants to play ping-pong?"

"Yes, it was his suggestion. Why?"

"No reason. I'll be over in ten minutes."

Playing partners against their friends proved strenuous. Despite his earlier discomfort, Eric had no problem meeting the challenge. He and Kathy won three of the five games.

While the foursome relaxed on the deck and drank lemonade, Kathy said, "When are you two going to have your one-on-one basketball match?"

Jeff glanced at Eric. "Didn't you tell her we decided to play ping-pong instead? Hey, if you forgot, then your winning doesn't count."

Eric marveled at Jeff's smoothness. "We beat you fair and square." He grinned. "However, to show you what a great guy I am, I'll pick up tomorrow night's dinner tab anyway."

"Let's split it fifty-fifty," Jeff replied.

"Okay."

The girls exchanged puzzled glances before they went to the kitchen to refill the glasses.

"Why'd you volunteer to pay the whole dinner bill?" Jeff asked. "You and Kathy beat us."

"But you got us off the hook."

"So splitting the bill does make us even."

Friday afternoon, Jeff and Eric studied the movie section of the paper. "How about having seafood at the dock restaurant," Jeff suggested and added in a creepy voice, "Afterward, we'll go see *Frankenstein Meets the Wolfman* and *Cat People.*"

"Why horror features? I figured we'd pick out a couple of love stories to put the girls in a romantic mood."

"You're behind the times. If you choose scary films, the girls cling to you all through the movie and all the way home. Trust me."

The all-you-can-eat restaurant proved an excellent choice. Eric sampled food he had never eaten, including his first shrimp. Remembering his night of discomfort, he curbed his desire to overeat and noticed Jeff doing likewise.

"What's wrong with your appetites?" Mary asked. "I thought you chose this place, Jeff, so you both could gorge yourselves."

Jeff and Eric exchanged glances and laughed.

"What's so funny?" Kathy asked.

"Private joke," Eric replied.

Kathy's brow furrowed. "What's with you two anyway? You've been acting weird lately."

Eric grinned. "Jeff and I are friends now, aren't we? What more do you want?"

That night, Eric smiled when he crawled into bed. He couldn't have asked for better friends and looked forward to watching them graduate and having fun at the evening beach party.

Graduation day dawned cloudy and cool. By noon, the predicted winds blew in like an ill omen. "Why today?" Kathy grumbled as she pushed hangers aside to find the floral print sundress she'd decided to wear under her gown.

Her father had pooh-poohed blue jeans, saying, "I want to take pictures of you before Jeff and Mary pick you up, and I plan to take some of you in front of the school, in and out of your cap and gown. Afterward, we're eating dinner at the Blue Ridge Inn. This is a big day for all of us."

Kathy hurried to get ready. Graduation would start at three o'clock, and those participating had to be there by two-fifteen.

Her father finished taking pictures a few minutes before Jeff's car pulled into the driveway. Kathy dashed down the porch steps and climbed into the backseat.

Mary turned. "Are your parents picking up Eric?"

"They don't have to. The Doles loaned him their car to drive to the school and later take me home."

Jeff asked, "Do you still want to ride with us to the beach?"

"I decided to drive the station wagon. That way, you and Mary can do what you want after the party and so can we."

Chuckling, Jeff turned. "And what do you want to do?"

Mary giggled.

Kathy felt her face redden. "Mary, what I told you was in confidential."

"Hey, the three of us are best friends. I couldn't help mentioning to Jeff how you hoped the night would end."

"Your wishes are safe with me," Jeff said. "I may think it's too soon for you to get serious about Eric, but if you're sure he's the one for you"—he shrugged—"far be it from me to put a damper on your dreams."

Kathy gave him a warning glare. "Don't you dare say anything to Eric."

"Me, give him encouragement? Not on your life."

The Arroyo Grande High School auditorium filled with seniors waiting for last-minute instructions. Confusion, mayhem, and jitters seemed ready to strangle all attempts by the teachers to organize the students. But on schedule, they marched in orderly fashion, and the ceremony proceeded without a hitch.

Kathy enjoyed dinner with her family at the fancy restaurant. When she glanced at Eric sitting next to her, the rapture on his face told her he was savoring the food, too. His closeness kept her mind drifting to the beach party. After her father paid the check, she asked Eric, "Dad will drop you off at the Dole's to change. Do you want to walk to our house or should I pick you up?"

"No, I'll walk over in half an hour. Is that enough time for you to get ready?"

"Perfect."

Kathy changed into jeans and a yellow sleeveless blouse. The serious part of graduation day had ended. Now the fun would begin—the evening beach party—a great finish to a wonderful day. *Tonight will be perfect if Eric tells me he loves me.*

When he arrived and kissed her, she shivered with excitement.

"Cold?" he asked.

"Of course not. The wind has quit, the sky has cleared, and there's going to be a full moon tonight." She flashed him her warmest smile.

He drew in a breath and let out a nervous laugh. "Then let's go,"

Kathy handed him the car keys. *Yes*, she thought as she watched him slide underneath the steering wheel, *tonight will end perfectly*.

On the road, he said, "I was so proud of you tonight. Did you know you were going to receive a scholarship to Cal Poly?"

"I didn't have a clue."

"Guess you'll have to go there now."

"I'd like to. You know, they have a good Ag program."

Eric chuckled. "Your father mentioned that."

"Why would he do that?"

"Maybe he thought if I went, you'd definitely decide to go."

"And?"

"It bears thinking about."

While he drove the beach highway, Kathy laid her head against his shoulder and pondered how tonight would end. *Will I want it to end?* She closed her eyes as she envisioned their kisses and the excitement they always evoked. Eric's pulling into a parking space jarred her back to reality.

"Have a good snooze?" he asked.

Tongue in cheek, she said, "I was resting up for tonight."

His eyes twinkled. "Are you expecting a strenuous evening?"

Kathy laughed as she climbed out of the car. "Who knows?"

Few had chosen to attend the beach party—six couples and about fifteen girls. "What's a party without beer?" was the remark she'd heard that summed up the feelings of most of the students.

Seven teachers chaperoned the students. Two men and the baseball coach joined those playing volleyball. Kathy, Eric, Mary and Jeff combined their skills to lead their team to victory twice.

The four women teachers worked in the snack stand and watched students swimming or playing in the water. When it grew dark, the snack stand provided music for jitterbugging. After dancing awhile, Kathy grabbed Eric's hand. "Let's take a breather."

"I'm all for that. Let's eat."

While she munched her hamburger, Kathy gazed at the sky and thought, *that moon will give us plenty of light for a walk along the water, but the teachers won't be able to see us clearly.* Kathy gave Eric a coy smile and whispered, "That moon will give us plenty of light for a walk along the water, but the teachers won't be able to see us clearly. "Want to take a long walk?"

Eric chuckled. "A long walk?" he said as if reading her mind. "Sure. It's a perfect night for one."

He kept his arm around her waist while they strolled the water's edge. When they were away from others, he turned and kissed her with so much passion Kathy felt giddy. He stopped and leaned back, breathing hard. She felt him tremble before he whispered, "We'd better go back."

They walked slowly enough for Kathy to regain her composure.

While the baseball coach strummed an old banjo and led the group in folk songs, Kathy cuddled close to Eric. His arm tightened around her waist, sending a shiver of excitement up her spine. Would he suggest a drive to somewhere romantic? Where? Would he propose? They wouldn't have much time. She had to be home by twelve.

Her thoughts scattered like the blowing sand when the coach began picking out *Mairzy Doats* as fast as he could and challenged the group to keep up. The jumbled words of the crazy song became more scrambled until the group began laughing so hard they could no longer sing.

The laughter died abruptly, cut down by shrill Indian-like war whoops and the din of revving motorcycles. Kathy stiffened with alarm. When six men on cycles roared into view, she clung to Eric. The men rode straight toward the girls without dates, skidding and spraying them with sand. The chaperones yelled for the girls to stay together, but they screamed and scattered like frightened chickens. The men corralled six and scooped them onto their cycles. When the chaperones tried to intervene, the bikers knocked them to the ground and roared off with the girls. It happened so quickly couples stood in shock.

Kathy screamed. "Do something!" She knew the terror and torture Mary had suffered when a cyclist raped her.

The coach yelled, "I'll call the police from the Warren's" and sprinted to the nearest house on the bluff.

Eric gathered Kathy into his arms. "The police will find them."

"It will be too late. Do something!"

"What? They're gone."

A teacher said, "All we can do is pray." She lifted her eyes heavenward. "Lord, protect them. Please don't let them be harmed."

The words rang hollow. Kathy pictured the girls fighting their attackers.

"They're coming back," Eric said.

Jeff yelled, "Get 'em, guys!"

The bikers roared in without the girls. They headed for the couples and laughed with contempt as each guy again stepped in front of his date.

Kathy backed away when one motorcyclist skidded close to her and Eric. Terrified, she watched the huge man whack the side of Eric's head so hard it sent him sprawling.

The man leaped from his bike. "So much for him," he laughed and headed for her.

Kathy saw Eric rise, looking dazed. "Eric! Help me!" When the brute grabbed her arm, Kathy yanked free and kicked him in the groin with all her might. Her bare foot hardly grazed him.

"So you want to play rough," he bellowed.

Eric lunged onto his back.

Like an enraged bronco, the roughneck tossed him off. Eric staggered but regained his balance. The man swore and charged, his buffalo weight knocking Eric to the ground. Eric rolled and evaded a vicious kick. He scrambled to his feet and dodged a blow to his head. The bully attacked again. Eric jumped aside. The man grabbed a driftwood log and rushed Eric.

Kathy shrieked when he swung the log. Eric reared backward and stumbled, but recovered in time to swerve and avoid being bashed. He clenched his hand and delivered an uppercut that smashed into the motorcyclist's jaw.

The man reeled and staggered toward Kathy. All the horror of seeing Mary raped and having to defend herself from Mary's attacker returned. When a man's hand touched her arm, Kathy raked her fingernails across his face. Part of her heard Eric's soothing voice. Above it rang her earlier assailant's obscenities and the stinging blows he'd dealt. "No," she cried again and again. Wailing police car sirens mingled with her screams. She fought to keep her arms from being pinned to her sides. Someone picked her up and forced her into a car. "No!" she shrieked and collapsed.

The incessant frantic ring of the doorbell brought Dr. Ryan to his feet, his book falling to the floor. "What in tarnation?" he grumbled. "Keep your shirt on; I'm coming." He yanked the door open. "Good, Lord," he cried, seeing Kathy in Eric's arms. A policeman stood at his side. "What happened?"

"She's not hurt," Eric blurted. "Passed out."

Dr. Ryan held open the screen door. "Put her on her bed. I'll get my bag." He ran to his study, grabbed his satchel, skirted around the officer and Eric to pull back the bed covers. "What happened?" he repeated as Eric laid her down.

The policeman explained. "A bunch of drunks rode up on motorcycles and crashed the party. Things got nasty." He put his hand on Eric, who was pale and breathing hard. "This young man fought to protect your daughter. He refused to go to the hospital to get his hand or head checked, said he was okay, that she needed to be at home where you could look after her."

"I want to stay with her," Eric pleaded, his voice frantic.

"You won't do her any good if she sees you like this." Dr. Ryan turned to the officer. "Take him to the kitchen and have him sit down. After I examine her, I'll come take care of him." Dr. Ryan was relieved to see Kathy had no apparent injuries, but he noticed blood under her fingernails. He had seen the scratches on Eric's face and arms and surmised he must have taken the brunt of her hysteria.

In the kitchen, Eric sat limp in the chair, his eyes dazed as he stared at the officer. His reddened right hand lay cradled in the other. "How's Kathy?" he said when Dr. Ryan hurried into the kitchen.

"She's okay. Let's see about you."

"I'm fine, just a little shaky. Kathy was hysterical. I couldn't calm her down."

"I'm glad you brought her home." Dr. Ryan touched a red area above Eric's temple. "What hit you here?"

"The drunk whacked me, but I'm okay."

"Let me be the judge of that." Dr. Ryan took his penlight and made Eric follow the beam. "No signs of a concussion, but let me know if you have any problems. Let me see your hand."

Eric flexed his fingers. "It's okay."

Dr. Ryan examined it closely. "I think you're right, but it will probably be stiff and sore tomorrow. Now for those scratches." He applied ointment, saying, "I don't want these getting infected. You should feel a whole lot better after a good night's rest. The officer can give you a ride to the Dole's."

"I want to stay near Kathy. I don't want her waking up terrified!"

"I'm going to give her a sedative so she'll sleep until morning. Officer, would you drive him home?"

"I'm not leaving!"

Eric's devotion tugged at Dr. Ryan's heart. "You may sleep on the couch. That way, you can go to her if she cries out. Fair enough?"

Eric nodded.

Dr. Ryan turned to the officer. "Do you need any more information?"

"No. I'll let myself out."

Dr. Ryan was thankful no one else had awakened. Eric stared ahead, his eyes dull. The doctor helped him to his feet and escorted him to the living room couch. Eric sank down in exhaustion, and Dr. Ryan said, "I'll get you a pillow and blanket and a cold pack for your hand."

He returned and found Eric asleep. Eric didn't flicker an eyelash when the doctor stretched him out and covered him with a blanket.

*Maybe it's good you're sleeping here so I can check on you too.* His thoughts returned to Kathy. *Lord, please don't let her nightmares return.*

# CHAPTER 13

Kathy's screams jarred Eric awake. He rolled off the couch, ran down the hallway, and entered Kathy's room a few steps ahead of her parents. Kathy sat in bed, shaking and shrieking. Eric sank beside her, pulling her close, and kissing her forehead. "It's okay. You're safe."

Mrs. Ryan asked above Kathy's terrified wail. "What happened? Why is Eric here?"

Eric vaguely heard the doctor tell her about the drunken motor-cyclists and say, "Kathy didn't get hurt, only hysterical."

"She's having a horrible nightmare," Mrs. Ryan said. "Can't you give her something?"

"First, let's see if Eric can calm her."

"Please stop crying," Eric implored. "You're safe." He gently massaged the back of her neck. "Go to sleep," he whispered. "I'm here." Her cries turned to quiet sobs before she fell asleep in his arms. Eric lowered her head to the pillow, tucked the covers under her shoulders, and kissed her cheek. Reluctant to leave, he gazed at her, wondering why so much pain should come to someone as sweet as Kathy.

Dr. Ryan tapped him lightly on the shoulder. "It's only five. I think you should try to get some more rest too."

Eric nodded, followed him into the living room, and sat on the couch. He searched Dr. Ryan's face, wondering if he should ask what he wanted to know.

"What is it, Eric?"

"Sir, I love Kathy." He paused to gather courage. "I . . . I need to know the truth. Two years ago did a motorcyclist—"

"Rape her? No. But one raped Mary on the beach in back of our house. Kathy was in the kitchen making sandwiches when she heard her screams. She dashed down the steps and fought the man. Kathy might have been raped, too, if my wife hadn't come home. She grabbed my shotgun and scared him off. The man is behind bars."

Eric glanced at the red streaks on his arms.

"Looks like you took the brunt of Kathy's hysteria last night. Try to get some sleep."

Eric lay back down and closed his eyes, but he agonized over Kathy's tormenting experience. No wonder she'd reacted like that. "Thank you, Lord, for protecting her."

Kathy sat upright in bed. *How did I get home?* She shuddered, remembering the bear-like man lunging toward her. Had he? She checked her arms and legs—not a mark, and she felt fine. Eric must have stopped the man. *Eric!* She jumped out of bed, threw on a robe, and dashed down the hallway to her parents' room. Through the doorway, she saw the bed covers neatly folded back and the room empty. Kathy ran into the living room. Stopped and stared.

Eric lay asleep on the couch, his swollen right hand cradled in the left on his stomach. His face and arms bore scratches as if he'd tangled with a mountain lion. Had the motorcyclist lashed out at him? Kathy tiptoed closer and knelt beside the couch but resisted the urge to stroke his forehead. If he'd fought that hard to protect her, he deserved his rest.

"Thank you, my gallant knight," she mouthed and walked to the kitchen where her parents sat drinking coffee.

Her mother stood and rushed to her side. "Are you all right?"

"Just confused. Everything is so nightmarish. What happened to Eric? I remember him fighting with that horrible man then . . ." Kathy trembled.

Her mother put a consoling arm around her and guided Kathy to the table.

"What else do you remember?" her father asked after Kathy slid onto a chair.

"It's so jumbled. I can picture that ape of a man lunging at me then I'm fighting the motorcyclist who attacked me two years ago. But that can't be. Can it?" When her parents exchanged knowing glances, Kathy blurted, "What happened last night?"

"You were so hysterical you fought Eric," her father said. "Look at your fingernails."

"Oh, no! I scratched Eric? How can I ever explain?"

Her father leaned back and regarded her. "Do you love him?"

"I do . . . even more than I loved Dennis."

"Maybe it's time to share what happened two years ago. You needn't go into details."

Her thoughts raced to her friend. "Mary! Is she okay?"

"Her mother said Mary's fine. She phoned earlier to see how you were."

Kathy pushed her chair away from the table. "I've got to call her."

Eric awakened to fingertips stroking his face. He opened his eyes and saw Kathy sitting on the floor next to the couch.

She smiled. "Good afternoon. How do you feel?"

"Not bad, considering last night, but I think I'll pass on tackling bears today."

"And wildcats?" She kissed the red marks on his arms, one by one.

"Those feel better already. How about doing the scratches on my face?"

She rose to sit on the edge of the couch, leaned over to kiss each scratch before seeking his lips.

"You know, I could get used to waking up like this. Since I doubt this scenario will be repeated, how about going through this act again?"

She kissed each mark briefly but her lips lingered on his, leaving no doubt in his mind she'd bounced back to her normal self.

"Lady, I love your bedside manner."

Jimmy and Tommy burst in on the tender scene. "Tell us about the fight!" Tommy blurted.

Jimmy glanced at Eric's swollen hand. His eyes widened with admiration. "Wow! You must have hit that guy hard. The policeman said you broke the man's jaw."

"Policeman?" Eric asked, sitting up.

Kathy nodded. "Dad said it was the same one who brought us home. He came over this morning to let us know the girls were found unharmed, and all the motorcyclists are in jail."

"Boys," Dr. Ryan called, entering the living room, "time to get washed and set the table."

Jimmy glanced at the wall clock. "It's not even eleven thirty."

Dr. Ryan pointed toward the doorway. "Out."

Tommy dashed from the room.

Jimmy stood, pouting. "How come Kathy gets all the fun?" When his father's brows came together in a scolding frown, he scurried after his brother.

"That should keep them out of here," Dr. Ryan said. "Lunch will be ready by noon. Eric, you can use the bathroom off our bedroom for cleaning up. Everything you'll need is on the counter, but there's no hurry." He gave Kathy a knowing smile.

Eric watched him leave. Was Dr. Ryan trying to communicate something to Kathy? He rose from the couch and stretched. "I can't believe I slept so late. Guess I'd better get washed."

Kathy touched his arm. "Not yet." She hesitated. "We need to talk."

Bewildered, he sat back down. "About what?"

Her lower lip quivered as she dropped beside him. "Last night." The words came barely above a whisper. "Why I became hysterical."

Eric longed to say it didn't matter, but he assumed her father wanted Kathy to tell him. Would it be therapeutic for her? When she didn't speak, he waited patiently. He understood the pain of sharing something traumatic.

"I'm sorry," she blurted. "Forgive me for raking my fingernails on your face and arms. I didn't know it was you. Everything was so weird." She sighed, again hesitant. "Two years ago, I fought off the

145

motorcyclist who . . . hurt Mary. In my mind, last night, I saw him. I don't know why."

"Maybe I can shed some light on that. When I slugged the drunk, he staggered toward you. Maybe you thought he was attacking you." Eric wrapped his arms around her. "It doesn't matter. It's over, but thank you for explaining. Try to forget the whole incident."

In the Ryan's bathroom, Eric shaved around the scratches. They weren't as deep as those on his arms but deep enough to extract more kisses from Kathy until they healed. Before joining the family in the dining room, he sent his mirror image a devilish lopsided grin.

Kathy's brothers monopolized conversation during lunch. Between mouthfuls, Eric answered their questions about the fight until Dr. Ryan said, "That's enough, boys. Let Eric eat." He leaned forward and offered him the platter of cantaloupe.

With his left hand, Eric speared a slice and tried to cut the firm melon with a fork.

"Here," Angela said, "let me help."

"Thanks, but I think I can manage." He brought the fork down harder on the unyielding cantaloupe. The piece shot across the table and landed in front of Dr. Ryan's plate. A moment of silence prevailed before laughter erupted. Eric's face grew hot.

Dr. Ryan cleared his throat. His eyes twinkled as he casually speared the elusive slice and studied it a moment before dropping it on Eric's plate. "This seems to have your name on it."

Kathy giggled. "Mother, men are so helpless. Where would they be without women?" She cut Eric's cantaloupe into smaller than bite-size pieces.

Eric frowned. "Are you looking for Round 3?"

"Whatever do you mean? Why would I want to spar with someone who is short-handed?" The mockery and smug confidence in her voice belied her wide-eyed innocence.

Eric glared at her a moment before turning his attention to his melon. He stabbed a tiny segment and gave her a super sweet smile. *Just you wait, Kathy Ryan, just you wait.*

Conversation returned to normal.

After lunch, while Kathy and Angela washed the dishes, Eric played with Jimmy and Tommy in the backyard and helped them train the dog to play hide and seek. Twenty minutes later, Kathy joined him. "Want to take a stroll on the beach?" Eric asked with a straight face.

"Sure. Mind if I change into shorts? It's getting hot outside."

"Take your time." He followed her back to the deck where her father sat reading the paper. "I'll talk to your dad while you change."

When she was out of sight, Dr. Ryan lowered the paper. "Are you going to let her get away with what she said at the table?"

"No. I'm planning to dunk her. Do you disapprove?"

"Not at all. Kathy deserves to be dunked, but you'd better be prepared. She's bound to be furious." Dr. Ryan returned to reading the paper.

Eric leaned on the deck railing. How angry would Kathy be? He sensed she wanted him to be masterful, but he also felt his mastery would last only as long as she desired it. Women! Uncle Jim told him once not to try and figure them out; it wasn't worth the effort. *Effort? Marriage should be a partnership.* Eric wanted to know Kathy intimately, wanted to be able to sense her moods, and know how to react whenever she looked downcast, worried, or scared, know when she needed to be held, and when she needed to be left alone. *Effort? No, Uncle Jim. Understanding the girl I love presents a challenge, one I willingly accept. She's worth it.*

Kathy strolled onto the deck.

"Ready?" Eric asked.

She nodded. Her eyes held his with a look of love and complete trust. He led the way down the cliff steps. Kathy's innocent smile almost dissuaded him from carrying out his plan.

Eric reached the bottom of the cliff and grasped Kathy's hand as she descended the last three steps. He took in her slim legs, her tiny waist, dwelt briefly on the yellow print blouse that accentuated her curves and gazed into her eyes. "You look terrific. Those yellow shorts really set off your tan." He put his left arm around the small of her back as they strolled toward the water's edge and stopped before the lapping waves. With his good hand, he lifted a few strands of auburn hair and let them slip through his fingers. "You really are beautiful."

She blushed. "I am not. I have freckles."

He ran the tip of his finger over the bridge of her nose. "I love every one of them. And I love you. You know that, don't you?" Her eyes, lit with expectation, almost dissuaded him again. "If I didn't love you, I wouldn't have to do this."

"Do what?" Her puzzled expression told him she didn't suspect a thing.

Despite his sore hand, he scooped her into his arms and grinned. "Remember the last time you laughed one time too many?"

"Eric, you wouldn't! I'll never forgive you!"

"Well, that's the chance I'll have to take." He ran into the water, dumped her, and waded back to shore.

Kathy came up sputtering and stomped toward him with venom shooting from her eyes. Before she could speak, Eric pinned her arms to her sides and kissed her.

Kathy struggled to free herself, but her will lost the war against her feelings. When Eric's arms encircled her waist, she melted in his embrace.

"Still angry?" he whispered and leaned back.

"I should hate you right now. My clothes and shoes are soaked. My hair's a mess." She gazed into his blue eyes that shimmered with tenderness. "But I can't."

"I'm glad."

"I'm sorry I embarrassed you." She giggled, "But it was so opportune."

"So was dunking you."

"Then you weren't embarrassed! Eric Stone, I'd like to—"

"Try for round 4?"

"Round 4? No, let's leave things as they are." Eric kissed her again, and Kathy snuggled close, reveling in his protective arms. "I can't go back into the house looking like this. Can we walk awhile so I can dry off?"

"Sure. It will give us a chance to talk."

But they didn't talk. Kathy wondered if Eric felt as tongue-tied as she did. Dennis had always made her feel secure by treating her like a goddess. Eric had the same knack of making her feel loved and protected, but he was more fun. She never knew what he'd do or say next. Dennis had been passive, predictable. She shivered, remembering the feel of Eric's lips against hers.

He drew her closer. "You've been awfully quiet. Are you sure you're not angry?"

She tried to keep the tremor of excitement out of her voice. "Positive."

"I'd like to make it up to you over dinner tonight. The sky's the limit. Your choice."

"That would be terrific, and I know the perfect place. Be here at seven."

Kathy eagerly awaited Eric's arrival. Would he approve of her choice? Before the mantel clock chimed the hour, the bell rang. Kathy dashed to answer.

Eric's blue eyes twinkled as he stood on the porch with one hand behind his back. "I was hoping you'd wear the yellow sundress I love." He presented her with a corsage, five orange, yellow-tipped rosebuds. "Let me pin these on."

"They're beautiful." The scent of *Old Spice* aftershave tantalized her as he deftly wove the corsage pin through her dress.

Trying not to crush the roses, Eric leaned down and kissed her. "I think I did something backward," he laughed. "Kisses should come before corsages. Are you ready?"

She nodded and handed him the car keys. "You drive. I'll navigate."

"Where are we going?"

"You'll see."

Eric followed her directions without comment until Kathy told him to turn off on a narrow, winding road. "Are you sure you're not leading me astray?"

"Could be."

When they reached the picturesque spot that looked like a bit of Switzerland, he glanced around with approval. "Some place."

Kathy loved the resort. The gift shop, the grocery store, and the bakery gave the illusion of being in an Alpine village.

After Eric parked, they followed a meandering path through the trees. Yellow lights marked side paths off the main trail. "Where do those go?" Eric asked.

"To little honeymoon cottages, or at least that's how I view them."

"Aha," he laughed. "I see."

Kathy felt her face turning crimson. Why couldn't she have just said vacation cottages? What must he be thinking?

The trees thinned near the top of the hill and revealed a gray stone lodge standing in majestic splendor. "Wow," Eric said, "it's like an ancient castle."

Kathy knew he would appreciate the smorgasbord restaurant too. The atmosphere was continental, each booth a romantic private arbor lit by one flickering candle on the table.

"I like your choice," he said.

While they took their time eating, Kathy told him she planned to work for her father during the summer. "Are you going to take the part-time job at the police garage?"

He nodded. "It was good of Captain Dole to recommend me. I'll only be working mornings so it won't hamper my surfing, but I'll miss your being there to grade my progress."

"I'll only be working four weeks while Dad's staff takes vacations. The rest of the time, I'll have free as well as weekends."

Eric reached across the table, took her hand, and stroked it with his thumb.

Kathy thought, *Now is the time to ask the question that's been burning in my mind.* She took a fortifying breath. "Did you mean what you said just before you dunked me?"

Eric released her hand, leaned forward to cup her chin, drew her lips to his, and kissed her with tenderness. "Does that answer your question?" He sat back as a smile crept across his face. "But I'll never understand why I love you so much. You are the most unpredictable woman I know."

Only with Eric had Kathy found herself at a loss for words. Again, as it had earlier today, her mind went blank. Embarrassed, a sudden attack of shyness struck her, and she waited for Eric's lead.

"I think we've monopolized this booth long enough. We'd better leave."

She nodded and followed him.

Halfway down the path, Eric stopped and laughed. "I didn't know my simple declaration of love would send you into shock." He dropped to one knee and spread his arms. "Speak to me, woman!"

His antics made her giggle. "It's a wonder you're not in perpetual shock from all the awkward situations I've created."

"As long as we're together, I can take anything." He rose, gathered her into his arms, and pressed his lips against hers.

She leaned back and gazed at him in wonder. Her words tumbled out, "I love you, Eric."

He winked. "I kinda figured you did." He gave her a light hug and kept his arm around her as they strolled down the trail.

Kathy glanced longingly up one of the narrow paths.

Eric leaned close and whispered, "Thinking about spending the night?"

Astonishment lit Kathy's eyes. "We're not married."

"Then why did you bring me here? Last night, I could have sworn you wouldn't have resisted if I'd tried to make love to you. Today, you melted in my embrace. Now you bring me here. What else am I to think?"

"Eric, I'm sorry. I didn't realize." *How could I have been such a fool?*

"Jill used to pressure me almost beyond endurance. I never succumbed to her charms, but I *love* you, Kathy, and a guy can only back off so long."

"Forgive me?"

He took her hands in his. "There's nothing to forgive. I love you, and you love me. That's all that's important right now."

\*     \*     \*

Dr. Ryan and his wife lay in bed. "Dear," she said, "I don't think you should have given Kathy permission to go to that restaurant. It's . . . it's so out of the way."

"She used to go there with Dennis."

"But Dennis was such a safe kid. We knew him and his family."

*Safe kid? That's how she saw him? Restrained maybe, but Dennis was a man. I'm sure he had appetites as keen as any other male. He just took things slow and easy.* "We may not know Eric as well as we'd like, but we do know our daughter."

"But she's in love with him. Girls in love do foolish things."

"Really? Did you?"

"Of course not! My mother told me—"

"Everything you've told Kathy?" he interjected.

She nodded and sighed before she closed her eyes, but he knew his wife wouldn't fall sound to sleep until she heard Kathy return. Neither would he.

Dr. Ryan lay awake, thinking. All day, he'd watched Kathy for signs that last night's ordeal had affected her adversely. He saw none. Being able to tell Eric about the motorcyclist showed she was gradually getting over the emotional trauma.

He thought about what he'd witnessed on the beach this afternoon. He would have to remember not to let Kathy know he'd seen Eric dunk her. She might suspect a conspiracy. Eric had handled her perfectly. She needed a man who could be assertive as well as tender. Dr. Ryan had liked Dennis but never felt he was the right person for Kathy, too easily manipulated. Eric would be good for her as well as good to her.

The doctor saw God's hand working in their lives. Would they someday marry? First, Eric needed to get over his phobia and start talking about the war. Kathy complained about his clowning. She didn't realize he joked to hide his aching heart.

*I know Eric loves her, and she loves him, but he needs open up soon and share his pain before that hole he's digging gets deeper.*

# CHAPTER 14

Friday, June 22, Eric glanced at the wall clock—four fifteen. In an hour, he would be walking to Kathy's for another evening of food and fellowship with her family. Mid-June, Dr. Ryan had been up-front with him. "Do not take Kathy out on Fridays. This is the one night we have for family togetherness. You're welcome to join us but please honor our wishes by not asking her out. Okay?"

Eric had readily agreed. How could he not? A month ago, he was a stranger. Treated now as a family member, he looked forward to becoming a permanent one.

He also felt accepted in the community and enjoyed his part-time job at the police garage. He liked the friendly mechanics, the good pay, and flexible hours. Today, his boss had asked him to work an eight-hour shift. While he rotated tires on a squad car, a sudden realization came to him. He hadn't had a nightmare for a week. Working, surfing, and spending time with Kathy must have kept his memories of the war at bay. Eric shook his head in wonder. A bus accident, of all things, had brought them together. If the incident hadn't happened, where would he be? Still traveling? Still searching? Still trying to find meaning to his life?

*Kathy, my dear, sweet, unpredictable Kathy, I love you. You've stilled my restlessness and given my life meaning. I long to ask you to marry me. Is it too soon?*

First, he needed to share his life with her, tell her about Dennis, the truth minus the gore. At times, he wished he'd killed the young soldier, but when he reflected on the incident and envisioned the kid's fear-glazed eyes, he wondered if even now he could shoot him.

*Kathy, is your love strong enough to weather the shocking revelation that I could have prevented Dennis's death? How will Jeff and Mary react? Will all three of you hate me?*

Eric pushed the thoughts aside Friday night while he went bowling with Kathy's family, but the minute he left her house, his mind returned to the problem of when and where to tell her about Dennis.

While he lay in bed, his hands behind his head, staring at the ceiling, he made his decision. *Wednesday is July fourth. Freedom did not come without risk, and I will never be free to ask for Kathy's hand until I risk telling her.*

Over the weekend and the next week, he looked for the right moment to talk with her, but none came. Every time he got up courage, something happened and the moment passed.

Saturday, lighter in spirit since he'd made a mental commitment, he bounded up her porch steps and rang the bell. He and Kathy were meeting Jeff and Mary and other friends at ten o'clock for a day on the beach. Later the town's young people planned to have an evening barbecue.

Kathy opened the door, and before he could say hi, she threw her arms around his neck but waited for him to kiss her.

Eric leaned back and grinned. "You know, I could get used to being greeted like this."

"So?"

He drew her closer and touched her nose with his. "I hear Eskimos rub noses to show affection."

Her eyes danced with mischief. "I'm not an Eskimo."

"Neither am I." Eric only intended to give her a light, good morning kiss, but her arms tightening around his neck and her pressing closer, sent his senses reeling. When they parted, her flushed face showed she, too, had felt the heat of the moment.

They gazed at each other in wonder.

"Wow," he said to break the awkward silence.

Breathless, she blinked. "I'm sure glad I'm not an Eskimo.

Eric glanced at his watch to make his thoughts go elsewhere. "Mary and Jeff will be on the beach in half an hour. Are you ready?"

"Almost. All that's left is the picnic basket."

After Eric helped Kathy pack sandwiches, chips and soda, he carried the picnic basket to the station wagon and set it beside their surfboards. He wished now they could be alone all day, drive someplace where they could talk. Until he told her about Dennis, he didn't dare propose.

When Kathy tossed him the car keys, she asked, "Something bothering you? You look preoccupied."

"You caught me wondering how we could be alone. No Jeff. No Mary. Just us."

"Why didn't you mention this earlier, before we finalized plans for spending the day with them?"

He shrugged. "The feeling just came over me."

"Will tomorrow do?"

"Sure." *Can I wait that long to learn she loves me enough to forgive me?*

By noon, while the foursome ate lunch, Eric knew he'd have to tell her tonight or he'd never sleep. He put his barely touched Spam sandwich down, nibbled on a chip, and took a swig of orange soda.

Jeff, who had already wolfed down his food, stared at him. "You ailing?"

"Why?"

"You're not eating."

"Just off my feed." *I wish you'd kept your mouth shut, Jeff, now the girls have noticed.*

"Do you feel okay?" Kathy asked.

"Yes," he answered more forcefully than he intended. "Can't a guy be off his feed once in a while?"

Jeff laughed. "Me, maybe. But you?"

Eric rolled his eyes. "You three are worse than mother hens. I'm fine." To prove it, he managed to eat his sandwich but needed the orange soda to wash down each bite.

An hour later, he and Jeff watched the girls paddle out on their surfboards. While Eric watched Kathy ride in on her wave, his heart thudded like the pounding surf. He envisioned her forgiving him, thus cementing their love.

Jeff nudged him. "Boy have you got it bad. I haven't seen such a syrupy grin since I last glanced in a mirror."

Eric shook his head. "I look as lovesick as you? Impossible." Both laughed.

Jeff gestured toward Kathy as she trudged through the sand with her surfboard. "Are you going to propose tonight?"

"I'd sure like to."

Jeff gave him a thumbs-up.

"What are you two plotting?" Kathy asked.

"Not a thing," Jeff said. "Eric's just decided he's ready to go on to bigger and better waves."

"I'm not ready," Eric interjected. "That's your idea, not mine." *Good grief, Jeff. Why did you have to say that? I know you're speaking figuratively, comparing marriage to the thrill of surfing, but I don't want to be pressured into tackling more than I can handle.*

Kathy looked as if she were trying to put two and two together and had come up with one.

Before she could speak, Jeff said, "You are ready. You're a natural. It took me much longer to make the progress you have."

"Thanks," Eric stammered and winked at Kathy. "She's a good teacher."

Jeff paddled out, and Kathy asked again, "What are you two plotting? I've known Jeff far too long not to know when he's up to something."

"I'll tell you tonight."

Her face beamed. "He's going to propose to Mary?"

Eric cupped her chin. "I'll tell you tonight."

Toward evening, most of the beach crowd packed up their belongings and left. The remaining young people gathered around the pit to grill hamburgers and hot dogs. After eating, they talked about vacation plans. Some who had never been out of California looked envious of those traveling to other states.

After listening a few minutes, Eric's mind drifted. He envisioned all the interesting places where he and his dad had lived in the United States. Sometimes, his father's civil engineering job only lasted three months. Eric hated having to change schools and make new friends, but he loved weekends with his father. Their longest stint was a year in the Washington DC area, the highlight of Eric's childhood. They walked many civil war battlegrounds, examined every museum, camped, fished, and hiked in the Blue Ridge Mountains. *Dad, I wish you were alive so you could meet Kathy.*

Why had his father crammed all the love and living he could into every moment they spent together? Did he have a premonition of his own death? Eric recalled the freak accident that claimed his father's life instantly—a rock tumbling down a mountainside, striking him in the head. When Eric ran for help, his mind told him his father had died, but his heart refused to accept this. Devastated, he'd cried himself to sleep for weeks after the funeral. Now he chose to remember only the good moments, their times of togetherness, all the places-

Kathy's voice jarred him from his reverie. "Eric spent the last three years traveling." She hooked her arm in his and beamed. "I bet he's seen all forty-eight states."

Caught off guard, Eric blurted, "Not hardly." Guilt plagued him for not explaining his seeing the United States happened during his childhood.

"What were you?" one young man asked. "A traveling salesman?"

Eric laughed to cover his uneasiness. "More like a traveling mechanic." He felt the mire of deceit pulling him deeper. His mind said, *Tell them you were overseas,* but he kept still. He heeded his inner voice that said, *You don't owe them an explanation* and ignored the one that said, *You stupid fool, you're only making matters worse.*

"What kind of a job is that?" a girl asked.

"I moved around a lot and earned money by fixing vehicles."

The captain of Jeff's baseball team said, "Sounds like a good deal. Maybe I'll try that. Have you had any interesting experiences?"

"I've seen most of the territory north of the Rockies, and I've been up and down the east coast, but the bus accident is the only unusual thing that's happened." One of Jeff's classmates stared at Eric, a frown deepening his brow. Uncomfortable under his scrutiny, Eric shifted his position, picked up a handful of sand, and watched the grains slip through his fingers. He wished the topic would change to take him out of the spotlight.

Talk turned to the war. Several young men mentioned they were going to enlist as soon as they could. One scowled at Eric. "You're older than we are. Didn't you ever get a draft notice?"

"If they sent one, I never received it. I think I'll go catch one last wave before dark." He scrambled to his feet, grabbed his surfboard, and scurried away like a lizard. In his heart, he felt like a slithering worm.

Incredulous, Kathy stared. *He dodged the draft? He wouldn't have run off if he'd just been lucky. And all this time I've felt sorry for him, thinking he was recovering from some serious illness.*

Discussion broke out in the group, and one of Jeff's friends said, "I don't know about the rest of you, but to me, he all but admitted he evaded the draft."

"Look," Jeff said, "don't be so quick to judge. I'm sure there's an explanation."

Along with her grief when Dennis was killed had come pride in knowing he died for a just cause. Kathy clenched her hands. "You heard him, Jeff. How can you sit there and defend him?"

"He may be hiding something, but I can't believe he dodged the draft."

"Then why did he run?" Kathy snapped. "I never want to see him again."

"Let's go to another beach," the captain of Jeff's baseball team said.

Everyone left except Kathy, Mary, and Jeff.

Shaking with fury, Kathy grabbed her surfboard. "I'm going home."

Jeff clutched her arm. "Kathy, wait. Let him explain."

"No! Dennis was proud to fight for his country. Dodging the draft makes Eric a traitor." She jerked her arm free and trudged toward the station wagon.

\* \* \*

Eric rode in on his wave, knowing he had to face the group and set things straight. He saw Jeff and Mary watching from the water's edge. He picked up his board and walked toward them. "Where's Kathy?"

"She went home. The others moved to another beach. Your remarks about the draft not catching up with you rubbed them the wrong way. They think you bummed around to evade the draft."

"And Kathy?"

"I've never seen her madder."

"Why are you both still here?"

"You owe us an explanation as well as Kathy and need someone to drive you to her house. What's your problem? Your clown act hasn't exactly fooled me."

"What makes you think it's an act?"

"You're working too hard."

Eric's reserve broke. He drew in a deep breath and slowly let it out. "You're right, and I've been a fool. My traveling for three years was in Europe, in uniform. Jeff, I don't want to think about the war, let alone talk about it. I should have been up-front with everyone. I apologize for not giving you guys credit for understanding my feelings. I had planned to tell Kathy everything tonight."

Jeff shook his head. "Well, what's done is done. Now it's time to undo it. Let's get you over to her house."

\*    \*    \*

Kathy lay across the bed, crying. The ringing of the doorbell startled her, bringing her bolt upright. The persistent buzzing compelled her to answer. If it was Eric, she would turn off the porch light, and he would get the message. She pulled back the shade on the heavy glass door, saw Mary, and unbolted the lock. Before she opened the door fully, Mary said, "Talk to him."

Eric stepped in her place and wedged his foot so Kathy couldn't close the door. "Let me explain."

"I want nothing to do with a draft dodger." Kathy glared at Eric. "Go away. No one asked you to come to Arroyo Grande. We don't need the likes of you."

"Let me explain."

"You made yourself perfectly clear. Leave!"

Eric backed away, looking stunned. Kathy slammed the door, ran to her bedroom and threw herself across the bed.

Eric gazed at Mary. "She won't listen."

"You know how Kathy is . . . she just needs more time to cool off."

Shoulders slumped, Eric followed Mary to the car. He slid onto the backseat and stared out the window.

"No luck?" Jeff asked.

Eric clenched his hands and pressed his head against the seat. "No."

"Give her a few more minutes to think things over and try again. She knows we brought you, and she'll realize there has to be an explanation."

"Not tonight, she's too angry. Frankly, so am I."

"Kathy loves you," Mary said. "She told me so."

"Sometimes, there's a fine line between love and hate. Take it from one who knows. I love her, and I'm afraid I've lost her."

"Then you need to tell her now."

"No. We need time to calm down and sleep on what's happened."

Jeff snorted. "Sleep? You think either of you will sleep? Go talk with her. I'll go with you."

"Get off my back! I know what I'm doing. I'll try again tomorrow."

Jeff drove Eric to the Dole's. "Good luck," he said.

"Thanks, I'll need it."

Kathy grew calmer and began to think. *Why did Mary come to the door? To make sure I opened it? Did Eric have a logical explanation?* Horrified, Kathy sat up. Why had she talked so hatefully to him? She recalled the devastated look on his face before she slammed the door. Could he forgive her for not listening? What if he packed up and left before she could talk to him? "Please, Lord, don't let him. I love him!" She scooted off the bed, ran to the door, and pulled back the blind. Jeff's car had already disappeared. In desperation, she called the Dole's house. No answer. She called Mary's. No answer. She called Jeff's and let the phone ring several times, but no one was home there either. Kathy sat on the couch and buried her face in her hands. She heard the garage door open and ran to her room.

"Okay, boys," Dr. Ryan said, "you need to get right to bed." He walked down the hallway with them, past Kathy's door, and heard her crying. The boys stopped, listened, and looked puzzled. "She's probably having a bad dream," he whispered and gave them each a hug. "Off to bed with you. Don't forget to brush your teeth and say your prayers." He waited until they closed their door before he tapped on hers. "May I come in?"

He heard a faint yes between sobs.

Kathy sat on the edge of the bed, her face so grief-stricken it scared him.

"Oh, Daddy," she cried and threw her arms around his neck.

"What happened?"

For a few moments, she could only sob like a small child who'd skinned both knees. But he knew it was her heart that was torn and bleeding. She'd cried like this when she learned of Dennis's death. He drew her closer but was unable to think of comforting words. If anything had happened to Eric, surely one of her friends would have stayed with her. "What happened?" he asked. "Did you and Eric have an argument?"

Kathy nodded. After she regained her composure, she told him about the incident on the beach and Eric's coming over to explain. "Daddy, I didn't give him a chance. I told him to go away." She broke into tears again.

"And you're afraid he'll leave town?"

She nodded. "I love him!"

"I know you do, and he loves you." He took her hands in his, closed his eyes, and silently asked for guidance before he prayed aloud, "Lord, please calm Kathy's heart. We often say things we regret. Eric was unwise in saying what he did. You and I know the truth and understand why. Fighting overseas has left him with a tormented heart, and he can't bring himself to talk about the war." Kathy moaned in anguish, but he continued. "Please intervene in their behalf. Bring them back together. Amen."

Kathy stared at him in shock. "He was in the war?"

Dr. Ryan nodded. "Every time he came here, I noticed how he manipulated the conversation away from himself. If he couldn't, he made evasive answers but in such a charming way I thought at first I was wrong. I confronted him. He shared his life with me, even his stint overseas. Kathy, he was wounded and imprisoned in Europe."

"Oh, Daddy, what can I do to help him?"

"Pray for him. When he comes again, listen with your heart."

"What if he doesn't come?"

Dr. Ryan gave her a hug. "He will."

# CHAPTER 15

After Jeff drove him to the Dole's, Eric stashed his surfboard in the shed. For a few moments, he stood outside the empty house, unable to force himself to enter. Even in the cool night air, he couldn't shake the stifling pressure building around and within him. He walked down the sloping bank to the beach and sat cross-legged near the water's edge.

Angry with himself but also with Kathy for not listening, he pounded the ground until his anger was spent and his hand ached. He hung his head. *How could I have been so stupid? Dr. Ryan told me weeks ago to tell Kathy I'd been in the war.* He looked up at the twinkling stars. They seemed to say, "You blew it."

"God, I really believe You led me to Arroyo Grande. This town, my friends, and especially Kathy have stilled my restlessness. But in one thoughtless panicky moment, I ruined everything, and I have no one to blame but myself."

He picked up a handful of sand and let it shift between his fingers. He thought about the kids on the beach. *If our roles were reversed, I would have probably reacted like they and Kathy did. How in the world did Jeff see through me? Not that it matters now.*

After Kathy told him to leave, his first thought was to pack his duffel bag, write a note to the Doles, and take off. He couldn't. His inner voice told him he belonged here. He had to make amends. Tomorrow, he would go to Kathy, somehow make her listen. *Oh, my precious Kathy, please give me another chance.* He turned his gaze heavenward. "Lord, help me say the right words."

Eric stayed outdoors until the Doles came home. He watched for their bedroom light and waited for it to go out before he rose and climbed the steps to the deck. Quietly, he unlocked the door and felt his way down the darkened hallway to his room. For a while, he stared out the window with a heavy heart, wishing he could erase his careless words.

Stretched out on the bed, he listened to the drone of the clock and the intermittent rumble of cars as they drove past the house. A night bird sending forth a mournful call deepened his gloom. Exhausted, he fell into a troubled sleep.

The violence of his nightmares came stronger than usual. On Omaha Beach, mutilated bodies fell around Eric. He cradled Mato in his arms and sobbed, "Somehow I'll learn to surf, my friend."

His mind carried him to the pillbox that exploded and killed Erin. Weeping in anguish, he buried his twin.

The scene changed to Aachen. Eric fell when the chubby, rosy-cheeked German shot him. The youth pulled the trigger again but nothing happened. Eric struggled to his knees, took aim to kill, but saw the fear-glazed eyes. He lowered his sights and shot the boy in the thigh. In the next instant, Dennis's face flashed before him and exploded into a red mass of mangled flesh. Eric screamed.

The bloody Rhine engulfed him. He fought to keep his head above the raging water. Bodies bobbed around him. Mato. Erin. Dennis. Jill stood on the embankment laughing. He saw Kathy running toward him and yelled, "Kathy! Help me!" Jill grabbed Kathy's arm and pushed her over the rocky cliff. "Kathy!" he cried. She lay on the rocks along the river's edge. Eric struggled to reach her before the water carried her away. An invisible force held him back. Horrified, he watched the current lift her and whirl her into the mainstream. "Kathy!"

"Eric, wake up. You're dreaming."

He opened his eyes. In the early morning light, he saw Capt. Dole sitting on the edge of the bed but couldn't blot out the image of Kathy lying crumpled on the rocks. He shut his eyes, trying to erase the nightmare. He couldn't stop shaking. Was the river carrying away

Kathy a foreboding forecast? Had he lost her forever? He stared at Capt. Dole in helplessness.

"Son, you kept screaming Kathy's name. What happened?"

Eric pressed his head into the pillow as his mind shed the last remnants of sleep. "Kathy and I had a fight." Calmer, he sat up and looked at his watch, five fifteen. "Sorry I awakened you." Eric told him about his blunder and Kathy's reaction. "I've been a fool, but a lot of good it does to realize that now."

"And all because you've kept your feelings bottled up." The captain studied Eric with a thoughtful gaze. "Think you can go back to sleep?"

Eric shook his head.

"Then let's get dressed and have some coffee. Annie's still asleep, and if you don't mind, I'd like to have a father-son chat."

*Father-son chat? More than anything, I need an understanding father right now, but after Capt. Dole hears what I must tell him, will he want me around? And what about Kathy?*

On the deck, the captain filled their cups and sat across from him. "You've had some bad nightmares since you've been here, but last night was the worst. At one point, you let out such a blood-curdling scream I had to force myself to stay in bed. When you started yelling Kathy's name, I decided I'd better wake you up. I know this won't be easy, but I want you to tell me about your nightmare."

Eric debated whether to do that or just blurt out what he needed to tell the captain. Maybe talking about his torment first would help Capt. Dole understand his frame of mind. Bit by bit, he shared his nightmare, his anguish.

The older man listened, his countenance thoughtful, compassionate, then sad when Eric talked about Dennis. After describing the raging red water scene, Eric said, "When I saw the current sweep Kathy away, I thought I'd lost her forever, and maybe I have."

"Why? Because she wouldn't let you explain about being in the service?" He shook his head. "I've known Kathy since she was three. She's always been quick to react before thinking. Right now she's probably sobbing her heart out. She loves you."

"That may be, but there's something else I need to share with her that may end our relationship."

"Like what?"

Eric drew in a breath and slowly let it out. His temples pounded. "I'm responsible for Dennis's death."

Captain Dole stiffened. His face paled. "How?"

"When I had the chance, I couldn't kill the German kid who shot me. I only wounded him. Captain, he barely looked out of puberty. He was so scared." Tears filled Eric's eyes. "That kid shot him! Your son died because I didn't do my job." He bit down on his lip. "I'd better leave town."

"Run away?"

"I got your son killed!"

"I won't pretend I'm not shocked by what you've said. Annie and I took Dennis's death hard, but God has comforted us. Have you kept this from us the whole time you've been here?"

Eric shook his head. "I only recently remembered."

"I can see why. You've had enough to deal with . . . Mato's death, Erin's, your being wounded, and going behind enemy lines. That's quite a load. More than I've ever carried."

Unable to shake his despair, Eric stared into the black depths of his untouched coffee.

"Son, look at me."

*How can he call me son?* Eric forced himself to meet the captain's searching gaze.

"You're not responsible for Dennis's death. God is sovereign. The German boy's gun not firing spared your life. Then perhaps it fired and killed Dennis. You had no control over this situation."

"And that gets me off the hook? I didn't do my job, and I'm going to have to live with that!"

"Then you're letting Satan have the last laugh instead of forgiving yourself for being human and allowing God to comfort you. Do you also blame yourself for Erin's death?"

"It was my platoon that destroyed the pillbox. I stood there cheering all the way."

"Oh," the captain said as he stared at Eric. "Then I guess you're the one who's really responsible for the bus accident."

"What?"

"You were there, weren't you? Aren't you the one responsible for it?"

"No."

"Then who was?"

"You know good and well who was . . . the man behind the wheel of the car."

"And who's behind the wheel of the German army? Who was instrumental in putting your brother in that pillbox?"

*Hitler*, Eric answered in his mind as the captain continued talking.

"Son, you've suffered more than most men twice your age, but I feel God has used your pain to work out His plan for your life. The war may be the root of your restlessness, but God used it to compel you to come to California so you could meet Kathy."

"But I've lost her."

"Nonsense. She loves you. Now would not be the right time to tell her about Dennis, but when it is, you'll know, and she'll understand. Trust me and trust God to guide you." He gazed at the mantel picture as if pondering how to say something before his attention turned back to Eric. "You said you recently remembered everything. I'd like you to tell me about that day. What did you do when you entered that building?"

"Why do you ask?"

"Bear with me, just try to recall the sequence of events."

Eric closed his eyes as he recalled the incident. "I went in with my rifle spewing, the noise so deafening I didn't hear the kid upstairs."

"When you'd searched other buildings, was the sound always that loud?"

"No."

"Why was it so loud that day? Think. Remember."

Wondering why, Eric closed his eyes and pictured the moment. His eyes went wide with realization as he gazed at the captain. "I was—"

"Being shot at by six Germans. You killed four and disabled two, either one of whom could have killed Dennis. The other soldier, who came to your aid and carried you out of that building, praised your heroic actions. You did your job well. Above and beyond."

"How'd you find out?"

"I made inquiries to the War Department. They told me you are a credit to your unit and your country. Think about this. And talk with Kathy as soon as she comes home from church."

After the Doles left to attend church, Eric sat on the deck, forcing himself to face his problems, deal with his torment. Had he been blaming himself needlessly? The thought that maybe another German could have killed Dennis, lifted a little weight from his heart. More confident about talking to Kathy, Eric visualized Jill fading away, her laughter dying on her lips as Kathy's smile soothed his troubled mind.

"Lord, thank you for giving Capt. Dole so much wisdom and understanding. Please let Kathy listen to me."

Apprehensive, Eric walked to Kathy's house and rang the bell. Her father opened the door. "Will Kathy hear me out?" Eric asked.

"She's on the deck."

Eric took that to mean she was available, but it was up to him to make her listen. When he stepped onto the deck, Kathy turned and opened her mouth.

"Don't say a word," Eric ordered. "Just listen. I won't leave here until you do. I know what I said angered you. For that I'm sorry. Kathy, I never got a draft notice because I enlisted right after high school, six months after Pearl Harbor. Last night, as soon as the words left my mouth, I knew I'd gone too far with my charade. Yes, charade. I'm not the foot-loose, fancy-free character I've pretended to be. Because Jeff saw through me. I thought you would too."

"Why the charade?"

"I was afraid . . . afraid of questions. I have nightmares about the war. Last night was the worst because I lost you." He related parts of his nightmare and told her how Capt. Dole had awakened him and helped him pinpoint his feelings. "When I saw Erin dead, part of me died too." He took Kathy's hands. "I feel I've come a long way since last night, but I've got a long way to go. Will you help me?"

Kathy pulled her hands from his and threw her arms around his neck, making Eric's apprehension vanish under her kiss.

"Let's go down to the beach where we can talk," Kathy said.

Eric followed her as she descended the cliff stairs. As soon as she stepped onto the sand, he said, "Forgive me for being such a jerk."

"And please forgive me for not listening."

In silence, they strolled along the water's edge, turning often to embrace. An hour later, they walked back and sat on the cliff steps. Kathy leaned her head against his shoulder. Content, she let her mind drift. The lapping waves became a soothing lullaby, and she closed her eyes.

When Kathy awakened, she cast Eric a side glance, expecting to see a big grin. She giggled.

Eric's eyes opened with a start. "Guess I fell asleep too. What would your father say if he knew we'd been sleeping together on the beach?"

"Should we go ask him?"

"I don't think that would be wise. After I made you miserable, I'm sure he wasn't thrilled to see me this afternoon."

"He was the one who told me to listen to you. He mentioned last night you were wounded and imprisoned in Europe." She laid her hand over his. "I love you, Eric."

"And I love you. I know I should tell you everything but not right now. One horror haunting me will be very difficult to share."

She longed to blot out his memories but knew she couldn't. With tenderness, she said, "Whenever you're ready to confide in me, I'll listen." The tension lines in his face softened, but Kathy wanted to erase them. "I couldn't eat much today, and suddenly, I'm hungry. Are you?"

His countenance brightened, and he laughed like a man released from prison. "Starved."

"Then let's raid the refrigerator."

\*    \*    \*

Dr. Ryan heard Kathy and Eric climbing the steps. He lowered the newspaper as they crossed the deck. "Have a good talk?"

Kathy giggled, and Eric gave her a warning glance as if they shared a secret.

"That good?" Dr. Ryan asked, wondering if Eric had proposed.

Kathy's eyes twinkled with mischief. "We didn't do much talking while we walked, and when we sat down on the cliff steps . . . we fell asleep."

Eric's face flushed as he gave her a you-would-have-to-say-that look.

Dr. Ryan folded the Sunday paper and set it aside. "That's understandable. I doubt if either of you slept much last night."

"We decided to fix something to eat," she said. "Would you like something too?"

"Sure."

The men sat at the table, while Kathy made roast beef sandwiches. "Where is everybody?" she asked.

"Your mother took Angela and the boys to a movie. We thought you'd like a quiet house since you might need to do some serious talking."

"I appreciate your thoughtfulness," Eric said.

An awkward silence descended, and Dr. Ryan felt they needed to talk about Eric's blunder. "I hope the mechanics at the police garage won't give you too hard a time tomorrow. They may have heard the rumor that you're a draft dodger."

"Probably everybody in town thinks I am. Guess I've got a lot of explaining to do."

# CHAPTER 16

**M**onday morning, when Eric rode his motorcycle to the police garage, the cold stares he received could have frozen the ocean. He worked diligently without comment, waiting for the other mechanics to bring up the incident on the beach. Most had sons in service or near draft age, and Eric knew the men would soon confront him. He cast a nervous glance at the clock—almost ten. The mechanics would probably say something during lunch break when he joined them outside.

The glares from the first men, who left to wash their hands, confirmed Eric's suspicion. After the last person, Eric scrubbed the grease from his hands, walked out to the grassy area, and scooted onto the brick ledge along the driveway. He opened his thermos and felt targeted for the gallows when the men rose from the grass and approached. Eric met their hostile faces without flinching. "You want an explanation, don't you?"

They nodded.

"I'm sorry my actions and words were misinterpreted. I had my reasons, but that doesn't matter now. To set the record straight, I fought in the war for three years. I just don't want to talk about it. Fair enough?"

Their expressions turned somewhat thoughtful, but the previous week's friendly atmosphere didn't return. Did they hold it against him because he hadn't been up-front with them, or were they skeptical? He dismissed the thought of asking Capt. Dole to speak to them and confirm his story. *This is my problem. I lost their respect, and it's up to me to gain it back.*

That week, the garage needed Eric's help in the afternoons as well as the mornings. By quitting time on Friday, he couldn't get away fast enough from the cold shoulders surrounding him. He doubted next week would be better, but he refused to quit his job. He'd find some way to regain their trust.

Friday night, Jeff and Mary joined Eric at Kathy's for dinner and games. When her brothers went to bed, the foursome played ping-pong. Afterward, Jeff asked Eric, "You going surfing tomorrow?"

"Of course. I haven't missed a Saturday yet."

"Good." His devious grin made Eric wonder what was going through his mind.

Saturday morning, Eric noticed more of the town's young people gathering on the beach. He remembered Jeff's sly grin the previous night and asked, "Why is everyone congregating here? Your doing by any chance?"

Jeff shrugged. "The more people who hear you apologize, the sooner rumors will cease."

"I guess you're right," he said as Jeff beckoned his friends. Eric shook his head and laughed. "You got my script written too?"

"Nope. You're on your own."

Eric felt like a sideshow spectacle when Jeff's friends stared, but their expressions turned thoughtful, some even compassionate after he explained and apologized. The rest of the day, when they acted as if nothing had happened, Eric relaxed.

Early Sunday morning, Eric said good-bye to the Doles when they left for San Francisco. Their son, Mark, was due to arrive at the Union Station on Tuesday. After picking him up, they planned to spend a few days with their daughter who lived in the area.

Kathy's parents left right after the morning church service to take Jimmy and Tommy to summer camp. Eric, Kathy, Mary, and Jeff planned to spend the day at the beach, surfing and later join other young people for a barbecue.

Eric knew the basics of surfing but longed to have the style and grace of his friends. Despite the rough water, he saw them handle each wave with full control.

He practiced again, but his meager skills weren't enough. Just as he felt he was getting the hang of it, he'd spill. Exhausted, he shed his diving suit and decided to sit on the beach and observe. Minutes later, Jeff joined him to watch Mary who rode her wave in perfectly, but Kathy's board shot out from under her.

"Well," Jeff said, "looks like she missed that one. It happens to the best."

"Jeff, she hasn't surfaced!" Eric scrambled to his feet and ran.

"I'll get help," Jeff called after him.

While Eric swam to Kathy, he saw her head bob up and go under several times. He panicked every time she disappeared. The rough water became a formidable foe, each wave a barrier. Salt spray stung his eyes and blurred his vision. He fought to keep them open and fastened on Kathy. He had to save her. Nothing else mattered. Eric thought he heard the whir of a motorboat, but the sound was too far away to hope help was coming.

He battled through another wave, the last one. Relief washed over him when he saw Kathy, but she sank again. Eric dove and searched frantically. Out of breath, he surfaced, gulped air, and dove again. When he resurfaced, and Kathy bobbed up near him, he swam to her.

Kathy threw her arms around his neck. "Seaweed," she gasped, "my leg!"

"Hold on. Help is coming." He saw a speeding motorboat with two men. The younger man pointed toward them and waved his hand with frantic gestures. His mouth moved equally fast, but Eric couldn't make out what he was yelling.

"Eric," Kathy screamed and tried to pull him out of the path of an empty wayward surfboard, but it bounced off the top of his head, the force knocking them apart. Eric submerged. Kathy made a grab for his pullover shirt but missed and struggled to keep herself afloat until the boat reached her. It drew close, and she lunged for the rim. "Find Eric!"

After the engine idled and men lifted her aboard, the younger one yanked off his shoes and dove. Kathy trembled. *Lord, please let*

*Eric be okay.* The sight of the long strand of kelp wrapped around her leg became the focal point of her fear and anger. All because of seaweed, Eric might die. Weeping, she ripped the kelp away and pounded it with her fists.

The surfer who had lost his board swam up, looking mortified. "I'm sorry," he said. "I was only trying to help. I thought I could reach you before he did."

Only half-listening, she nodded. "He found him!" The sight of Eric's limp body brought relief, then panic. Kathy helped the older man pull Eric into the boat while the other two boosted him. Once Eric was in, they hauled themselves aboard and laid him face down.

The surfer straddled Eric and started artificial respiration. Kathy probed Eric's mouth with her fingers to make sure nothing blocked his air passages. She shuddered when water spewed forth, but she leaned close to see if she could hear him breathing. The dark-haired man started the engine.

"Hurry," Kathy yelled. "I don't think he's breathing!"

The surfer kept working. Kathy heard the motor spring to life but had no awareness of movement until they bumped the dock. Glancing up, reality hit as if she'd suddenly been shaken from a sound sleep. People ran about shouting. She spotted her father's partner, Dr. Randolf, who was like a second father. Relief crossed his face when he reached her side.

"You're all right? Jeff said you were drowning."

"I'm fine, but a surfboard hit Eric."

Dr. Randolf's attention immediately turned toward Eric who was being lifted out of the boat. Stethoscope in hand, he dropped to examine him. Kathy climbed onto the dock and bit down on her lip. She shivered while she knelt beside Eric and watched the doctor examine him. Someone draped a blanket around her shoulders and laid one next to Eric.

"He's breathing," Dr. Randolf announced, "but we need to get him to the hospital." He grabbed the blanket and tucked it snugly around Eric whose lips were blue, his skin mottled. "Where's that ambulance? It should be here by now."

Jeff and Mary pushed their way through the crowd to Kathy. "I called Dr. Randolf from the First Aid Station because I thought you were hurt. What happened to Eric?"

While the doctor continued to examine Eric, Mary explained about the wayward surfboard.

Kathy looked up at the doctor. "Is Eric okay?"

"His pulse is strong. That's a good sign."

Eric opened his eyes but stared blankly at the sky as if he wasn't seeing, wasn't really aware of his surroundings, and said mechanically, "In dem Amerikanischen krankenhaus nannten sie mich Kapitan Erin von Harmon." He closed his eyes.

The crowd gasped then stood in silence. Jeff stared at Kathy, his mouth agape. She glanced at the doctor who looked equally stunned. "Do you know what he was saying?"

He shook his head. "I . . . I have no idea."

"I can tell you." Kathy recognized the gruff voice of the arrogant drugstore owner. He pushed his way through the crowd, planted his feet, and sneered down at her. "I learned German in college. That young man said, 'In the American hospital, they called me Captain Erin von Harmon.' He's a lousy Kraut!"

Kathy stood and glared at him. "No! He's not! He fought in Europe for three years."

"Yeah? What side? German soldiers speak German."

Kathy said in tears. "He's not a Nazi. I know he isn't."

Jeff put an arm around her. "Of course, he isn't." He released her and raised his arms to the crowd. "All of you. Listen to me. Mary, Kathy, and I know Eric. He was in the war and may have problems, but he's no Nazi. I'd stake my reputation on that. Now get out of the way and let that ambulance through."

The crowd stepped aside.

Tears streamed down Kathy's cheeks as she watched the attendants place Eric on a litter and carry him toward the ambulance. She ran beside Dr. Randolf who followed them.

"Please let me ride to the hospital with him."

He shook his head. "You know I can't. Eric's going to be all right. And remember, there has to be a logical explanation for what he said." He climbed in the back of the ambulance.

While it sped away, the angry crowd started discussing the matter.

"He's a lousy German!"

"Is he a spy or a soldier who sneaked into our country?"

"How did he get into the United States?"

The mood of those around Kathy grew uglier. Even the young people Eric had apologized to believed now he had fought for Germany.

The more Kathy heard, the more she wanted to scream at them to convince everyone Eric wasn't a traitor, but she knew in their present mind, the crowd would not listen. She had to squelch the rumors before they escalated. "Jeff, I can't stand this. I've got to drive to the hospital."

"Mary, can you drive her? She shouldn't be behind the wheel. I'll follow."

The three ran to the parking lot.

The minute Kathy climbed into her car, she burst into tears. "Mary, I'm scared. What if Eric is seriously hurt? Or worse," she sobbed. "What if he doesn't make it? And if he does, by morning, the people will be so angry they'll be ready to lynch him. We've got to stop the rumors."

"Kathy, you're overreacting, but I wish we could stop the rumors. If only Capt. Dole were here, I'm sure he could help."

"Daddy told me Eric shared his life with him, but there's no way I can contact him."

They reached the hospital, and Mary said, "I'll drop you off at the emergency entrance and catch up with you after I park."

As soon as Mary stopped, Kathy jumped out and ran, leaving her purse.

Mary parked and put Kathy's purse out of sight. After she locked the car, she lifted her eyes heavenward. "Lord, please give Kathy strength for whatever lies ahead." She saw Jeff pull into a parking space and dashed over to him.

"How's Kathy?" he asked as he climbed out.

"Her fears have her close to hysteria. She jumped out of the car so fast she didn't take her purse or her clothes so she can change."

He unlocked the trunk and retrieved Mary's beach bag. "You'd better get out of your wet duds. You can come back for Kath's things when she wants them."

They found Kathy in the emergency room, still in tears, and staring into space.

Mary hurried to Kathy, slid onto the seat next to her, and Jeff sat on the other side.

Jeff laid his hand over Kathy's. "Eric's going to be fine. I just know he is." When she didn't respond, he said, "On the way over, I got an idea how we can stop the rumors."

Her countenance brightened. "How?"

"Eric's family lives in Buena Vista, Colorado. I'll drive home and make phone calls. Surely, there can't be very many people with his last name living in such a small town."

Giving him a grateful smile, she said, "Of course! They can give us answers."

"Be back in a flash."

Mary saw a nurse approaching. "Maybe she can tell us how Eric is."

"Ms. Ryan, Dr. Randolf said you can come back and see your young man a few minutes before he's moved to the second floor."

"Eric's awake?"

"Not yet, but you can talk to Dr. Randolf while the room is being readied."

Mary said, "I'll change my clothes and wait here for you."

Kathy found the doctor sitting on a padded stool next to Eric. "How is he?"

"Either your young man has an extra hard head, or God padded that blow. He only received a mild concussion."

Weak and shaky, Kathy leaned against the wall.

Dr. Randolf rose, put his arm around her and pointed to a chair. You'd better sit. Are you sure you didn't get hurt?"

She nodded. "Just scared. He wasn't breathing, and I thought I'd lost him."

"When Jeff called and said you were drowning, my heart nearly stopped. You're like my own daughter. God was good to both of us." He winked. "Now if you don't want your young man dying of fright, you'd better do something with your hair and get out of that hideous diving suit."

Kathy reached up and ran her fingers through the tangled mess. "Good grief, I must look a wreck." She hurried to the waiting room and saw Mary reading a magazine.

"How is he?" Mary asked.

"He has a mild concussion and should be fine."

"After I changed, I brought in your clothes and purse—thought you might want to make yourself presentable before you see Eric."

"Thanks. I really must look a fright. Dr. Randolf said I better do something with my hair or I'd scare Eric to death."

Mary giggled. "I've got a comb, if you don't."

Kathy felt better after she changed and freshened up.

Mary said, "I'll take your things out to the car."

When she returned, Kathy said, "Dr. Randolf came by to let me know Eric has been taken to room 202."

While the girls rode the elevator to the second floor, Mary said, "I hope Jeff gets back soon. I'm on pins and needles wondering what he found out."

"Me too."

They located room 202 at the far end of the hall.

The minute they entered, the nurse smiled at Kathy. "You're Dr. Ryan's daughter, aren't you? I've seen you with him a few times. I think your young man's going to be fine. He surely was lucky."

Kathy leaned over Eric, feeling helpless. She stroked his face as she'd done the day he slept on their couch. That day the corners of his mouth had lifted in a half-smile of realization. Now not a muscle twitched. She kissed his forehead. "Eric. Please. Open your eyes. Tell me you're okay!" Tears streamed down her cheeks. "Mary, I'm scared."

Mary rose and came to her side. "Hey, he's going to be fine. The nurse and Dr. Randolf both said so."

Kathy pulled her chair next to the bed and held Eric's hand while they kept vigil.

Almost two hours later, they turned anxious faces toward the door as Jeff rushed into the room. "Kathy, I saw Dr. Randolf, and he gave me some money, said we should go down to the cafeteria. We may have a long wait before Eric wakes up. While we eat, I'll tell you what I learned."

Kathy didn't feel like eating, but she was eager to learn what Jeff had found out.

Seated across from her at a corner table, Jeff said, "I was gone so long because it took a while to reach Eric's aunt who called his uncle to the phone. Boy, am I glad I could talk to him. You've got quite a hero for a boyfriend."

Kathy stared in surprise. "Eric?"

Jeff chuckled. "Do you have another boyfriend?" Turning serious, he told them about Eric impersonating Erin.

Kathy's jaw dropped. "Eric was a spy?"

"You heard right." He grinned before turning serious. "A scar gave him away. The Germans beat and imprisoned him."

Kathy crumpled her napkin and threw it on the table. "I've got to be with him."

Mary and Jeff stayed with Kathy all afternoon and evening.

Around nine, Dr. Ryan hurried into the room. "We just got back and heard. I saw Dr. Randolf, and he filled me in on Eric's condition." Kathy's father started examining Eric and smiled. "He's doing fine."

"Daddy, when will he wake up?" Kathy asked.

"That's in the Lord's hands."

When her friends needed to leave, Dr. Ryan said, "Kathy, I want you to go home too."

She shook her head. "I'll stay here until he wakes up."

"You need to get some rest. The nurse will call you as soon as he stirs." When she started to protest, he said, "No arguments. You want to look your best, don't you?"

She sighed. "You win."

Dr. Ryan walked out with them. *Eric Stone, you've made some good friends.*

# CHAPTER 17

E ric groaned when he started to roll over in bed. His head felt as if someone had slammed him against a brick wall. Lying still, he waited for the pain to ease. It didn't, but he managed to open his eyes a slit and glance around the dimly lit room. *A hospital?* Through confusion and pain, floating strands of red hair flashed through his mind. "Kathy! Kathy!" Despite the throbbing, he tried to sit up.

The door flew open and a nurse rushed into the room. "Easy," she said, placing her hands on his shoulders to keep him down. "Kathy's fine."

"Where is she?"

"At home, probably sound asleep."

Relieved she hadn't drowned, he relaxed, letting his head sink into the pillow. He touched the lump on the right side of his head, not far from his scar. "What happened? My head aches like crazy."

"A surfboard knocked you out. If it hadn't been for two men in a nearby boat, you might have died. Kathy was so worried she refused to leave your side until Dr. Ryan promised someone would call the minute you regained consciousness.

He winced. "She's really okay?"

The nurse nodded. "I'll let her know you're awake." She handed him two white pills before she lifted his head and gave him a glass of water. "These should help."

He gulped down the tablets. "How long before these work?"

"Give them a few minutes and don't try to sit up again." She smiled. "Doctor's orders," she added before she left.

Eric equated a few minutes as meaning ten to twenty, but it seemed longer before the throbbing eased so he could relax and drift back to sleep.

In a dream-like state, Eric felt someone stroking his face and lightly run a finger over his lips until they tickled. He brushed the hand away.

Fingers again stroked his cheek, and he heard Kathy say, "Why don't you open your eyes?"

Through a slit, he saw her sitting next to the bed. The morning sun, streaming through the window, played on her auburn hair, casting a burnished gold halo around her head. Dressed in white, she looked ethereal, an angelic vision. He wanted to reach out and touch her but was afraid she would vanish.

"How do you feel?"

The concern in her voice snapped him out of his daze. "I'm not dreaming. You really are here. You're really okay?"

"Yes, thanks to you." Tears misting, she whispered, "But I thought I'd lost you." Kathy pressed her head against his chest and clung to him a few moments before she straightened and flashed her smile—the one that always made him feel like her special knight. "You're my hero, as well as a war hero."

His eyes widened as the remnants of sleep vanished. "Hero?"

She nodded. "We know all about your going behind enemy lines."

"What brought that about?"

She told him what had happened on the beach. "Your words didn't make sense. Do you have any idea why you said them?"

He nodded. "Allied Intelligence figured when the Germans found me, their first question would be, 'Who are you?' I rehearsed the answer over and over." He gazed at the ceiling thinking about the crowd's reaction. "No wonder people thought I was a German spy, but the Doles and your father were the only ones here who knew about my impersonating Erin. How'd you find out?" After she told him, he took her hand in his. "What did you think when I spoke in German?"

"I was stunned but knew there had to be a reason. I realize talking about the war is hard, but I would like to know more." She pulled the chair closer to the bed.

Eric stared out the window a moment, trying to gather his thoughts. "Kathy, probably like every other GI who's come back, I have nightmares. I wish I could dismiss the war, pretend it never happened, but I can't. I'll never be the carefree guy I was before I went overseas." In a faraway voice, he said, "On Omaha Beach, Mato—my Hawaiian friend—died in my arms."

"Don't torture yourself. Let's talk about something else."

He shook his head. "I need to share this part of my life with you especially one incident I didn't fully remember until last week. But first, I want to tell you about my family in Cologne and my short stint as a spy." He forced a smile. "Okay?"

She nodded and tilted her head. "Weren't you scared?"

"That's putting it mildly. I'd taken two bullets—one in the stomach and another had creased my scalp. In a field hospital, Allied Intelligence instructed me to feign amnesia since my head wound would give my story credibility. Despite my stomach injury, they smuggled me behind enemy lines."

"How long before the Germans found you?"

"Probably only a few hours, but it seemed like days. Sure enough, the first question they asked was, 'Who are you?' I repeated the phrase you heard on the beach and pretended to pass out before they laid me on the bed of a truck. The ride jarred my head so much, I did lose consciousness and awakened in a hospital, alone and scared. A doctor told me I'd made it to Cologne, and my father would be in to see me later. I almost blurted, 'My father's dead.'" Eric laughed dryly. "That would have been a sure giveaway. Even so, I thought I'd be caught soon. I didn't think I could fool my stepfather, Col. von Harmon. But I did, and also Mom and my sister, Elizabeth. It was easy to feign amnesia since I barely knew them, but deceit tore me up. To make matters worse, Erin's girl visited. Marlena placed her hands on either side of my face and kissed me, first tenderly, then hard. I didn't have to play-act. My shock was real! Every time she came, she kissed me again and again, trying to jog my memory."

Kathy eyed him with curiosity. "Did you fall in love with her?"

He shook his head. "But I did enjoy her company. She tried to bring back my memory by telling me all the things she and Erin had done. I asked her questions and learned a lot about my brother. When she shared some of their intimate moments, I tried not to appear shocked and embarrassed. How should I say this? Let's just say compared to my brother, I'm reserved."

"And you never succumbed to her charms?"

"Maybe if circumstances had been different, I might have." He grinned. "She was beautiful." He cleared his throat. "Anyway, while I recuperated at home, my mother and sister answered my endless questions with patience and good humor. They seemed pleased with my inquisitiveness. I learned more about Erin and our childhood, things I didn't remember." He shifted his position to get more comfortable. "Kathy, I felt happier than I'd been for a long time. I knew it couldn't last, but I relished every moment."

"Do you want to go back?"

Eric thought about the love they'd showered on him and nodded. "Someday, I'd like to visit so I can get to know them better, even my stepfather. Despite his being a German officer, he was a great guy."

"Jeff said a scar gave you away."

"It did. The first week in December, the doctors pronounced me fit for light duty. Assigned as an aide at German Headquarters in Cologne, I worked hard and kept my eyes and ears open. My instructions were simple. My contact was an old man who worked at a local pub. When he brought me a beer, I passed him information."

"But you don't drink."

"No one seemed to pay any attention. I'd nurse a beer half an hour or so and leave. The first week in January, vital information leaking to the enemy was pinpointed to have come from German Headquarters. Although scared, I knew Erin's records were clean. Two weeks later, the doctor who had taken care of me rechecked the medical records and discovered a discrepancy. Erin's records showed no scars, but I had an ugly one on my thigh. Col. von Harmon recalled my mother telling him that when we were little, Erin and I jumped from the barn loft into a pile of hay. I landed on a pitchfork."

Kathy shuddered. "Ouch."

"You bet it hurt," he laughed before turning somber, "but being uncovered as a spy hurt more. Called into General Roer's office, I never suspected a thing since I often ran errands for him."

Eric stared at the ceiling, remembering every detail of that day. Feelings flooded back. "Kathy, the moment I stepped into the office, I knew the game was over. General Roer sat behind his desk, his lips drawn tight as if he were too angry to speak. Three SS men along the wall glared at me. Praying I was wrong, I tried to appear normal and said, 'You wanted to see me, Sir?'

"Kathy, I didn't know my stepfather was there until his voice boomed behind me, 'Eric, why are you in Cologne?' In that hushed room, my name seemed to bounce off the walls."

"What did you do? Weren't you terrified?"

"Terrified? I stood like a frozen mummy, unable to move, speak, or think. My stepfather ordered me to face him. I pivoted and fought not to flinch under his penetrating gaze. In the ensuing silence, my chest ached as I held my breath. I had the oddest sensation of shrinking when he said, 'You are Eric, aren't you?' After I nodded, his eyes narrowed. 'And you've been passing information to the Allies.' When I denied it, he said, 'Then why are you here?'"

Tears blurred Eric's vision as he thought about Erin lying half-buried under chunks of concrete.

Kathy kissed his forehead. "There's no need to continue. I know how hard this must be."

"Hard? Telling my stepfather how Erin died tore at my guts. I had to force myself to reveal that my platoon destroyed the pillbox Erin defended, that he died in my arms, asking me to get his things to Mom.

"I was so torn by the anguish I saw in my stepfather's eyes I didn't hear General Roer's footsteps until he stepped between us. His face contorted with rage as he said, 'Admit you're a spy.' When the SS men closed in on me, I blurted I wasn't, that I only wanted to see my family. He whacked me across the face and said, 'You expect me to believe that?' I told him it didn't matter whether he shot me or my army did for desertion."

Kathy's eyes went wide. "Why did you say that?"

Eric shrugged. "I have no idea, but my stepfather's gaze softened as if he believed me. When he asked what I hoped to gain from this, I told him a home after the war, that even if I were shot, I had peace of mind, knowing Mom and Elizabeth were okay. General Roer let out a vicious snort. Kathy, I have never seen a more sadistic smile when he asked, 'How comforting will that knowledge be under further interrogation?'"

In remembrance, Eric's hand slipped across his midsection. "That's when the SS men moved in and dragged me away."

Kathy bit down on her lip as her eyes misted. "Daddy said they belted you in the stomach and also lashed your back."

"Now you know why I never go bare-chested. I'm not exactly in mint condition."

"But you're alive! That's all that matters." Leaning over, her lips against his, she pressed his head deep into the pillow.

From the corner of his eye, Eric saw Dr. Ryan enter, chart in hand.

Kathy said, "And you're here in Arroyo Grande where I can make you forget." She gave him another smothering kiss before she sat back in the chair.

"Wow, now I can't remember what I was telling you."

Dr. Ryan cleared his throat. "I think kisses like that would make me forget too."

Kathy whirled around. "Daddy! How long have you been standing there?"

He grinned. "Long enough. I came to check Eric, and if you haven't worn him out, I'd like to hear the rest of his story."

Looking with suspicion at Eric, she asked, "Did you know he was there?"

He nodded.

"Why didn't you say something?"

Eric winked. "My lips were occupied."

"You could have pointed." Kathy stood and faced her father, hands on hips. "And you could have cleared your throat sooner." When he shrugged, she said, "Do you want me to leave?"

"Not necessary." After she walked to the foot of the bed, Dr. Ryan checked Eric's vitals and gently examined the lump on the side of his head. "The swelling is already subsiding. You are fortunate that board didn't split your skull or strike you nearer your temple. With all you've been through these past years, your guardian angel must be frazzled."

A twinge of pain made Eric wince. "I'd sure like to give that angel a well-deserved rest."

"And you're due for medication." Dr. Ryan handed him pills and water. After Eric downed the tablets, the doctor said, "Are you up to finishing your story? If so, I'll stay awhile."

"I'm fine."

"Daddy said they imprisoned you."

He nodded. "Crammed in a rat-infested hole they called a cell. I only saw my stepfather who came to put salve on my back and make me take sips of water and warm broth, which were all I could keep down. Just before the Allies took Cologne in March, he somehow managed to get me out of there and took me home."

Dr. Ryan retrieved a chair and sat next to Kathy. "You told me in my office that he wanted you to protect your mother and sister."

"From what?" Kathy asked.

Her father looked hesitant to answer but said, "From being raped. Soldiers sometimes lose their heads when they invade a town and come across helpless women."

Eric drew in a breath and slowly let it out. "Sometimes, I look back on that as the scariest incident. I awakened one afternoon to the door being kicked in. My mother and sister screamed, and a loud lusty voice bellowed, 'Hey, Sarge, look what we have here . . . one for you and one for me.'

"Kathy, nothing I've faced in life has terrified me more than the thought of those men raping my mother and sister. I crawled out of bed, but the floor flew up and whacked me in the face. I recall being rolled over and hearing my mother scream, 'Don't shoot him! He's

187

an American!' I opened my eyes and found myself staring up the barrel of a rifle held by the lankiest sergeant I've ever seen. A corporal had my sister pulled close, his hand slipped under her blouse. She struggled, and the sergeant yelled, 'Corporal, we don't take advantage of helpless women. Let her go.' The man pushed her away, glaring at the sergeant. Mom rushed to my side and threw herself over me. 'Ma'am,' the sergeant said gently, 'we won't harm him.'"

Tired, Eric sank deeper into the pillow and closed his eyes a moment.

Kathy kissed his forehead. "We'd better leave so you can rest."

He gazed at her and forced exhaustion aside. "Not yet. There's one last thing I must tell you, and your father might as well stay too. You need to know about an incident that happened in Aachen."

Kathy's mouth dropped open as she stared at him. "You were there? That's where Dennis died. Did you know him?"

He gasped as his chest constricted. The hospital walls closed in, imprisoning him in a world void of sound except for the pounding of his heart.

"Eric! What's wrong? Daddy, do something."

"I can't help him, Kathy. He needs to fight through this by himself."

*Lord, help me! Kathy needs to know.* Gradually, the vise-like grip on his chest eased, and his breathing normalized. "Whew," he said, gazing at Kathy in relief.

"What happened? You scared me."

"Sometimes, thinking or talking about the horrors I've seen brings on a bout of claustrophobia or a panic attack."

"But you were fine earlier. Why now?"

"Because what I have to say may jeopardize our relationship; depends on how much you love me."

She stared at him, her head tilted.

"To answer your question—no, I didn't know Dennis." He drew in a deep breath. "Aachen was so traumatic I blocked out a lot of things. Guess I couldn't handle them after what I'd already been through." Eric gave more details about Erin's death. "From then on, I found it harder to pull a trigger. I realized I'd be killing someone's loved one. While searching a building in Aachen, I hesitated shooting a German youth. He shot me in the head and stomach and would have kept on firing, but his gun jammed. The kid was so young and so scared I couldn't take his life. I only wounded him."

Eric stared out the window, seeing flashes of gunfire mutilate a man's face—Kathy's Dennis, the Doles' Dennis. He blinked back tears.

Kathy placed her hand over his. "This is too hard on you. Tell us later."

"Not talking about this has landed me in enough hot water. I've got to tell you now. I remembered nothing of what happened after I shot the boy until the day of your bus accident. Part of the incident came back my first night at the Dole's. One of the men in their family portrait looked familiar."

"Dennis?"

He nodded. "When Capt. Dole told me Dennis was killed at Aachen, the face and name came together. Dennis was one of the two men who had come to my aid. I didn't feel the Doles would want me around as a reminder so I told them I'd leave town. They asked me to stay. Both felt the Lord had led me to Arroyo Grande for a reason. They agreed to keep everything confidential, including my having been in service."

"Why?"

"Because I asked them. I couldn't deal with what I'd been through. I desperately wanted to forget."

She nodded. "I can understand that. The war loused up your life just like the motorcyclist did mine for a while."

Afraid to stop and comment, Eric continued. "My memory of Dennis's death only returned fully a few days ago. It was then I realized I was responsible. The German youth I didn't kill shot Dennis. I'd give anything to take those moments back. I . . . I'm sorry, Kathy. Please don't hate me."

Her shocked expression turned to one of concern. "Hate you? You were badly wounded. How could you have controlled the situation? I loved Dennis, but I love you more. Don't blame yourself for his death."

"That's what Capt. Dole said, but I didn't know how you'd react."

"Afraid I'd rant and rave, tell you to leave town?"

"Something like that."

"I grew up a lot after that incident. I learned what my bad temper could cost me."

"I've come a long way too."

Dr. Ryan glanced at his watch and stood. "You both have. And I think this is a good time for me to exit. Kathy, before I leave, there's one thing Eric didn't mention, something Capt. Dole told me. There were six other Germans in that building firing at Eric. He killed four of them and wounded two. Either one could have shot Dennis." He placed a hand on Eric's shoulder. "You, young man, did your job well." He started to leave but turned. "Kathy, don't stay much longer. He needs rest. I'll make arrangements for you to eat with Eric tonight."

After he left, Kathy rose to sit on the edge of the bed. "You still look depressed. No one blames you for Dennis getting killed. I wish you'd opened up sooner."

"I realize now what not sharing my feelings can do. Aunt Jean told me once that communication is essential to a good relationship. Guess I'd better work on that."

"But not now. You should rest, and I need to leave. I'm working at Dad's office this afternoon."

"How about a kiss?"

As before, her lips pressed hard against his with another smothering kiss. "Did Marlena ever kiss you like that?" she asked, smiling as if she realized the effect she'd had on him.

"Never."

"I'm glad. See you tonight."

Eric's mind drifted back to the day they beat him. He was sure the only reason the Germans hadn't shot him was because his stepfather had intervened. He wished he could have thanked him the day he was taken from the prison cell, but he'd been too weak.

He thought about his mother and sister. His pain and suffering had been worth the chance to see them. Someday, he would return to visit but not stay. Germany wasn't his home, but neither did he feel at home in Colorado.

*Where do I belong?*

Kathy rushed home after work and changed into the yellow sundress Eric liked. She applied fresh make-up and hurried to the hospital.

"I made it," she said, entering his room a few steps ahead of the aide carrying their dinners. Kathy gave Eric a quick kiss before she put a tray on her lap. "This actually looks good. I haven't had meat-loaf for a long time."

"The food's pretty good here," Eric replied, but while they ate, he seemed subdued.

*Does he have a headache, or does he have something on his mind?*

After they finished, Kathy put their trays outside the door. He looked so serious when she returned, she quipped, "Penny for your thoughts?"

Eric's face brightened. "Surely, they're worth a kiss."

Wrapping her arms around his neck, she kissed him. "Now why so sober?"

"You really expect me to tell you?"

"You'd better. I just paid the price."

"What if my thoughts aren't worth that much?"

"Then you'll have to repay me twofold."

Eric chuckled. "Sounds fair. I was just wondering where I belong."

"I don't follow."

"In Colorado, after my father died, my aunt and uncle took good care of me, but I don't feel that's my home. In Germany, I was a stranger feeling welcomed in a home that wasn't mine. And living with the Doles, I feel the same way. Was that worth a kiss?"

"Yes, but I still don't see what your problem is. Where is your heart? Surely, you've heard the saying, 'Home is where the heart is?' Well, where is your heart?"

"My heart isn't in any of those places."

"Then where is it?"

"I told you. I don't belong anywhere."

Frustrated he couldn't see her point, she said each word emphatically. "*Eric! Where is your heart?*"

He stared at her as if trying to figure out what she was driving at before he rolled his eyes and said, "Boy am I dense. That surfboard must have addled my brain." He took her hands into his. "It takes two to make a home," he whispered. "Will you marry me?"

"Any time, any place."

"Well, it can't be for a while. Can you be content knowing my future plans include you?"

"I can wait." When his lips drew tight, she realized what she'd said. "Oh, Eric, Jill said those same words, didn't she? But I really can wait, and you have the power to make sure I do. Just never let me out of your sight."

"Make you my prisoner? What kind of a relationship would that be? If I can't trust you and you can't trust me, we'll both be miserable. I need to return to Colorado for Nancy's wedding. Jill will be in the wedding party. Can you trust me?" When she nodded, he relaxed.

# CHAPTER 18

Released from the hospital Friday morning, Eric spent two days resting at the Dole's and spent Sunday with Kathy. After attending church, her father insisted he should still take it easy—no ping-pong, so he and Kathy played Monopoly with her brothers. That night on the porch, he said, "You didn't tell your folks, did you?"

"I thought it would be more proper for you to ask Dad on Monday when he gives you a check up."

"Does he suspect?"

She nodded. "They both do."

*   *   *

Monday morning, when Eric entered the examination room, he found it hard to hide his nervousness. He knew he'd failed when Dr. Ryan chuckled and said, "You look like a stallion chomping at the bit to run a race. You're either eager to get back to practicing for the surf competition next month, or there's another reason you're wound up." His lopsided grin suggested he already knew the answer.

"Would I be rushing matters if I said I'd like to start practicing Saturday? Also, I'd like your permission to marry Kathy."

Dr. Ryan laughed as he shook his head. "Is my daughter an afterthought?"

Feeling his face grow hot, Eric stammered, "Sir . . . I didn't mean that."

"I know you didn't. Forgive me for laughing." He laid a fatherly hand on Eric's shoulder. "I'll answer your first question before we discuss the second." He gave Eric a sympathetic smile. "Since I haven't examined you, I can't give the go-ahead for surfing. As to Kathy, we knew long ago she'd given you her heart. Even though you haven't known each other long, we approve. Out of curiosity, did you ask her, or did she ask you? At times, she can be quite forward, especially when she's made up her mind."

The question took Eric by surprise, and he hesitated answering.

"She asked you, didn't she?"

"Not exactly."

After Eric explained, her father nodded and said, "Have you discussed a date?"

"Not yet."

With the go-ahead to start practicing for the August 4 competition, Eric spent every moment he could surfing.

One day in the middle of July, Eric's suspicious nature surfaced when Kathy said, "Mary, Jeff and I have a beach outing planned for tomorrow night from eleven fifteen to one fifteen. Are you game?"

Eric raised an eyebrow. "Doing what?"

"Grunion hunting or as some call it surf fishing."

"In the dark?"

"There will be a full moon."

Tongue in cheek, he asked, "Is grunion hunting anything like snipe hunting?"

"I don't know. What are snipe?"

"Game fowl. You hunt them at night by beating the bushes, flushing them out, and catching them in a large bag." His Midwest cousins had conned him into doing this and left him hitting the underbrush with a stick while they went home. He didn't' plan to be conned again.

"Except for the night hunting, I don't see any similarity. Grunions are little fish that swim in on high tide to lay eggs on the beach and afterward swim back. You have to scoop them up in nets or, more sporting, catch them bare-handed."

She looked so serious he was almost inclined to believe her. *To make sure I'm not being conned by those three, I'd better, check with the Doles.*

"What are you thinking?"

"Should I wear my diving suit to stay dry?"

Kathy shook her head. "Shorts and a sweatshirt should be fine. We'll bring the nets and buckets."

The Doles confirmed what Kathy had said, but it still surprised Eric to see so many people on the beach, carrying pails and fishing nets. The moon glistened on the water as he watched the rolling waves, but nothing was happening. "What if the fish don't come?" he asked Jeff.

"Then we'll return tomorrow night or the next, only half an hour later each night."

The first sighting transformed the beach. Groups of talking people scattered—every man for himself, each vying to scoop fish as fast as possible. Eric was shoved out of the way several times before he managed to net a fish to put in their bucket.

While he walked Kathy home, carrying their full pail, he asked, "How do you cook these? You certainly can't filet them."

"Come over after work tomorrow and see."

The next evening, Eric watched Mrs. Ryan deep fry the tiny fish that were no bigger than smelt. As she took the first batch out, she said, "You eat these whole."

Eric enjoyed his first fish fry and looked forward to the next big event—his first surfing competition.

Saturday, August 4, Eric changed into dark blue shorts and studied the bedroom calendar. He'd circled today's date for the surf competition at Pismo Beach. *I can't believe time has passed so quickly. Working, surfing, and spending hours with Kathy have made it fly faster than the surfboard I can now control.*

He'd regained his health, and his muscles no longer screamed from carrying the board, or did he feel exhausted after a day's work-out. Eric felt alive and ready to tackle the waves he'd meet today in his first and probably only competition he would participate in this summer. *Jeff, I may not beat you, but I'll give you a run for that trophy Mr. Watkins carved.*

Eric glanced at his watch. *It's almost one fifteen. Kathy will be here soon.* Pismo Beach was a nice walk from the Doles' but not when you had to lug surfboards. He hurried to the living room to wait for Kathy.

Mr. and Mrs. Dole stood by the couch. "Won't be long now," he told Eric. "Annie and I will be in the crowd, rooting for you."

"I'll need all the encouragement I can get. I'm not sure I have enough skill for competing, but I'll do my best."

Mrs. Dole placed her hands on his shoulders. "Kathy says you're good, really good."

Eric laughed. "I think she watches through rose-colored glasses."

The captain nodded. "Could be," he said and cocked his head. "I think I hear her car pulling in the driveway. Good luck."

"Thanks."

"On the way to the beach, Kathy said, "Ready for this?"

"Ready or not, here I come."

Twelve young people had signed up for Mr. Watkins surf meet—five women and seven men.

After Kathy parked, she grabbed the *Brownie* box camera. "I want to take your picture before we go down and get suited up."

"And I want to take one of you to show everyone back home."

Kathy gave him one of her you-are-special smiles. "When you first came to Arroyo Grande, I told Mom if you weren't so pale and thin, you'd be the most handsome man on the beach." She appraised him head to foot. "Now look at you . . . tan and with muscles equal to Jeff's. You've become quite a hunk."

Eric laughed to cover his embarrassment. "Hunk of what? Liverwurst or Baloney?"

She gave him a playful swat. "Don't you dare compare the man I love to lunch meat." Kathy squeezed his biceps. "You are one hunk of man."

"And I'm all yours." He pulled her close and planted a quick kiss. "That's for good luck to you today." Pulling her into tighter embrace, his lips closed over hers again and lingered. "That kiss is for me."

"For good luck?"

"Just pleasure."

"Let me give you one for good luck. I hope you beat Jeff. Dennis is the only person who ever did."

With her lips pressing against his, her mentioning Dennis didn't faze him. When she released him, he cupped her chin. "Someday, I will beat Jeff."

Though he knew he lacked Jeff's grace and style, Eric finished his two competitive rides, satisfied he'd done his personal best. As he expected, Jeff took first place. Kathy had looked super riding her waves, but she came in second to Mary. While their friends received their trophies, he whispered, "Next summer, Kathy, you and I will take first place. Deal?"

Her smile erased the shadow of disappointment he'd seen. "Deal."

That night, back at the Doles', Eric slipped between the sheets and thought about going home. *By this time next month, I'll be in Colorado. If I hadn't promised Cindy I'd take her to Lakeside Park, I'd stay here.* He wondered if his nightmares would return. He hadn't had one for three weeks. The horrors of war were gradually becoming a distant memory.

During the previous weeks, thoughts of war remained pushed to the back of his mind, only to return with sharp reality Monday, August 6.

Eric shuddered while he listened to the news on the radio and tried to comprehend the destructive power of an atomic bomb. Reportedly, the one dropped on Hiroshima obliterated half the population, 75,000. Three days later, another devastated Nagasaki, killing 40,000. Eric couldn't fathom a bomb that powerful. So much havoc, so many people killed or maimed. Was an atom bomb the only way to bring the Japanese leaders to their knees? *The Japanese started this war. We didn't ask for it. Doesn't President Truman have the right to bring it to a close, put a stop to the human carnage on both sides? Still . . .*

Visualizing the destruction made Eric sick at heart. He turned off the radio and picked up the paper. It didn't help. The front page carried a more vivid account. Pictures of the mushroom clouds and the appalling devastation stunned Eric. Surely this had to be the war to end all wars. Who could survive another? He folded the paper and tossed it on the coffee table. *I need air.*

On the deck, Eric breathed in deeply and tried to push the news aside by concentrating on packing his motorcycle. Tomorrow, he would follow the Ryan's and go camping with them in Sequoia National Park. When they left the campground to return home, he would head for Colorado. He had to be home August 24 to be fitted for a tux. Perfect timing.

To Eric, the Ryan's invitation showed they already considered him part of their family. He marveled how God had blessed him, taken the broken threads of his life, and rewoven them into something extraordinary. Restlessness no longer plagued him. He knew where he belonged. Eyes heavenward, he whispered, "Thank you, Lord."

The wonder and joy that filled him remained while he combed the Redwoods with the Ryans. Each day, they walked a new trail or viewed the forest from horseback. From fire-scarred trees to those unscathed, each giant Redwood held a beauty all its own. As much as Eric enjoyed being with Kathy's family, he longed to have her to himself. *Someday, Kathy, we're coming back here.*

August 14, VJ day, Japan surrendered. The blare of car horns shattered the forest's stillness. Campers flocked to the road in their vehicles and drove bumper to bumper, shouting, waving, and doing everything they could to show their exuberance over Japan's surrender. Eric hugged and kissed Kathy. The war was over.

On their last night together, Eric held Kathy's hand while they strolled a moonlit path meandering between the trees. Her quietness made him wonder if she were worried about him seeing Jill. He pointed to a fallen log. "Want to sit a while?"

"Sure." She brushed away a scattering of pine needles and sat beside him. "It's so beautiful here. I don't want to go home, and I hate to see you leave tomorrow."

"I won't be gone long. Have you made any wedding plans?"

"We haven't even set a date."

"True, but surely the wheels have been turning in that pretty head of yours."

She laughed. "They haven't stopped, but I thought we should make plans after you return. Nancy's wedding may give you some ideas."

"I'm not keen on dressing like a penguin, but it will be good practice. Have you thought any more about us attending Cal Poly after we're married?"

"You're really serious about us going the second semester?"

"Yes."

"What if I get pregnant?"

"Then we have a baby."

"But we could have twins."

He laughed. "Then we'll both be up for night feedings."

She put her hands on her hips. "You're not taking me seriously."

"Kathy, I'm sorry, but I can't worry about all the 'what ifs' that might come into our lives. Look, I want you to start college with me. If you get pregnant, then we'll decide what to do. Okay?"

She nodded but stared past him, her brow furrowing as if she were reluctant to say what was on her mind. Finally, Kathy said, "What's Jill like?"

"I won't lie to you, Kathy. She's the most provocative woman I've ever known. I really thought I loved her, but no more. I hope she gracefully accepts the fact that I love you."

"What if she doesn't?"

He laughed. "Then I may have a wildcat on my hands. You'd better pray for me. I'll need all the help I can get." Her tightly drawn lips told him it was no laughing matter. "Think your folks would let you ride with me to Colorado?"

"You know the answer to that. Why even ask?"

"Because I'd love to have you along. I hate leaving you, but Nancy and Cindy would be devastated if I didn't return. I'll call you every day and tell you my schedule so you'll know the best time to call me. Maybe if we can talk often, we won't feel so lonely. Okay?"

"That will help some."

The next morning, when they said good-bye, she clung to him as if she were afraid he wouldn't return.

"I love you, Kathy," he whispered. "Nothing Jill says or does will keep me from coming back to you. I don't have a ring to seal our engagement, but let's get married in October. Is that too soon?"

She leaned back and gave him her special smile. "October would be perfect."

"You pick the date and let me know when."

"Oh how I love you," she said, throwing her arms around him. They kissed one last time, a lingering kiss.

After Kathy climbed in the car, Eric followed the Ryans to the park exit and waved until they were out of sight.

\*     \*     \*

Eric took no side trips on the way to Colorado and pushed himself to cover as many miles a day as he could. Early Tuesday evening, his motorcycle roared up the ranch driveway and stopped in front of the back door.

The screen flew open, and Cindy dashed down the steps. "Eric!" she squealed.

He picked her up and whirled her around. "Ready for our special day at the amusement park?"

"You didn't forget!"

He put her down and hugged her. "Of course not. Next week after Nancy's wedding, we're going to Lakeside. We'll ride the roller coaster as many times as you want."

Aunt Jean came out wiping her hands on her apron. "What are you two yakking about? I thought you'd be right in."

Eric kissed her. "How's my favorite girl? Am I too late for dinner? I'm famished."

"Come on in. Nancy and Ann ate early. They had to meet the organist to go over the music, but the rest of us waited for you."

Eric followed her into the kitchen. Uncle Jim stood next to the table, looking completely out of character in bib overalls and a long-sleeved gray shirt. His uncle may have shed the uniform of a commanding officer, but his imposing, straight-backed stance remained.

"Welcome home," he said, grabbing Eric's shoulders in a manly embrace.

Eric stiffened. "I'd better get washed."

After dinner, his uncle said. "From the way you ate, I'd say your stomach's completely healed."

"I feel fine." Eric turned to his aunt and smiled. "Thanks, Aunt Jean. That was a great meal. Before I get too content, I'd better unpack my Harley and put it in the barn."

"Want some help?" his uncle asked.

"No, thanks. I don't have much." Just seeing his uncle had revived his bitterness, but at the moment, he wasn't up to the confrontation bound to come.

Eric carried his gear into the bedroom and dropped it on the floor. He fingered the items on his dresser, each where he had left them. All three basketball trophies shone from a recent polishing. The glass case, housing his seventh grade bug collection, glistened. Eric smiled, picturing Aunt Jean's loving care over all he'd left behind.

Stacks of labeled boxes stood against the wall—his father's books, school mementos. Aunt Jean probably wanted him to sort through them. He opened the one marked mementos and found his old cigar box. Eric chuckled. He'd stashed so many odds and ends here: fountain pens, pencil stubs, rubber bands, and paper clips. He shook his head in wonder. Even the five Indian head pennies remained where he had buried them years ago. He dug out the treasured coins and clutched them, fondly remembering his father's words. "Hold onto these. Someday, they'll be worth something." The memory contained far more value. These would go with him to California.

*California*, he repeated to himself while he rode his Harley to the barn and parked it in the empty horse stall. *Soon, I'll be with Kathy. Soon, we'll be married.*

He leaned against the wall and glanced around. The barn remained as he remembered it. Nothing had changed. He headed for the open doorway.

Jill burst in and threw her arms around him. "Welcome home."

"Where . . . where'd you come from?"

"I stopped at the house, and your uncle said you were out here. Aren't you glad to see me?"

"Let's just say I'm surprised."

"Still angry?" she asked.

"No, I got over that."

"Then, you're still hurt."

"You might say that."

"Can't you forgive and forget?"

He snorted. "I'm not God."

"Eric, I've changed."

"Me too. My feelings for you are gone."

"You just think they are. Kiss me. Prove to me you don't love me."

He gave her a peck on the cheek.

She stamped her foot. "I said, kiss me!"

She pressed him against the wall and kissed him harder than she'd ever done before. Stunned but aroused, Eric shoved her away. "You she-devil," he declared, angry for the way his body had responded.

She laughed. "You do still love me. I could tell."

"That wasn't love! And maybe I've mistaken my feelings all these years."

Cindy ran into the barn. "Mom wants to know if you two want some ice cream."

"Sure," Eric said.

"Eric," Jill purred, "you'll want to spend your first night home with only your family. I'll see you tomorrow."

Eric fumed while he walked back with Cindy. Sitting at the kitchen table, he stared at his bowl of ice cream.

"Problems?" Uncle Jim asked.

"Jill isn't taking no for an answer."

Cindy piped up, "I don't like Jill. Go throw her in a lake."

"Not a bad idea. I'll keep that in mind."

Later, while Aunt Jean and Cindy went outdoors to pick vegetables from the Victory garden, Uncle Jim asked, "Do you think Jill's going to be a problem?"

"She already is. I was totally unprepared for her kiss in the barn. I felt like a fool, and she's convinced I still love her."

"You're sure you don't?"

"Positive!"

"Then I think you'll be able to handle her." He filled two coffee cups, handed one to Eric, and sat across from him. "We're looking forward to meeting Kathy. How does she feel about becoming a lieutenant's wife?"

Eric stared in disbelief. "I've only been back a few hours and already you're mapping out my life. Not only mine but Kathy's. I'm not reenlisting. From now on, I'm running my own life. I hope that doesn't shock or disappoint you."

His uncle barely raised an eyebrow. "Not really. I've sensed your discontent for some time. In the hospital, you were understandably depressed, but something more was bothering you. Son, I love you, and I'm concerned. I'd like to know what's troubling you."

Eric snorted. "Now you call me son? Now you say you love me? You sure had a strange way of showing it in the hospital. Love isn't insensitive. You were! You never asked how I felt or expressed one ounce of sympathy." Eric clenched his hands. "You just gave orders!"

"And that's how you saw everything?"

The sudden mist that clouded his uncle's eyes stopped Eric from delivering a bitter reply and continuing his discourse. He could only nod and wonder if he'd misread Uncle Jim.

"They weren't my orders, Eric, but they were made mine to give. You were so close to a nervous breakdown, I didn't want you sent behind enemy lines. Allied Intelligence saw the situation differently. They said your chance to see your mother and sister would pull you through." His eyes filled with sadness. "I guess they were right, but how you regard me now really hurts."

Eric lowered his head a few moments, trying to sort out his feelings before he could meet his uncle's searching gaze. "I . . . I'm sorry. I didn't realize."

"Think we can begin again?"

Eric nodded. "I'd like that. You've done a lot for me. You took a snotty-nosed kid and raised him to be a man. I'm grateful."

"Do you still resent the times I was hard on you?"

Only Nancy knew about his resentment. Did she tell Uncle Jim or had he sensed it? "It wasn't your sternness I minded but the way you barked orders and never gave me the chance to volunteer."

His uncle nodded. "I guess I was too intent on making sure you didn't grow up to be a sissy. I'm sorry. I'll try to do better with my grandchildren. Have you and Kathy set a wedding date?"

"It will be sometime in October. I'd like for all of you to come."

"Son, we'd be proud to."

The love that shone from his eyes and his words spoken with deep conviction touched Eric, but a tendril of past bitterness remained clamped on his heart. "Twice tonight, you've called me son. For years, I longed for that. Do I finally measure up to your standards?"

His uncle smiled with the tenderness of a loving father. "Measure up?" he said choked. "You've surpassed all my expectations. I've never called you 'son' because I sensed your resentment. You and your father were close. The love between you was something I'd have given my eyeteeth to have. I wanted a son desperately, and when you came to live with us, I yearned to make you my own but didn't know how. I felt I had to earn your respect before I could hope to gain your love so I treated you like a new recruit." He shook his head. "Obviously that was not the way to go. Forgive me?"

Eric nodded as the last strand of bitterness disappeared. He now found it easier to share his feelings. They talked about the past, about the war, about love, and marriage. When they finally said good night, Eric crawled into bed feeling he understood his uncle better. His respect now bordered on love.

## CHAPTER 19

E ric found his relationship with Jill a continual problem. Every day, she drove over to see him. Since Jill was Nancy's best friend, Eric suspected a conspiracy. Was he targeted for Cupid's arrows with Nancy pulling the bow string? She had paired them in the wedding party.

During the rehearsal, Jill clung to his arm every chance she had, gave him alluring glances, and thanked Eric in a super sweet voice for the slightest gesture. The day of the wedding, while they strolled down the aisle, Jill flashed him a dreamy smile and whispered. "We could be doing this." Afterward, she remarked how handsome he looked in his tuxedo and praised or flattered him in front of family and friends.

At the house, after Nancy and her husband left under a shower of rice for their honeymoon, Ann mentioned she and her boyfriend were looking forward to a day at Lakeside with Eric and Cindy. Interest sparked Jill's eyes. When she was ready to leave, she purred, "I'd love to go to Denver with you."

"You won't be able to. I promised Cindy that Wednesday would be *our* special day."

Eric enjoyed showering Cindy with attention at the amusement park. Ann's boyfriend, Steve, had driven his car, and on the way home, Cindy laid her head on Eric's lap and fell asleep. After midnight, when Steve dropped them off, Eric carried Cindy to her room. She stirred and opened sleep-filled eyes as he laid her on the bed. "Thank you for taking me," she said with a smile. "I love you."

He kissed her forehead. "And I love you."

Eric rose early Thursday to help Uncle Jim finish painting the barn. Around eleven thirty, Jill pulled into the driveway in her red convertible and stopped near them. "Are you free? I packed a huge picnic lunch and dinner on the chance you'd join me. The aspen trees are turning early, and I thought you'd like to see their brilliant splash of colors before you return to California."

Before Eric could open his mouth, his uncle said, "You're free. You've worked enough. Go have some fun. Besides, this way you won't have to fix your own dinner tonight since everyone's going to be gone."

Eric hesitated.

"Please," she said. "I know I've been a pest, and I'd like to make it up to you. I don't want to part on a bad note."

"Okay," he agreed, "but first I need to get out of these paint-duds."

Jill drove him to the house. "Hurry," she urged.

Catching her eagerness, he dashed up the steps, took long strides to his room, and hurried to change before stopping in his tracks. He smacked the side of his head. *Good grief, what a numbskull I am. I'm responding to Jill's maneuvering ways like a stupid wooden puppet.* Eric wanted to kick the puppet across the room for being so gullible. He flopped on the bed and glanced at his watch. *She can just wait ten minutes.*

Outside, Eric opened the car door and slid onto the seat, wondering if Jill had packed his favorite foods.

"I thought we'd drive up to the lake," she said, turning the car around.

While she drove, Eric gradually relaxed. Maybe he and Jill could part as friends.

They ate ham sandwiches at a roadside picnic table. Afterward, she drove a scenic winding road to the lake where aspen abounded. A forest fire had ravished the area years ago, and large groves of young aspens had sprung up among the evergreens. Jill pulled over and parked.

"Want to take a hike?"

"Great idea."

All afternoon, they followed a well-worn forest trail that meandered around the lake. The contrast between the white-trunk flaming aspens and the dark green firs and pines, equaled the best of nature's offerings. In a clearing blue sky back-dropped a mountain where the crimson leaves wove a trail through its dark green neighbors.

It was the next grove they entered that astounded Eric—fiery red leaves formed a canopy overhead blocking out the sky. As far as he could see, he and Jill were encased among a mass of white trunks. *I've got to bring Kathy here next year. Together, we'll stretch out on a blanket and marvel at the beauty above. Oh, my precious Kathy, what a wonderful setting for two lovers. I wish I had a camera. A picture would only give you a taste of what I'm seeing, but I'm sure it would whet your appetite.*

"You have such an enraptured look on your face. What are you thinking?"

His reverie disrupted, he had the urge to tell her, but that would have started a fight and disturbed nature's tranquility. "I was wishing I had a camera. Thanks for suggesting we come here."

She linked her arm in his, flashed him a syrupy smile, and like a Southern belle who'd snagged a beau, she said, "I just knew you'd like this. We could do this again next year."

Eric held his tongue but thought, *I should have never thanked her. Even being polite encourages Jill.*

Leaving the area, she drove to a picnic ground where they could build a fire. While she laid out the food on a blanket, he gathered wood. In a rock enclosed area, he crisscrossed the logs and lit them. It was only a little after six, but the air had already turned nippy.

For dinner, Jill had brought all his favorite foods—fried chicken, Rocky Ford cantaloupe, baked beans, potato salad, and fresh peach pie. Finished eating, he leaned back against a rock and basked in the fire's warmth. He had to give Jill credit. She'd been super all day. He watched her walk to the car to get a sweater. Her trim hips swung tantalizingly, her tight jeans emphasizing every curve. She was still the most beautiful woman he'd ever known, but one he no longer desired. He pictured Kathy and smiled. Thinking about marrying her made his heart quicken. October 26 was the date they'd set. Now he wished he'd asked her to plan a September wedding.

Jill returned and knelt in front of him, her hands resting on his thighs. "You look content," she said. "Maybe you realize now how much I've changed. Please stay another week or two. Give yourself a chance to know for sure who you love."

"Jill . . ."

She pressed two fingers against his lips. "Don't say anything." She slipped her arms around his neck, brushed her lips gently over his, and kissed him with tenderness. "Give me a chance to prove I've changed." Her lips sought his once more.

Eric put his hands on her shoulders to prevent her from kissing him again. "Jill, I've changed too. It's over between us. I've enjoyed the day, but I'm going to marry Kathy."

She reared back as if he'd slapped her. "No," she shrieked, with tears streaming down her cheeks. "You can't!" Jill scrambled to her feet, ran to the car, and drove away.

Eric sat dumbfounded. What did Jill think she would accomplish by pulling this stunt? He shook his head in disgust, gathered up the picnic items, and put them in the basket. Surely she would return any moment. She didn't. Disgruntled, he kicked dirt on the fire and hiked the two miles to the ranger station.

The ranger chuckled over his predicament. "I'll give you a ride home. I'm off duty in ten minutes."

Halfway down the mountain, they saw a car tilted in a shallow ditch. "That's her," Eric told the ranger.

Jill leaned out the window and raised her hand as if to flag them for help but jerked her arm down and turned her face away.

The ranger chuckled. "I think she spotted you. Doesn't look like she's happy about having you rescue her. Want to drive past and let her squirm?"

"No. I may be upset, but I think she's been humiliated enough."

The ranger pulled in front of her car and backed up to the bumper. Eric climbed out of the Jeep and approached Jill. After she opened the door and climbed out, he said, "You okay?"

Jill nodded, gritting her teeth as if to keep from crying, did an about-face, and hurried away to sit on a rock.

Eric vented his anger by concentrating on helping the ranger hook a chain to her convertible to pull it back on the road. Afterward, Eric tried the engine. "Sounds okay," he told the ranger and thanked him as Jill walked toward them. He stared at her, fighting the urge to turn her over his knee and whack her good. "Get in. I'll drive. You're too angry." *And I'm not?*

Jill cast her eyes down and obeyed. She sat silent. Although thoroughly disgusted, Eric kept his mouth shut.

When he pulled into her driveway and stopped, Jill blurted, "Eric, I'm sorry!"

He shoved the car keys in her hand. "That was a dumb stunt, really dumb."

She ran into the house, sobbing.

Eric walked to the nearest gas station, called his uncle, and fumed all the way home. Before going to bed, he gave Aunt Jean and Ann a brief rundown on what had happened.

The next morning when ten-year-old Cindy heard how Jill had treated him, she said, "Why didn't you throw her in the lake like I told you?"

Her remark brightened Eric's spirits. "Believe me, Cindy, I wanted to."

After breakfast, Eric rode into town to look over a 1940 Chevy he'd seen advertised. He bought it when the man offered a good price for his motorcycle as part of the deal. Next, he stopped at the jewelry store.

At dinner, he showed everyone the rings he'd purchased. "Think Kathy will like them?"

"What girl wouldn't?" Ann exclaimed. She lifted the engagement ring from its blue velvet nest and slipped the three-quarter solitaire on her finger. "Wish I had a rich boyfriend."

Eric laughed. "I guess I did go overboard, but with my back pay finally catching up with me, I had the money and couldn't resist." He'd talked with Kathy this morning, but he longed to hear the sound of her voice. He excused himself from the table and took quick strides toward the living room phone. The Buena Vista operator placed the call, and Eric drummed his fingers on the telephone stand, waiting for someone to answer. He prayed it would be Kathy. Her voice made his heart pound with yearning. "I'm leaving next Tuesday," he told her. "I'd leave tomorrow, but I want to spend Labor Day here since Nancy will be back from her honeymoon. I'll be home Thursday evening." After he hung up he realized what he'd said—home. *At last, my sweet Kathy, I know where I belong.*

Eric left Tuesday morning at five. This time, saying good-bye to his loved ones wasn't nearly as painful. Now he wasn't running away, searching for something intangible. He had a definite purpose, a positive destination. He'd told Kathy to expect him Thursday, but he planned to drive straight through. Eric reached San Luis Obispo around six Wednesday morning. Bushed, he pulled into the deserted city park and slept three full hours. He awakened refreshed and ravenous. In a small diner, Eric ordered breakfast before he hurried into the restroom to wash, shave, and change into his uniform, complete with medals and campaign ribbons. The waitress's smile told him he was indeed ready to surprise Kathy.

Eric rang the Ryan's doorbell and waited. When Angela opened the door and gasped, he laid a finger on his lips and whispered, "I want to surprise Kathy."

Angela yelled, "Kathy, your cake with all the trimmings is here."

Eric gave her a thumbs-up.

"What are you talking about," he heard Kathy say, "I didn't . . ." Her hair was piled with curlers, and she wore paint-splattered green shorts, a stained yellow blouse, and a pair of dirty saddle shoes. "Oh, no," she shrieked, covering her hair with her hands. "You're not supposed to be here."

"Want me to leave?"

"No," she said, red-faced, but by the time he kissed her, she appeared composed. "You look like a million. Angela's description is perfect. You certainly do have all the trimmings."

"I came early because I wanted to have lunch at that fancy resort. Okay by you?"

"That sounds terrific."

"While you get ready, I'll drive to the Dole's and unpack my car."

"You bought a car?" She glanced in the driveway. "It's blue, my favorite color."

"I thought you'd be pleased. "I'll be back in half an hour. How about wearing your yellow sundress that transforms you into a ravishing princess?"

"You don't like my Cinderella rags?" Her pout belied the glint in her eyes. Before he could answer, she said, "I'll be on the porch, awaiting my blue carriage."

While Eric and Kathy walked the trail to the Lodge restaurant, he fingered the velvet box in his pocket and pointed down one of the side paths. "Want to honeymoon in one of those cottages?"

"I'd love to."

"Before we leave, let's make a reservation. First, come sit on this rock." He brushed it off and spread his handkerchief across the surface. Kathy lowered herself with the daintiness of a queen. He retrieved the small box from his pocket, and her eyes widened when he opened it. "I think we need to make our engagement official."

Kathy gasped as he slipped the solitaire on her finger. "It's . . . it's gorgeous." She jumped up and threw her arms around him.

They sealed their engagement with a lingering kiss that grew increasingly more passionate. Breathless, Eric drew back. Kathy nestled her head in the crook of his shoulder, clinging to him as if she didn't want their embrace to end.

Eric knew they should separate before he carried her off into the woods and yielded to the desire spreading through him. Was Kathy feeling what he felt? What if he were to suggest . . . His army buddies had mocked him when he let it slip he hadn't made love to Jill before shipping out.

"Forbidden fruit is sweeter," one claimed.

"Don't you try on shoes before you buy them?" another had said.

"Jill's not a shoe to be walked on," Eric remembered countering.

Neither was Kathy. She might be vulnerable enough to agree to spend a few hours in one of the cottages, but he wasn't about to bring up the idea. "We'd better go," he whispered.

Kathy smiled as she gazed at him intently. "Be sensible?" she said as if she'd read his thoughts.

Eric couldn't help chuckling. "Something like that."

Over lunch in their private arbor booth, they discussed their wedding day.

"Could we have a military ceremony?" Kathy asked. "You said you didn't like wearing a tuxedo, and you look so dashing in your uniform, I think you should wear it. Jeff has his ROTC uniform and so do all the ushers I've chosen. We could even exit with swords crossed over our heads. It would be romantic."

"I like the idea."

\*       \*       \*

October 26 dawned foggy, but by two o'clock, the sun high-lighted the cross on the church's stained glass window. From the side room at the front, Eric could hear the sanctuary organ playing. He ran a comb through his hair one last time while Jeff paced opening and closing his hands. "Why are you pacing," Eric asked, "when this is my wedding day?"

"I'm thinking about mine six weeks from now."

"Well, stop it. You're making me nervous." He put the comb in his pocket and drew in a breath when he heard strains of the wedding march. "This is it," he said. He brushed his sweaty palms over his trousers while his heart thudded.

Jeff grinned. "Now who's nervous? After you," he gestured.

Eric viewed the packed sanctuary with mild panic. When he saw his family and Uncle Jim gave him a thumbs-up, Eric smiled and tried to relax. He gazed toward the back of the church, longing to see Kathy. He vaguely saw the six bridesmaids in blue floral dresses, gliding down the aisle, but after the last one, he drew in a breath, knowing Kathy was next. His heart quivered with anticipation when she appeared in the doorway, her arm tucked through her father's.

212

Her white puffed-sleeved gown trimmed with blue daisies emphasized her innocence. Like a knight of old, Eric silently vowed to protect his lady-fair, guard her from all adversity. That she had chosen to leave the security of her home and its comforts for a life of uncertainty made him feel both humble and proud.

After they recited their vows and he kissed Kathy, his overwhelming love brought tears to his eyes. "I love you, Mrs. Stone," he whispered, pulling her into a tighter embrace and kissing her again as if only the two of them existed.

He yearned to leave immediately with Kathy but endured with good humor the seemingly endless number of pictures taken and the lengthy reception. Finally, their moment came. Under crossed swords and a shower of rice, he and Kathy ran for the car.

For Kathy, the following hour was a reenactment of her dream— the drive to the mountain resort, the stroll up the narrow path to their cottage, Eric carrying her over the threshold. But once inside, she tensed.

Eric kissed her with tenderness. "I know you're nervous," he said. "We have forever, Kathy. Why don't we change clothes and go stretch our legs. You can use the bathroom; I'll change out here."

She nodded with relief.

*       *       *

Eric felt her relax as they walked arm-in-arm to the top of the mountain. This night would be one of the most important in their lives. He wouldn't allow his impatience to ruin it. They watched the sky turn ablaze with color and ate dinner by candlelight in the same arbor booth where he had declared his love. After they strolled back to the cottage, Eric picked her up to carry her over the threshold.

Kathy giggled. "You already did this."

"I know, but I want to do it again."

"Why?"

"Because your dainty feet shouldn't touch the doorway until after our marriage is consummated."

"But I walked out earlier. Remember?"

213

"Leaving doesn't count."

Kathy laughed. "That doesn't make sense."

"Doesn't have to. It's my tradition."

"You're still holding me. Is that part of your tradition too?"

"Yep. Can't put you down, except on the bed." He searched her face, hoping this nonsensical discussion had erased her apprehension. "I can hold you forever."

Smiling, she brushed back a lock of his hair. "You don't have to. I'd like to sit on the bed." When he set her down, Kathy wrapped her arms around his neck. "I love you," she whispered.

She responded to his tender kisses and gentle touches. For Eric, there was no need to rush. It was enough to have her next to him. In this cottage, nestled among tall pines, he felt at home embracing the one who held his heart.

At the first whisper of daylight, Eric opened his eyes. Resisting the urge to snuggle against Kathy, he listened to the forest sounds, birds chirping their welcome song to the new day, the rustle of leaves. A hint of wood smoke drifted in through the half-open window. He thought about lighting the logs in their fireplace, but he was too comfy to move, and returning to bed might disturb Kathy. He could see her chest rise and fall in the even rhythm of sleep, make out her cute upturned nose, her mouth curved in a relaxed smile as if she were having a wonderful dream. *No, I don't want to disturb her, and yet I do. Last night was fantastic.* Eric lifted his eyes heavenward. "Thank you, Lord, for bringing Kathy into my life. Marrying her has made my life complete, and I know where I belong."

He thought about his family in Cologne, about the letter he had received from his mother.

Dearest son and my new daughter-to-be, Kathy,

What joy filled my heart when I received your long letter and the invitation to your wedding. Oh, how I wish it were possible for us to attend, but peace between our countries is only on paper. Time will mend hostilities, and as soon as we feel the emotional climate change, we will travel to America. Eric, your stepfather is very proud of you, and I know your father has watched from heaven with pride. I'm glad you made peace with your uncle. He's proud of you too. He managed to visit us and told your stepfather he harbors no resentment toward him, and his face glowed with pride when he talked about your stepping up to the plate—whatever that means. There's no need to dwell on how proud I am of you and Erin. We miss him dearly but know he is at peace, safe in the arms of Jesus. May God bring you peace and unspeakable joy.

Love, Mom

Kathy rolled over and gazed at him. "Eric, are you okay?"

"Of course. Why do you ask?"

She snuggled close. "You looked a million miles away."

He chuckled. "Not quite that far. I was thinking about Mom's letter, her asking God to bring me peace and unspeakable joy."

"And?"

Pulling her into tight embrace, he whispered, "He has."

Born, raised and married in Colorado, Donna moved with her husband, Ernest, in 1957 to southern California where they raised two boys and two girls. Their oldest girl was married before they moved north to Redding California. Their sons met their perspective brides and married in 1982. That same year, God pushed her into writing fiction. She resisted. Two bad school experiences convinced her that wasn't her field. She tried to ignore the story rummaging through her mind and told no one about it, but God knew. In His own unique way He compelled her to write it down. Once He hooked Donna on the fun of creating, He led her every step of the way in learning to write well. God is Awesome. What He initiates He completes.

CPSIA information can be obtained
at www.ICGtesting.com
Printed in the USA
BVHW031939160119
537994BV00001BA/28/P

9 781635 254846